This book belongs to

....

First published in 2009 by Miles Kelly Publishing Ltd
Harding's Barn, Bardfield End Green, Thaxted, Essex, CM6 3PX, UK

This edition printed in 2010

2 4 6 8 10 9 7 5 3

Editorial Director *Belinda Gallagher*
Art Director *Jo Brewer*
Managing Editor *Rosie McGuire*
Editorial Assistant *Claire Philip*
Designer *Michelle Foster*
Production Manager *Elizabeth Collins*
Reprographics *Stephan Davis, Ian Paulyn*
Assets Manager *Bethan Ellish*

ISBN 978-1-84810-109-8

Printed in China

British Library Cataloguing-in-Publication Data
A catalogue record for this book is available from the British Library

ACKNOWLEDGEMENTS
The publishers would like to thank the following artists
who have contributed to this book:

Beehive Illustration: Elena Selivanova

The Bright Agency: Christine Pym, Jasmine Foster,
Katy Wright, Patricia Moffett (inc. cover), Zdenko Basic

All other artwork from the Miles Kelly Artwork Bank

Made with paper from a sustainable forest

www.mileskelly.net   info@mileskelly.net

www.factsforprojects.com

Self-publish your
children's book

buddingpress.co.uk

50 Fairy Stories

Compiled by Tig Thomas

Contents

Enchantments

READING
TIME

(10)	*A Midsummer Night's Dream*	12
(10)	*Melisande*	24
(10)	*Rosanella*	36
(5)	*The Fairy Blackstick*	46
(5)	*Connla and the Fairy Maiden*	51
(6)	*The Smith and the Fairies*	56
(10)	*The Maiden of the Green Forest*	62
(12)	*The Prince with the Nose*	70
(12)	*The Man who would not Scold*	82

Children and Fairies

READING
TIME

8   *Sweet-One-Darling and the Dream-Fairies*   96

15   *Eva's Visit to Fairyland*   104

12   *Betty and the Wood Maiden*   118

15   *The Counterpane Fairy*   129

20   *Puck of Pook's Hill*   143

6   *My Own Self*   163

10   *The Boy Who Wanted More Cheese*   168

Fairy Helpers

READING
TIME

15   Mrs Bedonebyasyoudid and
Mrs Doasyouwouldbedoneby   180

10   The Touch of Iron   194

15   Graciosa and Percinet   205

4   Whippety Stourie   220

12   The Phantom Vessel   224

20   The Story of Wali Dad, the Simple-Hearted   235

4   Farmer Mybrow and the Fairies   251

Magic and Mischief

READING TIME

3	*Paddy Corcoran's Wife*	258
7	*The Fairy Cure*	261
12	*Master and Man*	267
4	*A French Puck*	279
4	*The Fairy Fluffikins*	283
5	*Iktomi and the Ducks*	288
5	*Iktomi and the Muskrat*	294
12	*Adventures of a Brownie*	299
2	*The Fairies and the Envious Neighbour*	310
8	*Drak, the Fairy*	313
3	*The Hillman and the Housewife*	322

Visitors to Fairyland

READING
TIME

10	*A Boy that Visited Fairyland*	328
12	*Murdoch's Rath*	338
6	*Billy Beg, Tom Beg, and the Fairies*	349
7	*The Fairy Cow*	355
5	*Fairy Ointment*	361
20	*Bruno's Revenge*	366
10	*The Fiddler in the Fairy Ring*	386
8	*The Fairy Wife*	396
10	*The Treasure Stone of the Fairies*	404
20	*Guleesh*	413

I Wish, I Wish

READING TIME

20	Beautiful as the Day	434
12	Christmas Every Day	452
6	Under the Sun	465
20	The Magic Pitcher	471
10	The Laird and the Man of Peace	488
15	Peter's Two Wishes	499

About the artists   512

A Midsummer Night's Dream 12

Melisande 24

Rosanella 36

The Fairy Blackstick 46

Connla and the Fairy Maiden 51

The Smith and the Fairies 56

Enchantments

The Maiden of the Green Forest 62

The Prince with the Nose 70

The Man who would not Scold 82

A Midsummer Night's Dream

Retold by E Nesbit

READING TIME: 10 MINUTES

Hermia and Lysander were lovers, but Hermia's father wished her to marry another man, named Demetrius.

Now, in Athens, where they lived, there was a wicked law, by which any girl who refused to marry according to her father's wishes, might be put to death. Hermia's father was so angry with her for refusing to do as he wished, that he actually brought her before the duke of Athens to ask that she might be killed, if she still refused to obey him. The duke gave her four days to think about it, and, at the end of that time, if she still refused to marry Demetrius, she would have to die.

Lysander of course was nearly mad with grief, and the best thing to do seemed to him for Hermia to run away to his aunt's house at a place beyond the reach of that cruel law, and there he would come to her and marry her. But before she started, she told her friend, Helena, what she was going to do.

Helena had been Demetrius' sweetheart long before his marriage with Hermia had been thought of, and being very silly, like all jealous people, she could not see that it was not poor Hermia's fault that Demetrius wished to marry her instead of his own lady, Helena. She knew that if she told Demetrius that Hermia was going, as she was, to the wood outside Athens, he would follow her, 'and I can follow him, and at least I shall see him,' she said to herself. So she went to him, and betrayed her friend's secret.

Now this wood where Lysander was to meet Hermia, and where the other two had decided to follow them, was full of fairies, as most woods are, if one only had the eyes to see them, and in this wood on this night were the king and queen of the fairies, Oberon and Titania. Now fairies are very wise people, but now and then they can be quite as foolish as mortal folk. Oberon and Titania, who might have been as happy as the days were long, had thrown away all their joy in a foolish quarrel. They never met without saying disagreeable things to each other, and scolded each other so dreadfully that all their little fairy followers, for fear, would creep into acorn cups and hide there.

So, instead of keeping one happy court and dancing all night through in the moonlight as is fairies' use, the king with his attendants wandered through one part of the wood, while the queen with hers kept state in another. And the cause of all this trouble was a little Indian boy whom Titania had taken to be one of her followers. Oberon wanted the child to follow him and be one of his fairy knights, but the queen would not give him up.

On this night, in a mossy moonlit glade, the king and queen of the fairies met.

"Ill met by moonlight, proud Titania," said the king.

"What! Jealous, Oberon?" answered the queen. "You spoil everything with your quarrelling. Come, fairies, let us leave him. I am not friends with him now."

"It rests with you to make up the quarrel," said the king. "Give me that little Indian boy, and I will again be your humble servant and suitor."

"Set your mind at rest," said the queen. "Your whole fairy kingdom buys not that boy from me. Come, fairies."

And she and her train rode off down the moonbeams.

"Well, go your ways," said Oberon. "But I'll be even with you before you leave this wood."

Then Oberon called his favourite fairy, Puck. Puck was the spirit of mischief. He used to slip into the dairies and take the cream away, and get into the churn so that the butter would not come, and turn the beer sour, and lead people out of their way on dark nights and then laugh at them, and tumble people's stools from under them when they were going to sit down, and upset their hot ale over their chins when they were going to drink.

"Now," said Oberon to this little sprite, "fetch me the flower called Love-in-idleness. The juice of that little purple flower laid on the eyes of those who sleep will

make them, when they wake, love the first thing they see. I will put some of the juice of that flower on my Titania's eyes, and when she wakes she will love the first thing she sees, were it lion, bear, or wolf, or bull, or meddling monkey, or a busy ape."

While Puck was gone, Demetrius passed through the glade followed by poor Helena, and still she told him how she loved him and reminded him of all his promises, and still he told her that he did not and could not love her, and that his promises were nothing. Oberon was sorry for poor Helena, and when Puck returned with the flower, he bade him follow Demetrius and put some of the juice on his eyes, so that he might love Helena when he woke and looked on her, as much as she loved him. So Puck set off, and wandering through the wood found, not Demetrius, but Lysander, on whose eyes he put the juice, but when Lysander woke, he saw not his own Hermia, but Helena, who was walking through the wood looking for the cruel Demetrius. Directly he saw her, he loved her, and left his own lady, under the spell of the purple flower.

When Hermia woke she found Lysander gone, and wandered about the wood trying to find him. Puck went back and told Oberon what he had done, and Oberon soon found that he had made a mistake, and set about looking for Demetrius, and having found him, put some of the juice on his eyes. And the first thing Demetrius saw when he woke was also Helena. So now Demetrius and Lysander were both following her through the wood, and it was Hermia's turn to follow her lover as Helena had done before. The end of it was that Helena and Hermia began to

quarrel, and Demetrius and Lysander went off to fight. Oberon was very sorry to see his kind scheme to help these lovers turn out so badly. So he said to Puck:

"These two young men are going to fight. You must overhang the night with drooping fog, and lead them so astray, that one will never find the other. When they are tired out, they will fall asleep. Then drop this other herb on Lysander's eyes. That will give him his old sight and his old love. Then each man will have the lady who loves him, and they will all think that this has been only a midsummer night's dream. Then when this is done, all will be well with them."

So Puck went and did as he was told, and when the two had fallen asleep without meeting each other, Puck poured the juice on Lysander's eyes, and said:

> "*When thou wakest,*
>   *Thou takest*
>   *True delight*
>   *In the sight*
>   *Of thy former lady's eye:*
>   *Jack shall have Jill;*
>   *Nought shall go ill.*"

Meanwhile Oberon found Titania asleep on a bank where grew wild thyme, oxlips, and violets, and woodbine, musk-roses and eglantine. There Titania always slept a part of the night, wrapped in the enameled skin of a snake. Oberon stooped over her and laid the juice on her eyes, saying:

"*What thou seest when thou wake,*
  Do it for thy true love take."

Now, it happened that when Titania woke the first thing she saw was a stupid clown, one of a party of players who had come out into the wood to rehearse their play. This clown had met with Puck, who had clapped an ass's head on his shoulders so that it looked as if it grew there. Directly Titania woke and saw this dreadful monster, she said, "What angel is this? Are you as wise as you are beautiful?"

"If I am wise enough to find my way out of this wood, that's enough for me," said the foolish clown.

"Do not desire to go out of the wood," said Titania. The spell of the love-juice was on her, and to her the clown seemed the most beautiful creature on the earth.

"I love you," she went on. "Come with me, and I will give you fairies to attend on you."

So she called four fairies, whose names were Peaseblossom, Cobweb, Moth, and Mustardseed.

"You must attend this gentleman," said the queen. "Feed him with apricots and dewberries, purple grapes, green figs, and mulberries. Steal honey-bags for him from the bumble-bees, and with the wings of painted butterflies fan the moonbeams from his sleeping eyes."

"I will," said one of the fairies, and all the others said, "I will."

"Now, sit down with me," said the queen to the clown, "and let me stroke your dear cheeks, and stick musk-roses in your smooth, sleek head, and kiss your fair large ears, my gentle joy."

"Where's Peaseblossom?" asked the clown with the ass's head. He did not care much about the queen's affection, but he was very proud of having fairies to wait on him.

"Ready," said Peaseblossom.

"Scratch my head, Peaseblossom," said the clown. "Where's Cobweb?"

"Ready," said Cobweb.

"Kill me," said the clown, "the red bumble-bee on the top of the thistle yonder, and bring me the honey-bag. Where's Mustardseed?"

"Ready," said Mustardseed.

"Oh, I want nothing," said the clown. "Only just help Cobweb to scratch. I must go to the barber's, for methinks I am marvellous hairy about the face."

"Would you like anything to eat?" said the fairy queen.

"I should like some good dry oats," said the clown – for his donkey's head made him desire donkey's food – "and some hay to follow."

"Shall some of my fairies fetch you new nuts from the squirrel's house?" asked the queen.

"I'd rather have a handful or two of good dried peas," said the clown. "But please don't let any of your people disturb me – I am going to sleep."

Then said the queen, "And I will wind thee in my arms."

And so when Oberon came along he found his beautiful queen lavishing kisses and endearments on a clown with a donkey's head.

And before he released her from the enchantment,

he persuaded her to give him the little Indian boy he so much desired to have. Then he took pity on her, and threw some juice of the disenchanting flower on her pretty eyes, and then in a moment she saw plainly the donkey-headed clown she had been loving, and knew how foolish she had been.

Oberon took off the ass's head from the clown, and left him to finish his sleep with his own silly head lying on the thyme and violets.

Thus all was made plain and straight again. Oberon and Titania loved each other more than ever. Demetrius thought of no one but Helena, and Helena had never had any thought of anyone but Demetrius.

As for Hermia and Lysander, they were as loving a couple as you could meet in a day's march, even through a fairy wood.

So the four mortal lovers went back to Athens and were married; and the fairy king and queen live happily together in that very wood at this very day.

Melisande

By E Nesbit

READING TIME: 10 MINUTES

*W*hen the Princess Melisande was born, her mother, the queen, wished to have a christening party, but the king put his foot down and said he would not have it.

"I've seen too much trouble come of christening parties," said he. "However carefully you keep your visiting-book, some fairy is sure to get left out, and you know what that leads to. We'll have no nonsense about it. We won't ask a single fairy, then none of them can be offended."

"Unless they all are," said the queen.

And that was exactly what happened. When the king and the queen and the baby got back from the christening the great throne room was crammed with fairies, of all ages and of all degrees of beauty and ugliness – good fairies and bad fairies, flower fairies and moon fairies, fairies like spiders and fairies like butterflies – and as the queen opened the door they all cried, with one voice, "Why didn't you ask me to your christening party?"

"I'm very sorry," said the poor queen, but Malevola pushed forward and said, "Hold your tongue," most rudely.

Malevola is the oldest, as well as the most wicked, of the fairies. "Don't begin to make excuses," she said, shaking her finger at the queen. "You know well enough what happens if a fairy is left out of a christening party. We are all going to give our

christening presents now. As the fairy of highest social position, I shall begin. The princess shall be bald."

The queen nearly fainted as Malevola drew back. But the king stepped forward too.

"No you don't!" said he. " How can you be so unfairylike? Have none of you been to school? Have none of you studied the history of your own race?"

"How dare you?" cried a fairy in a bonnet. "It is my turn, and I say the princess shall be—"

The king actually put his hand over her mouth.

"Look here," he said, "I won't have it. A fairy who breaks the traditions of fairy history goes out – you know she does – like the flame of a candle. And all tradition shows that only one bad fairy is ever forgotten at a christening party and the good ones are always invited; so either this is not a christening party, or else you were all invited except one, and, by her own showing, that was Malevola. Try it, if you don't believe me. Give your nasty gifts to my innocent child – but as sure as you do, out you go, like a candle flame. Now, then, will you risk it?"

No one answered, but one by one all the fairies said goodbye and thanked the queen for the delightful afternoon they had spent with her.

When the very last fairy was gone the queen ran to look at the baby. She tore off its lace cap and burst into tears. For all the baby's downy golden hair came off with the cap, and the Princess Melisande was as bald as an egg.

"Don't cry, my love," said the king. "I have a wish lying by, which my fairy godmother gave me for a wedding present, but since then I've had nothing to wish for!"

"Thank you, dear," said the queen, smiling through her tears.

"I'll keep the wish till the baby grows up," the king went on. "And then I'll give it to her and if she likes to wish for hair she can."

"Oh, won't you wish for it now?" said the queen.

"No, dearest. She may want something else more when she grows up. And besides, her hair may grow by itself."

But it never did. Princess Melisande grew up as beautiful as the sun and as good as gold, but never a hair grew on that little head of hers. The queen sewed her little caps of green silk, and the princess's pink and white face looked out of these like a flower peeping out of its bud. And every day as she grew older she grew dearer, and as she grew dearer she grew better, and as she grew more good she grew more beautiful.

Now, when she was grown up the queen said to the king:

"My love, our dear daughter is old enough to know what she wants. Let her have the wish."

So the king unlocked his gold safe with the seven diamond-handled keys that hung at his girdle, and took out the wish and gave it to his daughter.

Then the queen said:

"Dearest, for my sake, wish what I tell you."

"Why, of course I will," said Melisande. The queen whispered in her ear, and Melisande nodded. Then she said, aloud:

"I wish I had golden hair a yard long, and that it would grow an inch every day, and grow twice as fast every time it was cut, and—"

"Stop," cried the king. And the wish went off, and the next moment the princess stood smiling at him through a shower of golden hair.

"Oh, how lovely," said the queen. "What a pity you interrupted her, dear. What's the matter?"

"You'll know soon enough," said the king. "Come, let's be happy while we may. Give me a kiss, little Melisande, and then go to nurse and ask her to teach you how to comb your hair."

"I know," said Melisande, "I've often combed mother's."

"Your mother has beautiful hair," said the king, "but I fancy you will find your own less easy to manage."

And, indeed, it was so. The princess's hair began by being a yard long, and it grew an inch every night. If you know anything at all about the simplest sums you will see that in about five weeks her hair was about two yards long. This is a very inconvenient length. It trails on the floor and sweeps up all the dust. And the princess's hair was growing an inch every night. When it was three yards long the princess could not bear it any longer – it was so heavy and so hot – so she cut it all off, and then for a few hours she was comfortable. But the hair went on growing, and now it grew twice as fast as before, so that in thirty-six days it was as long as ever. The poor princess cried with tiredness. When she couldn't bear it anymore she cut her hair and was comfortable for a very little time. For the hair now grew four times as fast as at first, and in eighteen days it was as long as before, and she had to have it cut and so on, growing twice as fast after each cutting, till the princess would go to bed at night with her hair clipped short, and wake up in the morning with yards and yards and yards of golden hair flowing all about the room, so that she could not move without pulling her own hair, and nurse had to come and cut the hair off before she could get out of bed.

"I wish I was bald again," sighed poor Melisande.

And still the hair grew and grew. Then the king said:

"I shall write to my fairy godmother and see if something cannot be done."

So he wrote and sent the letter by a skylark, and by return of bird came this answer:

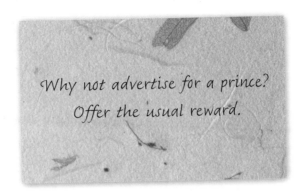

Why not advertise for a prince?
Offer the usual reward.

So the king sent out his heralds all over the world to proclaim that any respectable prince with proper references should marry the Princess Melisande if he could stop her hair growing.

Then from far and near came trains of princes anxious to try their luck, and they brought all sorts of nasty things with them in bottles and round wooden boxes. The princess tried all the remedies, but she did not like any of them, and she did not like any of the princes, so in her heart she was rather glad that none of them made the least difference to her hair.

The princess had to sleep in the great throne room
now, because no other room was big enough to hold her
and her hair. When she woke in the morning the long
high room would be quite full of her golden hair, packed
tight and thick like wool in a barn. And every night
when she had had the hair cut close to her head she
would sit in her green silk gown by the window and cry,
and kiss the little green caps she used to wear, and wish
herself bald again. It was as she sat crying there on
Midsummer Eve that she first saw Prince Florizel.

He was walking in the garden in the moonlight, and
he looked up and she looked down, and for the first time
Melisande, looking on a prince, wished that he might
have the power to stop her hair from growing. As for the
prince, he wished many things, and the first was
granted him. For he said, "You are Melisande?"

"And you are Florizel?"

"There are many roses round your window,"
said he to her, "and none down here."

She threw him one of three white roses
she held in her hand. Then he said:

"If I can do what your father asks, will you
marry me?"

"My father has promised that I shall," said Melisande, playing with the white roses in her hand.

"Dear princess," said he, "your father's promise is nothing to me. I want yours. Will you give it to me?"

"Yes," said she, and gave him the second rose.

"I want your hand."

"Yes," she said.

"And your heart with it."

"Yes," said the princess, and gave him the third rose.

"Then," said he, "stay by your window and I will stay down here in the garden and watch. And when your hair has grown to the filling of your room call to me, and then do as I tell you."

"I will," said the princess.

So at dewy sunrise the prince, lying on the turf beside the sundial, heard her voice. "Florizel! Florizel! My hair has grown so long that it is pushing me out of the window."

"Get out on to the windowsill," said he, "and twist your hair three times round the great iron hook that is there."

And she did.

Then the prince climbed up the rose bush with his naked sword in his teeth, and he took the princess's hair in his hand about a yard from her head and said:

"Jump!"

The princess jumped, and screamed, for there she was hanging from the hook by a yard and a half of her bright hair. The prince tightened his grasp of the hair and drew his sword across it.

Then he let her down gently by her hair till her feet were on the grass, and jumped down after her.

They stayed talking in the garden till all the shadows had crept under their proper trees and the sundial said it was breakfast time.

Then they went in to breakfast, and all the court crowded round to wonder and admire. For the princess's hair had not grown.

"How did you do it?" asked the king, shaking Florizel warmly by the hand.

"The simplest thing in the world," said Florizel, modestly. "You have always cut the hair off the princess. I just cut the princess off the hair."

"You are a young man of sound judgment," said the king, embracing him.

The princess kissed her prince a hundred times, and the very next day they were married. Everyone remarked on the beauty of the bride, and it was noticed that her hair was quite short – only five feet five and a quarter inches long – just down to her pretty ankles.

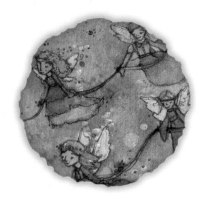

Rosanella

By Comte de Caylus

READING TIME: 10 MINUTES

Inconstant, fickle, faithless – these are all words to describe someone who cannot stay true to one love, but is always finding a new person to fall in love with. But what happens when an incurably fickle prince meets a princess no one can resist?

*E*verybody knows that though the fairies live hundreds of years they do sometimes die, and especially as they pass one day in every week under the form of some animal, when of course they are liable to accident. It was in this way that death once overtook the queen of the fairies, and it became necessary to elect a new sovereign.

After much discussion, it appeared that the choice lay between two fairies, one called Surcantine and the other Paridamie, and their claims were so equal that it was impossible to choose one over the other.

In the end, the fairy court decided that whichever of the two could show to the world the greatest wonder should be queen, but it was to be a special kind of wonder, no moving of mountains or any such common fairy tricks would do. Surcantine, therefore, decided that she would bring up a prince whom nothing could make faithful and constant to one love. While Paridamie decided to display to admiring mortals a princess so charming that no one could see her without falling in love with her. They were allowed to take their own time, and meanwhile the four oldest fairies were to attend to the affairs of the kingdom.

Now Paridamie had for a long time been very friendly with King Bardondon, who was a most noble monarch, and whose court was the model of what a court should be. His queen, Balanice, was also charming – indeed it is rare to find a husband and wife so perfectly of one mind about everything.

They had one little daughter, whom they had named

'Rosanella', because she had a pink rose birthmark upon her throat.

On the the night following the assembly of fairies, Queen Balanice woke up with a shriek, and when her maids of honour ran to see what was the matter, they found she had had a frightful dream.

"I thought," said she, "that my little daughter had changed into a bouquet of roses, and that as I held it in my hand a bird swooped down suddenly and snatched it from me and carried it away."

"Let someone run and see that all is well with the princess," she added.

So they ran, but they found the cradle empty, and though they sought high and low, not a trace of

Rosanella could they find. The queen was beside herself with grief, and so, indeed, was the king, only being a man he did not say quite so much about his feelings.

He presently suggested to Balanice that they should spend a few days at one of their palaces in the country, and she agreed, since in her sorrow she no longer enjoyed the pleasures of town. One summer evening, as they sat together on a shady lawn shaped like a star, from which radiated twelve splendid avenues of trees, the queen looked round and saw a charming peasant girl approaching by each path, and that each girl carried something in a basket with the greatest care. As each girl drew near she laid her basket at Balanice's feet, saying:

"Charming queen, may this be some slight comfort to you in your unhappiness!"

The queen hastily opened the baskets, and found in each a lovely baby girl, about the same age as the little princess for whom she sorrowed so deeply. At first the sight of them renewed her grief, but presently their charms so gained upon her that she forgot her sadness in looking after the babies, providing them with maids, cradle-rockers, and ladies-in-waiting, and in sending hither and thither for swings and dolls and tops.

Oddly enough, every baby had upon its throat a tiny pink rose. The queen found it so difficult to decide on suitable names for all of them, that until she could settle the matter she chose a special colour for each girl, pink for one, purple for another and, so that when they were all together they looked like nothing so much as a nosegay of flowers. As they grew older it became clear that though they were all remarkably intelligent, they differed one from another in character, so much so that they gradually ceased to be known as 'Ruby,' or 'Primrose,' or whatever might have been their colour, and the queen instead would say: "Where is my Sweet?" or "my Kind," or "my Happy."

Of course, with all these charms they had lovers by the dozen. Not only in their own court, but princes from afar, who were constantly arriving, attracted by the reports which were spread abroad; but these lovely girls, the first maids of honour, were as sensible as they were beautiful, and favoured no one.

But let us return to Surcantine. She had fixed upon the son of a king who was cousin to Bardondon, to bring up as her fickle prince. She had before, at his christening, given him all the graces of mind and body that a prince could possibly require, but now she redoubled her efforts, and spared no pains in adding every imaginable charm and fascination. So that whether he happened to be cross or amiable, splendidly or simply attired, serious or frivolous, he was always perfectly irresistible! In truth, he was a charming young fellow, since the Fairy had given him the best heart in the world as well as the best head, and had left nothing to be desired except faithfulness. For it cannot be denied that Prince Mirliflor was a desperate flirt, and as fickle as the wind. By the time he arrived at his eighteenth birthday there was not a heart left for him to conquer in his father's kingdom – they were all his own, and he was tired of everyone! Things were in this state when he was invited to visit the court of his father's cousin, King Bardondon.

Imagine his feelings when he arrived and was presented at once to twelve of the loveliest creatures in the world, and they all liked him as much as he liked each one of them, so that things came to such a pass that he was never happy a single instant without them. For could he not whisper soft speeches to Sweet, and laugh with Joy, while he looked at Beauty? And in his more serious moments what could be pleasanter than to talk to Thoughtful upon some shady lawn, while he held the hand of Loving in his own, and all the others lingered near? For the first time in his life he really loved, though the object of his devotion was not one person, but twelve, to whom he was equally attached, and even Surcantine was deceived into thinking that this was indeed the height of inconstancy. But Paridamie said not a word. One day the queen gave a large garden party, and just as the guests were all assembled, and Prince Mirliflor was as usual dividing his attentions between the twelve beauties, a humming of bees was heard. The Rose-maidens, fearing their stings, uttered little shrieks, and fled to a distance from the rest of the company. Immediately, to the horror of all who were looking on, the bees pursued them, and, growing suddenly to an enormous size, pounced each upon a maiden and carried her off into the air, and in an instant they were all lost to view. This amazing occurrence plunged the whole court into the deepest sadness, and Prince Mirliflor, after giving way to the most violent grief at first, fell gradually into a state of such deep dejection that it was feared if nothing could rouse him he would certainly die.

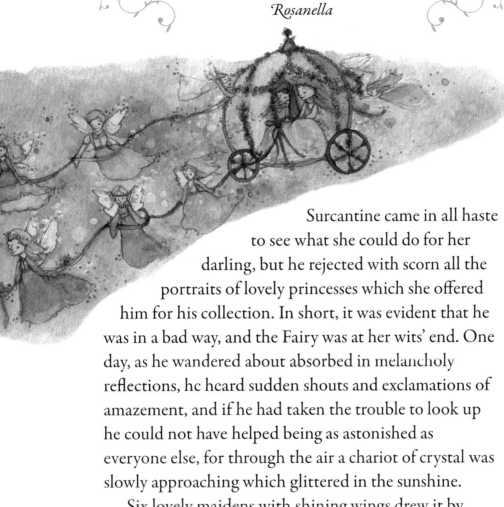

Surcantine came in all haste to see what she could do for her darling, but he rejected with scorn all the portraits of lovely princesses which she offered him for his collection. In short, it was evident that he was in a bad way, and the Fairy was at her wits' end. One day, as he wandered about absorbed in melancholy reflections, he heard sudden shouts and exclamations of amazement, and if he had taken the trouble to look up he could not have helped being as astonished as everyone else, for through the air a chariot of crystal was slowly approaching which glittered in the sunshine.

Six lovely maidens with shining wings drew it by rose-coloured ribbons, while others, equally beautiful, were holding long garlands of roses crossed above it, so as to form a canopy. In it sat the Fairy Paridamie, and by her side a princess whose beauty positively dazzled all who saw her.

At the foot of the great staircase they descended, and proceeded to the queen's apartments, though everyone had run together to see this marvel, till it was quite difficult to make a way through the crowd, and exclamations of wonder rose on all sides at the loveliness of the strange princess. "Great queen," said Paridamie, "permit me to restore to you your daughter Rosanella, whom I stole out of her cradle."

After the first transports of joy were over the queen said to Paridamie, "But my twelve lovely ones, are they lost to me for ever? Shall I never see them again?"

But Paridamie only said:

"Very soon you will cease to miss them!" in a tone that evidently meant 'Don't ask me any more questions.' And then mounting again into her chariot she swiftly disappeared.

The news of his beautiful cousin's arrival was soon carried to the prince, but he had hardly the heart to go and see her. However, it became absolutely necessary that he should pay his respects, and he had scarcely been five minutes in her presence before it seemed to him that she combined in her own charming person all the gifts and graces which had so attracted him in the twelve

Rose-maidens whose loss he had so truly mourned.

And after all it is really more satisfactory to be in love with one person at a time. So it came to pass that before he knew where he was he was entreating his lovely cousin to marry him, and the moment the words had left his lips, Paridamie appeared, smiling and triumphant, in the chariot of the queen of the fairies, for by that time they had all heard of her success, and declared her to have earned the kingdom. She had to give a full account of how she had stolen Rosanella from her cradle, and divided her character into twelve parts, that each might charm Prince Mirliflor, and when once more united might cure him of his inconstancy once and for ever.

And as one more proof of the fascination of the whole Rosanella, I may tell you that even the defeated Surcantine sent her a wedding gift, and was present at the ceremony which took place as soon as the guests could arrive. Prince Mirliflor was faithful only to his adored Rosanella for the rest of his life. And indeed who would not have been in his place?

As for Rosanella, she loved him as much as all the twelve beauties put together, so they reigned in peace and happiness to the end of their long lives.

The Fairy Blackstick

From *The Rose and the Ring*

By William Makepeace Thackeray

READING TIME: 5 MINUTES

Between the kingdoms of Paflagonia and Crim Tartary, there lived a mysterious personage, who was known in those countries as the Fairy Blackstick, from the ebony wand which she carried, on which she rode to the moon sometimes, and with which she performed her wonders.

When she was young, and had been first taught the art of conjuring by the sorcerer, her father, she was always practising her skill, whizzing about from one

kingdom to another upon her black stick, and conferring
her fairy favours upon this prince or that. She had scores
of royal godchildren, turned numberless wicked people
into beasts, birds, millstones, clocks, pumps, boot jacks,
umbrellas, or other absurd shapes, and, in a word, was
one of the most active of the whole College of Fairies.

But after two or three thousand years of this sport,
I suppose Blackstick grew tired of it. Or perhaps she
thought, 'What good am I doing by sending this
princess to sleep for a hundred years? By fixing a black
pudding on to that fool's nose? By causing diamonds and
pearls to drop from one little girl's mouth, and vipers
and toads from another's? I might as well shut my
incantations up, and allow things to take their natural
course.' So she locked up her books in her cupboard,
declined further magical performances, and scarcely
used her wand at all except as a cane to walk about with.

When the Princess Angelica was born, her parents
not only did not ask the Fairy Blackstick to the
christening party, but gave orders to their porter to
absolutely refuse her if she called. This porter's name was
Gruffanuff, and he had been selected for the post by
their Royal Highnesses because he was a very tall fierce

man, with a rudeness which frightened most such persons away.

Now this fellow tried his rudeness once too often, as you shall hear. For the Fairy Blackstick coming to call upon the prince and princess, who were actually sitting at the open drawing-room window, Gruffanuff not only denied them, but made the most odious vulgar sign as he was going to slam the door in the fairy's face! "Get away, hold Blackstick!" said he. "I tell you, Master and Missis ain't at home to you." And he was, as we have said, *going* to slam the door.

But the fairy, with her wand, prevented the door being shut, and Gruffanuff came out again in a fury, swearing in the most abominable way, and asking the fairy 'whether she thought he was a going to stay at that there door all day?'

"You *are* going to stay at that door all day and all night, and for many a long year," the fairy said, very majestically.

Gruffanuff, coming out of the door, straddling before it with his great calves, burst out laughing, and cried, "Ha, ha, ha! This is a good un! Ha – ah – *what's this? Let me down –O–o–H'm!*" and then he was dumb!

For, as the fairy waved her wand over him, he felt himself rising off the ground, and fluttering up against the door, and then, as if a screw ran into his stomach, he felt a dreadful pain there, and was pinned to the door, and then his arms flew up over his head, and his legs, after writhing about wildly, twisted under his body. He felt cold, cold, growing over him, as if he was turning into metal.

He was turned into metal! He was neither more nor less than a knocker! And there he was, nailed to the door in the blazing summer day, till he burned almost red-hot, and there he was, nailed to the door all the bitter winter nights, till his brass nose was dropping with icicles. And the postman came and rapped at him, and the boy with a letter came and hit him up against the door. And the king and queen (princess and prince they were then) coming home from a walk that evening, the king said, "Hello, my dear! You have had a new knocker put on the door. Why, it's rather like our porter in the face! What has become of that boozy vagabond?" And the housemaid came and scrubbed his nose with sandpaper, and once, some larking young men tried to wrench him off, and put him to the most excruciating

agony with a screwdriver. And then the queen had a
fancy to have the colour of the door altered, and the
painters dabbed him over the mouth and eyes, and
nearly choked him, as they painted him pea-green. I
warrant he had leisure to repent of having been rude to
the Fairy Blackstick!

As for his wife, she did not miss him, and when the
prince and princess chose to become king and queen,
they left their old house, and nobody thought of the
porter any more.

Connla and the Fairy Maiden

By Joseph Jacobs

READING TIME: 5 MINUTES

Connla of the Fiery Hair was son of Conn of the Hundred Fights. One day as he stood by the side of his father on the height of Usna, he saw a maiden clad in strange attire coming towards him.

"Whence comest thou, maiden?" said Connla.

"I come from the Plains of the Ever Living," she said, "there where there is neither death nor sin. There we keep holiday always, nor need we help from any in our joy. And in all our pleasure we have no strife. And because we have our homes in the round green hills, men call us the Hill Folk."

The king and all with him wondered much to hear a voice when they saw no one. For save Connla alone, none saw the Fairy Maiden.

"To whom art thou talking, my son?" said Conn the king.

Then the maiden answered, "Connla speaks to a fair maid, whom neither death nor old age awaits. I love Connla, and now I call him away to the Plain of Pleasure, Moy Mell, where Boadag is king, nor has there been complaint or sorrow in that land since he has held the kingship. Oh, come with me, Connla of the Fiery Hair. A fairy crown awaits thee to grace thy comely face and royal form. Come, and never shall thy comeliness fade, nor thy youth, till the last awful day of judgment."

The king in fear at what the maiden said, which he heard though he could not see her, called aloud to his druid, Coran by name.

"Oh, Coran of the many spells," he said, "and of the cunning magic, I call upon thy aid. A task is upon me too great for all my skill and wit, greater than any laid upon me since I seized the kingship. A maiden unseen has met us, and by her power would take from me my dear, my comely son. If thou help not, he will be taken from thy king by woman's wiles and witchery."

Then Coran the druid stood forth and chanted his spells towards the spot where the maiden's voice had been heard. And none heard her voice again, nor could Connla see her longer. Only as she vanished before the druid's mighty spell, she threw an apple to Connla.

For a whole month from that day Connla would take nothing, either to eat or to drink, save only from that apple. But as he ate it grew again and always kept whole. And all the while there grew within him a mighty yearning and longing after the maiden he had seen.

But when the last day of the month of waiting came, Connla stood by the side of his father on the Plain of Arcomin, and again he saw the maiden come towards him, and again she spoke to him.

"'Tis a glorious place that Connla holds among short-lived mortals awaiting the day of death. But now the folk of life beg and bid thee come to Moy Mell, the Plain of Pleasure, for they have learnt to know thee, seeing thee in thy home among thy dear ones."

When the king heard the maiden's voice he called to
his men, "Summon swift my druid, for I see she has
again this day the power of speech."

Then the maiden said "Oh, mighty Conn, fighter of a
hundred fights, the druid's power is little loved; it has
little honour in the mighty land, peopled with so many
of the upright. When the Law will come, it will do away
with the druid's magic spells that come from the lips of
the false black demon."

Then the king observed that since the maiden came
Connla his son spoke to none that spake to him. So
Conn of the hundred fights said to him, "Is it to thy
mind what the woman says, my son?"

"'Tis hard upon me," then said Connla; "I love my
own folk above all things, but yet a longing seizes me for
the maiden."

When the maiden heard this, she answered, "The
ocean is not so strong as the waves of thy longing. Come
with me in my curragh, the gleaming, crystal canoe.
Soon we can reach Boadag's realm. I see the bright sun
sink, yet far as it is, we can reach it before dark. There is,
too, another land worthy of thy journey, a land joyous to
all that seek it. Only wives and maidens dwell there. If

thou wilt, we can seek it and live there together in joy."

When the maiden ceased to speak, Connla of the Fiery Hair sprang into the curragh, the gleaming crystal canoe. And then they all, king and court, saw it glide away over the bright sea towards the setting sun. Away and away, till eye could see it no longer, and Connla and the fairy maiden went their way on the sea, and were no more seen.

The Smith and the Fairies

By Kate Douglas Wiggin

READING TIME: 6 MINUTES

It was a superstition in Celtic lands that fairies stole babies and left fairy babies (changelings) in their place. In this story the fairies are called by their Gaelic name of Daione Sith, *and the word for a changeling is* Sibhreach. *A dirk is a short knife.*

Years ago there lived in Crossbrig a smith of the name of MacEachern. This man had an only child, a boy of about thirteen or fourteen years of age, cheerful, strong, and healthy. All of a sudden he fell ill, took to his bed and moped whole days away. No one could tell what was the matter with him, and the boy himself could not, or would not, tell how he felt. He was wasting away fast – getting thin, old, and yellow – and his father and all his friends were afraid that he would die.

After the boy had been lying in this condition for a long time, getting neither better nor worse (but with an extraordinary appetite) an old man, well known for his knowledge of out-of-the-way things, walked into the smith's workshop. Forthwith the smith told him the occurrence which had clouded his life.

The old man looked grave as he listened; and after sitting a long time pondering over all he had heard, gave his opinion thus:

"It is not your son you have got. The boy has been carried away by the Daione Sith, and they have left a Sibhreach in his place."

"Alas! And what then am I to do?" said the smith. "How am I ever to see my own son again?"

"I will tell you how," answered the old man. "But, first, to make sure that it is not your own son you have got, take as many empty eggshells as you can get, go into his room, spread them out carefully before his sight, then proceed to draw water with them, carrying them two and two in your hands as if they were a great weight, and arrange them when full, around the fire."

The smith proceeded to carry out all his instructions. He had not been long at work before there arose from the bed a shout of laughter, and the voice of the seeming sick boy exclaimed:

"I am eight hundred years of age, and I have never seen the like of that before." The smith returned and told the old man.

"Well, now," said the old man to him, "did I not tell you that it was not your son you had: your son is in Borracheill in a digh there (that is, a round green hill frequented by fairies). Get rid as soon as possible of this intruder, and I think I may promise you your son. You must light a very large and bright fire before the bed on which this stranger is lying. He will ask you, 'What is the use of such a fire as that?' Answer him at once, 'You will see that presently!' and then seize him, and throw him into the middle of it. If it is your own son you have got, he will call out to you to save him, but if not, the thing will fly through the roof."

The smith again followed the old man's advice:

kindled a large fire, answered the question put to him as he had been directed to do, and seizing the child flung him in without hesitation. The Sibhreach gave an awful yell, and sprang through the roof, where a hole had been left to let the smoke out.

The old man told the smith that on a certain night the green round hill, where the fairies kept the boy, would be open. On that date the smith, having provided himself with a Bible and a dirk, was to proceed to the hill. He would hear singing and dancing, and much merriment going on, but he was to advance boldly – the Bible he carried would be a safeguard to him against danger from the fairies. On entering the hill he was to stick the dirk in the threshold, to prevent the hill from closing upon him. "And then," said the old man, "on entering you will see a spacious apartment before you, and there, standing far within, working at a forge, you will also see your son. When you are questioned, say you come to seek him, and will not go without him."

Not long after this, the time came round, and the smith sallied forth, prepared as instructed. Sure enough as he approached the hill, there was a light where light was seldom seen before. Soon after, a sound of piping, dancing, and joyous merriment reached the anxious father on the night wind.

Overcoming every impulse of fear, the smith approached the threshold steadily, stuck the dirk into it as directed, and entered. Protected by the Bible he carried on his breast, the fairies could not touch him, but they asked him, with a good deal of displeasure, what he wanted there. He answered, "I want my son, whom I see down there, and I will not go without him."

The fairies, incensed, seized the smith and his son, and throwing them out of the hill, flung the dirk after them, and in an instant all was dark.

For a year and a day the boy never did a turn of work, and hardly ever spoke a word. At last one day, sitting by

his father and watching him finishing a sword, he suddenly exclaimed, "That is not the way to do it," and taking the tools from his father's hands he set to work himself in his place, and soon fashioned a sword, the like of which was never seen in the country before.

From that day the young man wrought constantly with his father, and became the inventor of a peculiarly fine and well-tempered weapon,

the making of which kept the two smiths, father and son, in constant employment, spread their fame far and wide, and gave them the means in abundance, as they before had the disposition, to live content with all the world and very happily with each other.

The Maiden of the Green Forest

By William Elliot Griffis

READING TIME: 10 MINUTES

$\mathcal{M}$any a palace lies under the waves that wash Cymric land, for the sea has swallowed up more than one village, and even cities.

When Welsh fairies yield to their mortal loves and consent to become their wives, it is always on some promise. Sometimes there are several of these, which the fairy ladies compel their mortal lovers to pledge them, before they agree to become wives. In fact, the fairies in

Cymric land are among the most exacting of any known.

A prince named Benlli, of the Powys region, found this out to his grief, for he had always supposed that wives could be had simply for the asking. All that a man need say, to the girl to whom he took a fancy, was this:

'Come along with me, and be my bride,' and then she would say, 'Thank you, I'll come,' and the two would trot off together. This was the man's notion.

Now Benlli was a wicked old fellow. He was already married, but wrinkles had gathered on his wife's face. She had a faded, washed-out look, and her hair was thinning out. She would never be young again, and he was tired of her, and wanted a mate with fresh rosy cheeks, and long, thick hair. He was quite ready to fall in love with such a maiden, whenever his eyes should light upon her.

One day, he went out hunting in the Green Forest. While waiting for a wild boar to rush out, there rode past him a young woman whose beauty was dazzling. He instantly fell in love with her.

The next day, while on horseback, at the same opening in the forest, the same maiden reappeared, but it was only for a moment, and then she vanished.

Again, on the third day, the prince rode out to the

appointed place, and again the vision of beauty was there. He rode up to her and begged her to come and live with him at his palace.

"I will come and be your wedded wife on three conditions: You must put away the wife you now have, you must permit me to leave you, one night in every seven, without following after or spying upon me, and you must not ask me where I go or what I do. Swear to me that you will do these three things. Then, if you keep your promises unbroken, my beauty shall never change, no, not until the tall vegetable flag-reeds wave and the long green rushes grow in your hall."

The Prince of Powys was quite ready to swear this oath and he solemnly promised to observe the three conditions. So the maiden of the Green Forest went to live with him.

'But what of his old wife?' one asks. Ah! He had no trouble from that quarter, for when the newly-wedded couple arrived at the castle, she had already disappeared.

Happy, indeed, were the long bright days, which the prince and his new bride spent together, whether in the castle, or outdoors, riding on horseback, or in hunting the deer. Every day, her beauty seemed diviner, and she more lovely. He lavished various gifts upon her, among others that of a crown of beryl and sapphire. Then he put on her finger a diamond ring worth what was a very great sum – a king's ransom. He loved her so dearly that he never suspected for a moment that he would ever have any trouble in keeping his three promises.

But without variety, life has no spice, and monotony wearies the soul. After nine years had passed, and his wife absented herself every Friday night, he began to wonder why. His curiosity, to know the reason for her going away, so increased that it so wore on him that he became both miserable in himself and irritable towards others. Everybody in the castle noticed the change in their master, and grieved over it.

One night, he invited a learned monk from the white monastery, not far away, to come and take dinner with him. The table in the great banqueting hall was spread with the most delicious food, the lights were magnificent, and the music gay.

But Wyland, the monk, was a man of magic and could see through things. He noticed that some secret grief was preying upon the prince's mind. He could see

that, amidst all this splendour, he, Benlli, the lord of the castle, was the most miserable person within its walls. So Wyland went home, resolved to call again and find out what was the trouble.

When they met, some days later, Wyland's greeting was this:

"Christ save thee, Benlli! What secret sorrow clouds thy brow? Why so gloomy?"

Benlli at once burst out with the story of how he met the maiden of the Green Forest, and how she became his wife on three conditions.

"Think of it," said Benlli, groaning aloud. "When the owls cry and the crickets chirp, my wife leaves my bed, and until the daystar appears, I lie alone, torn with curiosity, to know where she is, and what she is doing. I fall again into heavy sleep, and do not awake until sunrise, when I find her by my side again. It is all such a mystery, that the secret lies heavy on my soul. Despite all my wealth, and my strong castle, with feasting and music by night and hunting by day, I am the most miserable man in Cymric land. No beggar is more wretched than I."

Wyland, the monk, listened and his eyes glittered. There came into his head the idea of enriching the monastery. He saw his chance to win a bride for himself, and acted on it it at once. He could make money by solving the secret for a troubled soul.

"Prince Benlli," said he, "if you will bestow upon the monks of the White Minster, one tenth of all the flocks that feed within your domain, and one tenth of all that flows into the vaults of your palace, and hand over the maiden of the Green Forest to me, I shall warrant that your soul will be at peace and your troubles end."

To all this, Prince Benlli agreed, making solemn promise. Then the monk Wyland took his book, leather bound, and kept shut by means of metal clasps, and hid himself in the cranny of a rock near the Giant's Cave, from which there was an entrance down into Fairyland.

He had not long to wait, for soon, with a crown on her head, a lady, royally dressed, passed by out of the silvery moonlight into the dark cave. It was none other than the maiden of the Green Forest.

He moved forward to the mouth of the cave. Then summoning into his presence the spirits of the air and the cave, he informed them as to Benlli's vow to enrich the monastery, and to deliver the Green Forest Maiden to himself. Then, calling aloud, he said:

"Let her forever be, as she now appears, and never leave my side. Bring her, before the break of day, to the cross near the town of the White Minster, and there will I wed her, and swear to make her my own."

Then, by the power of his magic, he made it impossible for any person or power to recall or hinder the operation of these words. Leaving the cave's mouth, in order to be at the cross, before day should dawn, the first thing he met there was a hideous woman, grinning and rolling her bleared red eyes at him.

On her head seemed what was more like moss, than hair. She stretched out a long bony finger at him. On it flashed the splendid diamond, which Benlli had given his bride, the beautiful maiden of the Green Forest.

"Take me then, monk Wyland," she shrieked, laughing hideously and showing what looked like green snags in her mouth. "For I am the wife you are sworn to wed. Thirty years ago, I was Benlli's blooming bride and first wife. When my beauty left me, his love flew away but I won it back by my magic. Now I am a foul ogress, but magic makes me young again every seventh night. I promised that my beauty should last until the tall reeds and the long green rushes grow in his hall."

Amazed at her story, Wyland drew in his breath.

"And this promise, I have kept. It is already fulfilled. Your spell and mine are both completed. Yours brought to him the peace of the dead. Mine made the river floods rush in. Now, waters lap to and fro among the reeds and rushes that grow in the banqueting hall, which is now sunk deep below the earth. With the clash of our spells, no charm can redress our fate.

"Come then and take me as thy bride, for oath and spell have both decreed it as thy reward. As Benlli's promise to you is fulfilled, for the waters flow in the palace vaults, the pike and the dace feed there."

So, caught in his own dark, sordid plot, the monk, who played conjurer, had become the victim of his own craft.

They say that Wyland's Cross still recalls the monk, while fishermen on the Welsh border, can, on nights with smooth water, see towers and chimneys far below, sunk deep beneath the waves.

The Prince with the Nose

By Dinah Maria Mulock Craik

READING TIME: 12 MINUTES

*T*here was once a king who was passionately in love with a beautiful princess, but she could not be married because a magician had enchanted her. The king went to a good fairy to inquire what he should do. Said the fairy, after receiving him graciously:

"Sir, I will tell you a secret. The princess has a great cat whom she loves so well that she cares for nothing and nobody else; but she will be obliged to marry any person who is adroit enough to walk upon the cat's tail."

"That will not be very difficult," thought the king to

himself, and departed, resolving to trample the cat's tail to pieces rather than not succeed in walking upon it. He went immediately to the palace of his fair mistress and the cat; the animal came in front of him, arching its back in anger as it was wont to do. The king lifted up his foot, thinking nothing would be so easy as to tread on the tail, but he found himself mistaken. Minon – that was the creature's name – twisted itself round so sharply that the king only hurt his own foot by stamping on the floor. For eight days did he pursue the cat everywhere: up and down the palace he was after it from morning till night, but with no better success; the tail seemed made of quicksilver, so very lively was it. At last the king had the good fortune to catch Minon sleeping, when – *tramp, tramp* – he trod on the tail with all his force.

Minon woke up, mewed horribly, and immediately changed from a cat into a large, fierce-looking man, who regarded the king with flashing eyes.

"You must marry the princess," cried he, "because you have broken the enchantment in which I held her, but I will be revenged on you. You shall have a son with a nose as long as this," – he made in the air a curve of half a foot – "yet he shall believe it is just like all other noses, and shall be always unfortunate till he has found out it is not. And if you ever tell anybody of this threat, you shall die on the spot." So saying, the magician disappeared.

The king, who was at first much terrified, soon began to laugh at this adventure. 'My son might have a worse misfortune than too long a nose,' thought he. 'At least it will hinder him neither in seeing nor hearing. I will go and find the princess, and marry her at once.'

He did so, but he only lived a few months after, and died before his little son was born, so that nobody knew anything about the secret of the nose.

The little prince was so much wished for that when he came into the world they agreed to call him Prince Wish. He had beautiful blue eyes, and a sweet little mouth, but his nose was so big that it covered half his face. The queen, his mother, was inconsolable, but her ladies tried to satisfy her by telling her that the nose was not so large as it seemed, that it would grow smaller as the prince grew bigger, and that if it did not, a large nose was indispensable to a hero. All great soldiers, they said, had great noses, as everybody knew. The queen was so very fond of her son that she listened eagerly to all this comfort. She grew so used to the prince's nose that it did not seem to her any larger than ordinary noses of the court, where, in process of time, everybody with a long nose was very much admired, and the unfortunate people who had only snubs were taken little notice of.

Great care was observed in the education of the prince, and as soon as he could speak they told him all sorts of amusing tales, in which all the bad people had short noses, and all the good people had long ones. When he was old enough his tutor taught him history, and whenever any great king or lovely princess was referred to, the tutor always took care to mention that he or she had a long nose. All the royal apartments were filled with pictures and portraits having this peculiarity, so that at last Prince Wish began to regard the length of his nose as his greatest perfection.

When he was twenty years old his mother and his people wished him to marry. They procured for him the portraits of many princesses, but the one he preferred was Princess Darling, daughter of a powerful monarch and heiress to several kingdoms. Alas! With all her beauty, this princess had one great misfortune, a little turned-up nose, which, everyone else said, made her only the more bewitching. But here, in the kingdom of

Prince Wish, the courtiers were thrown by it into the
utmost perplexity. They were in the habit of laughing at
all small noses, but how dared they make fun of the nose
of Princess Darling?

They would have found themselves in constant
difficulties, had not one clever person struck out a bright
idea. He said that though it was necessary for a man to
have a great nose, women were different, and that a
learned man had discovered in a very old manuscript
that the celebrated Cleopatra, queen of Egypt, the
beauty of the ancient world, had a turned-up nose. At
this information Prince Wish was so delighted that he
immediately sent off ambassadors to demand Princess
Darling in marriage.

She accepted his offer at once, and returned with the
ambassadors. He made all haste to meet and welcome
her, but when she was only three leagues distant from his
capital, before he had time even to kiss her hand, the
magician who had once assumed the shape of his
mother's cat, Minon, appeared in the air and carried her
off before the lover's very eyes.

Prince Wish, almost beside himself with grief,
declared that nothing should induce him to return to his

throne and kingdom till he had found Princess Darling.
He mounted a good horse, laid the reins on the animal's
neck, and let him take him wherever he would.

The horse entered a wide, extended plain, and trotted
on steadily the whole day without finding a single house.
Master and beast began almost to faint with hunger, and
Prince Wish might have wished himself safe at home
again, had he not discovered, just at dusk, a cavern,
where sat beside a bright
lantern, a little woman who
might have been more than
a hundred years old.

She put on her spectacles
the better to look at the
stranger, and he noticed that
her nose was so small that
the spectacles would hardly
stay on. Then the prince
and the fairy – for it was a
fairy – burst into a mutual
fit of laughter.

"What a funny nose!" cried the one.

"Not so funny as yours, madam," returned the other.

"But pray let us leave our noses alone, and be good enough to give me something to eat, for I am dying with hunger, and so is my poor horse."

"With all my heart," answered the fairy. "Although your nose is ridiculously long, you are no less the son of one of my best friends. I loved your father like a brother. He had a very handsome nose."

"What is wanting to my nose?" asked Wish, rather savagely.

"Oh! Nothing at all. On the contrary, there is a great deal too much of it, but never mind, one may be a very honest man, and yet have too big a nose.

"I will give you some supper directly, and while you eat it I will tell you my history in six words, for I hate much talking. A long tongue is as insupportable as a long nose; and I remember when I was young how much I used to be admired because I was not a talker, indeed, my mother, for poor as you see me now, I am the daughter of a great king, who always—"

'Hang the king your father!' Prince Wish was about to exclaim, but he stopped himself, and only observed that however the pleasure of her conversation might make him forget his hunger, it could not have the same effect upon his horse, who was really starving.

The fairy, pleased at his civility, called her servants and bade them supply him at once with all he needed. "And," added she, "I must say you are very polite and very good-tempered, in spite of your nose."

"What has the old woman to do with my nose?" thought the prince. "If I were not so very hungry I would soon show her what she is – a regular old gossip and chatterbox. She fancies she talks little, indeed! One must be very foolish not to know one's own defects. This comes of being born a princess. Flatterers have spoiled her, and persuaded her that she talks little."

While the prince thus meditated, the servants were laying the table, the fairy asking them a hundred unnecessary questions, simply for the pleasure of hearing herself talk. 'Well,' thought Wish, 'I am delighted that I came hither, if only to learn how wise I have been in never listening to flatterers, who hide from us our faults, or make us believe they are perfections. But they could never deceive me. I know all my own weak points, I trust.' And truly he believed he did.

So he went on eating contentedly, nor stopped till the old fairy began to address him.

"Prince," said she, "will you be kind enough to turn a little? Your nose casts such a shadow that I cannot see what is on my plate. And, as I was saying, your father admired me and always made me welcome at court. What is the court etiquette there now? Do the ladies still go to assemblies, promenades, balls? I beg your pardon for laughing, but how very long your nose is."

"I wish you would cease to speak of my nose," said the prince, becoming annoyed. "It is what it is, and I do not desire it any shorter."

"Oh! I see that I have vexed you," returned the fairy. "Nevertheless, I am one of your best friends, and so I shall take the liberty of always—"

She would doubtless have gone on talking till midnight, but the prince, unable to bear it any longer, here interrupted her, thanked her for her hospitality, bade her a hasty adieu, and rode away.

He travelled for a long time, half over the world, but he heard no news of Princess Darling. However, in each place he went to, he heard one remarkable fact – the great length of his own nose. The little boys in the streets jeered at him, the peasants stared at him, and the more polite ladies and gentlemen whom he met in society

used to try in vain to keep from laughing, and to get out
of his way as soon as they could. So the poor prince
became gradually quite forlorn and solitary. He thought
all the world was mad, but still he never thought of there
being anything queer about his own nose.

At last the old fairy, who, though she was a
chatterbox, was very good-natured, saw that he was
almost breaking his heart. She felt sorry for him, and
wished to help, for she knew the enchantment, which
hid from him the Princess Darling, could not be broken
till he discovered his own defect. So she went in search
of the princess, and being more powerful than the
magician, she took her away from him, and shut her up
in a palace of crystal, which she placed on the road
which Prince Wish had to pass.

He was riding along, very melancholy, when he saw
the palace, and at its entrance was a room made of glass,
in which sat his beloved princess, smiling and beautiful
as ever. He leaped from his horse, and ran towards her.
She held out her hand for him to kiss, but he could not
get at it for the glass. Transported with eagerness and
delight, he dashed his sword through the crystal, and
succeeded in breaking a small opening, to which she put

up her beautiful rosy mouth. But it was in vain, Prince Wish could not approach it. He twisted his neck about, and turned his head on all sides, till at length, putting up his hand to his face, he discovered the impediment.

"It must be confessed," exclaimed he, "that my nose is too long."

That moment the glass walls all split asunder, and the old fairy appeared, leading Princess Darling.

"Admit, prince," said she, "that you are very much

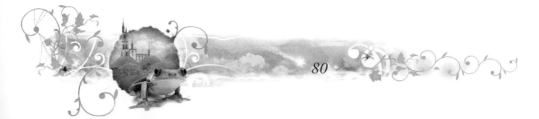

obliged to me, for now the enchantment is ended.
You may marry the object of your choice. But," added
she, smiling, "I fear I might have talked to you forever
on the subject of your nose, and you would not have
believed me in its length, till it became an obstacle to
your own inclinations. Now behold it!" and she held up
a crystal mirror. Are you satisfied to be no different from
other people?"

"Perfectly," said Prince Wish, who found his nose had
shrunk to an ordinary length. And, taking the Princess
Darling by the hand, he kissed her, courteously,
affectionately, and satisfactorily. Then they departed to
their own country, and lived very happy all their days.

The Man who would not Scold

By Norman Hinsdale Pitman

READING TIME: 12 MINUTES

Old Wang lived in a village near Nanking. He cared for nothing in the world but to eat good food and plenty of it. His greatest pleasure was to eat at someone else's table when he knew that the food would cost him nothing, and you may be sure that at such times he always licked his chopsticks clean. But when he was spending his own money, he tightened his belt and drank a great deal of water, eating very little but scraps such as his friends would have thrown to the dogs.

One day while Wang was lying half asleep on the bank of a stream that flowed near his house he saw a flock of ducks swimming in the river. He knew that they belonged to a rich man named Lin who lived in the village. They were fat ducks, so plump and tempting that it made him hungry to look at them. 'Oh, for a boiled duck!' he said to himself with a sigh. 'Why is it that the gods have not given me a taste of duck during the past year? What have I done to be thus denied?'

Then the thought flashed into his mind: 'Here am I asking why the gods have not given me ducks to eat. Who knows but that they have sent this flock thinking I would have sense enough to grab one? Friend Lin, many thanks for your kindness. I think I shall accept your offer and take one of these fowls for my dinner.' Of course Mr Lin was nowhere near to hear old Wang thanking him.

By this time the flock had come to shore. The miser picked himself up lazily from the ground, and, after tiring himself out, he at last managed to pick one of the ducks up, too. Once in his own yard, he lost no time in killing and preparing it for dinner. He ate it, laughing to himself all the time at his own slyness, and wondering what his friend Lin would think if he chanced to count his ducks that night. 'No doubt he will believe it was a hawk that carried off that bird. I think I will repeat the dose tomorrow. It would be a pity to leave the first one to pine away in lonely grief. I could never be so cruel.'

So old Wang went to bed happy. For several hours he snored away noisily. At midnight, however, he was wakened from his sleep by an unpleasant itching. His whole body seemed to be on fire, and the pain was more than he could bear. He got up and paced the floor. At early dawn he stepped outside his shanty. Lo, and behold, he found little red spots all over his body. Before his very eyes he saw tiny duck feathers sprouting from these spots. As the morning went by, the feathers grew larger and larger, until his whole body was covered with them from head to foot. Only his face and hands were free of the strange growth.

With a cry of horror, Wang began to pull the feathers out by handfuls, flinging them in the dirt and stamping on them. "The gods have fooled me!" he yelled. "They made me take the duck and eat it, and now they are punishing me for stealing." But the faster he jerked the feathers out, the faster they grew in again, longer and more glossy than before. Then, too, the pain was so great that he could scarcely keep from rolling on the ground. At last, completely worn out by his useless labour, and moaning with despair, he took to his bed. He tossed about on his bed but he could not sleep. His heart was sick with fear. Finally he fell into a troubled sleep, and, sleeping, had a dream.

A fairy came to his bedside, it was Fairy Old Boy, the friend of the people. "Ah, my poor Wang," said the fairy, "all this trouble you have brought upon yourself by your shiftless, lazy habits. When others work, why do you lie down and sleep your time away? Why don't you get up and shake your lazy legs? There is no place in the world for such a man as you except the pig-sty."

"I know you are telling the truth," wailed Wang, "but how, oh, how can I ever work with all these feathers sticking out of me? They will kill me! They will kill me!"

"Hear the man!" laughed Old Boy. "Now, if you were a hopeful, happy fellow, you would say, 'What a stroke of luck! No need to buy garments. The gods have given me a suit of clothes that will never wear out.' You are a pretty fellow to be complaining, aren't you?"

After joking in this way for a little while, the good fairy changed his tone of voice and said, "Now, Wang, are you really sorry for the way you have lived, sorry for your years of idleness, sorry because you disgraced your old Father and Mother? I hear your parents died of hunger because you would not help them."

Wang, seeing that Old Boy knew all about his past life, and, feeling his pain growing worse and worse every minute, cried out at last: "Yes! Yes! I will do anything you say. Only, I pray you, free me of these feathers!"

"I wouldn't have your feathers," said Old Boy, "and I cannot free you of them. You will have to do the whole thing yourself. What you need is to hear a good scolding. Go and get Mr Lin, the owner of the stolen duck, to scold freely. The harder he scolds, the sooner will your feathers drop out."

Mr Wang woke up very happy. He would go to Mr Lin, confess everything and take the scolding. Then he would be free of his feathers and would go to work. Truly he had led a lazy life. What the good Fairy Old Boy had said about his father and mother had hurt him very badly, for he knew that every word was true. From this day on, he would not be lazy. He would take a wife and become the father of a family.

Miser Wang meant all right when he started out from his shanty. From his little hoard of money he took enough cash to pay Mr Lin for the stolen duck. He would do everything the fairy had told him and even more. But this doing more was just where he got into trouble. As he walked along the road jingling the string of cash, and thinking that he must soon give it up to his neighbour, he grew very sad. He loved every copper of his money and he disliked to part with it. After all, Old Boy had not told him he must confess to the owner of the duck – he had said he must go to Lin and get Lin to give a good scolding. "Old Boy did not say that Lin must scold me," thought the miser. "All that I need do is to get him to scold, and then my feathers will drop off and I shall be happy. Why not tell him that old Sen stole his duck, and get him to give Sen a scolding? That will surely do just as well, and I shall save my money as well as my face. I shall fool Fairy Old Boy too. Really he had no right to speak of my father and mother in the way he did. After all, they died of fever, and I was no doctor to cure them. How could he say it was my fault?"

The longer Wang talked to himself, the surer he became that it was useless to tell Lin that he had stolen the duck. By the time he had reached the duck man's house he had fully made up his mind to deceive him. Mr Lin invited him to come in and sit down. He was a plain-spoken, honest kind of man, this Lin. Everybody liked him, for he never spoke ill of any man and he always had something good to say of his neighbours.

"Well, what's your business, Wang? You have come out early, and it's a long walk from your place to mine."

"Oh, I had something important I wanted to talk to you about," began Wang slyly. "That's a fine flock of ducks you have over in the meadow."

"Yes," said Mr Lin smiling, "a fine flock indeed." But he said nothing of the stolen fowl.

"How many have you?" questioned Wang more boldly.

"I counted them yesterday morning and there were fifteen."

"But did you count them again last night?"

"Yes, I did," answered Lin slowly.

"And there were only fourteen then?"

"Quite right, Wang, one of them was missing, but one duck is of little importance. Why do you speak of it?"

"What, no importance! Losing a duck? How can you say so? A duck's a duck, isn't it, and surely you would like to know how you lost it?"

"A hawk most likely."

"No, it wasn't a hawk, but if you would go and look in old Sen's duck yard, you would likely find feathers."

"Nothing more natural, I am sure, in a duck yard."

"Yes, but your duck's feathers," persisted Wang.

"What! You think old Sen is a thief, do you, and that he has been stealing from me?"

"Exactly! You have it now."

"Well, well, that is too bad! I am sorry the old fellow is having such a hard time. He is a good worker and

deserves better luck. I should willingly have given him the duck if he had only asked for it. Too bad that he had to steal it."

Wang waited to see how Mr Lin planned to punish the thief, feeling sure that the least he could do, would be to go and give him a good scolding.

But nothing of the kind happened. Instead of growing angry, Mr Lin seemed to be sorry for Sen, sorry that he was poor, sorry that he was willing to steal.

"Aren't you even going to give him a scolding?" asked Wang in disgust.

"What use, what use? Hurt a neighbour's feelings just for a duck? That would be foolish indeed."

By this time the Miser King had begun to feel an itching all over his body. The feathers had begun hurting again, and he was frightened once more. He became excited and threw himself on the floor in front of Mr Lin.

"Hey! What's the matter, man?" cried Lin, thinking Wang was in a fit. "What's the matter? Are you ill?"

"Yes, very ill," wailed Wang. "Mr Lin, I'm a bad man, and I may as well own it at once and be done with it. There is no use trying to dodge the truth or hide a fault.

I stole your duck last night, and today I came sneaking over here and tried to put the thing off on old Sen."

"Yes, I knew it," answered Lin. "I saw you carrying the duck off under your garment. Why did you come to see me at all if you thought I did not know you were guilty?"

"Only wait, and I'll tell you everything," said Wang, bowing still lower. "After I had boiled your duck and eaten it, I went to bed. Pretty soon I felt an itching all over my body. I could not sleep and in the morning I found that I had a thick growth of duck's feathers from head to foot. The more I pulled them out, the thicker they grew in. I could hardly keep from screaming. I took to my bed, and after I had tossed about for hours a fairy came and told me that I could never get rid of my trouble unless I got you to give me a thorough scolding. Here is the money for your duck. Now for the love of mercy, scold, and do it quickly, for I can't stand the pain much longer."

Wang was grovelling in the dirt at Lin's feet, but Lin answered him only with a loud laugh which finally burst into a roar. "Duck feathers! Ha! Ha! Ha! and all over your body? Why, that's too good a story to believe!

You'll be wanting to live in the water next. Ha! Ha! Ha!"

"Scold me! Scold me!" begged Wang, "For the love of the gods scold me!"

But Lin only laughed the louder. "Pray let me see this wonderful growth of feathers first, and then we'll talk about the scolding."

Wang willingly opened his garment and showed the doubting Lin that he had been really speaking the truth.

"They must be warm," said Lin, laughing. "Winter is soon coming and you are not over fond of work. Won't they save you the trouble of wearing clothing?"

"But they make me itch so I can scarcely stand it! I feel like screaming out, the pain is so great,"

"Be calm, my friend, and give me time to think of some good scold-words," said Lin at last. "I am not in the habit of using strong language, and very seldom lose my temper. Really you must give me time to think of what to say."

By this time Wang was in such pain that he lost all power over himself. He seized Mr Lin by the legs crying out, "Scold me! Scold me!"

Mr Lin was now out of patience with his visitor. Besides Wang was holding him so tightly that it really

felt as if Lin were being pinched by some gigantic crawfish. Suddenly Lin could hold his tongue no longer:

"You lazy hound! You whelp! You turtle! You lazy, good-for-nothing creature! I wish you would hurry up and roll out of this!"

Now, in China, this is very strong language, and, with a cry of joy, Wang leaped from the ground, for he knew that Lin had scolded him. No sooner had the first hasty words been spoken than the feathers began falling from the lazy man's body, and, at last, the dreadful itching had entirely stopped. On the floor in front of Lin lay a great pile of feathers, and Wang, freed from his trouble, said, "Thank you kindly, my dear friend, for the pretty names you have called me. You have saved my life, I have learned my lesson well, I hope, and I shall go out from here a better man. Fairy Old Boy told me that I was lazy. You agree with the fairy. From this day, however, you shall see that I can bend my back like a good fellow. Goodbye, and many thanks for your kindness."

So saying, with many low bows and polite words, Wang left the duck owner's house, a happier and a wiser man.

Sweet-One-Darling and the Dream-Fairies 96

Eva's Visit to Fairyland 104

Betty and the Wood Maiden 118

The Counterpane Fairy 129

Children and Fairies

Puck of Pook's Hill 143

My Own Self 163

The Boy Who Wanted More Cheese 168

Sweet-One-Darling and the Dream-Fairies

By Eugene Field

READING TIME: 8 MINUTES

A wonderful thing happened one night. Sweet-One-Darling was lying in her cradle, and she was trying to make up her mind whether she should go to sleep or keep awake. Sweet-One-Darling was ready for sleep and dreams. She had on her nightgown and her nightcap, and her mother had kissed her goodnight. But the day had been so very pleasant, with its sunshine and its play, that Sweet-One-Darling was unwilling to give it up. It was high time for the

little girl to be asleep. A cricket was chirping, and some folk believe that the cricket is in league with the Dream-Fairies. They say that what sounds to us like a faint chirping is actually the call of the cricket to the Dream-Fairies to let those creatures know that it is time for them to come with their dreams. I more than half believe this myself, for I have noticed that it is while the cricket is chirping that the Dream-Fairies come with their wonderful sights that seem oftentimes very real.

Then, all of a sudden, there was a faint sound as of the rustle of gossamer, silken wings, and the next moment two of the sweetest fairies you ever saw were standing upon the windowsill, just over the honeysuckle.

They had come from Somewhere, and it was evident that they were searching for somebody, for they peered cautiously and eagerly into the room. One was dressed in a bright yellow suit of butterfly silk and the other wore a suit of dark-grey mothzine, which (as perhaps you know) is a dainty fabric made of the fine strands which grey moths spin. Both of these fairies together would not have weighed much more than the one-sixteenth part of four dewdrops.

"Sweet-One-Darling! Oh, Sweet-One-Darling!" they cried softly. "Where are you?"

Sweet-One-Darling pretended that she did not hear, and she cuddled down close in her cradle and laughed, all to herself. The mischievous little thing knew well enough whom they were calling but she meant to fool them and hide from them awhile – that is why she did not answer. But nobody can hide from the Dream-Fairies, and least of all could Sweet-One-Darling hide from them, for presently her laughter betrayed her and the two Dream-Fairies perched on her cradle – one at each side – and looked smilingly down upon her.

"Hello!" said Sweet-One-Darling.

This was the first time I had ever heard her speak, and

I did not know till then that even wee little babies talk
with fairies, particularly Dream-Fairies.

"Hello, Sweet-One-Darling!" said Gleam-of-the-
Dark, for that was the name of the Dream-Fairy in the
dark-grey mothzine.

"And hello from me, too!" cried Frisk-and-Glitter,
the other visitor – the one in the butterfly-silk suit.

"You have come earlier than usual," suggested Sweet-
One-Darling.

"No, indeed," answered Frisk-and-Glitter, "But the
day has been so happy that it has passed quickly. For that
reason you should be glad to see me, for I bring dreams
of the day – the beautiful golden day, with its sunlight,
its grace of warmth, and its mirth and play."

"And I," said Gleam-o'-the-Dark, "I bring dreams,
too. But my dreams are of the night, and they are full of
the gentle, soothing music of the winds, of the pines, and
of the crickets! And they are full of fair visions in which
you shall see the things of Fairyland and of Dreamland
and of all the mysterious countries that compose the vast
world of Somewhere away out beyond the silvery mist
of night."

"Oh!" cried Sweet-One-Darling. "I should never be

able to make a choice between you two. I would love to have the play of the daytime brought back to me, and I am quite as sure that I want to see all the pretty sights that are unfolded by the dreams which Gleam-of-the-Dark brings."

"You have no need to feel troubled," said Frisk-and-Glitter, "for you are not expected to make any choice between us. We have our own way of solving the question, as you shall presently understand."

Then the Dream-Fairies explained that whenever they came of an evening to bring their dreams to a little child they seated themselves on the child's eyelids and tried to rock them down. Gleam-of-the-Dark would sit and rock upon one eyelid and Frisk-and-Glitter would sit and rock on the other. If Gleam-of-the-Dark's eyelid closed first, the child would dream the dreams Gleam-of-the-Dark brought it. If Frisk-and-Glitter's eyelid closed first, why, then, of course, the child dreamt the dreams Frisk-and-Glitter brought.

"But suppose," suggested Sweet-One-Darling, "suppose both eyelids close at the same instant? Which one of you fairies has his own way, then?"

"Ah, in that event," said they, "neither of us wins, and,

since neither wins, the sleeper does not dream at all, but awakes next morning from a sound, dreamless, refreshing sleep."

Sweet-One-Darling was not sure that she fancied this alternative, but of course she could not help herself. So she let the two little Dream-Fairies flutter across her shoulders and clamber up her cheeks to their proper places upon her eyelids.

Gracious! How heavy they seemed when they stood on her eyelids! As I told you before, their actual combined weight hardly exceeded the sixteenth part of four dewdrops, yet when they are perched on a little child's eyelids (tired eyelids at that) it really seems sometimes as if they weighed a tonne! It was just all she could do to keep her eyelids open, yet Sweet-One-Darling was determined to be strictly fair. She loved both the Dream-Fairies equally

well, and she would not for all the world have shown either one any favouritism.

Well, there the two Dream-Fairies sat on Sweet-One-Darling's eyelids, each one trying to rock his particular eyelid down, and each one sung his little lullaby in the pipingest voice imaginable. This was very soothing, as you would suppose. It was the most exciting contest (for an amicable one) I ever saw. As for Sweet-One-Darling, she seemed to be lost presently in the magic of the Dream-Fairies, and although she has never said a word about it to me I am quite sure that, while her dear eyelids drooped and drooped and drooped to the rocking and the singing of the Dream-Fairies, she enjoyed a confusion of all those precious things promised by her two fairy visitors. Yes, I am sure that from under her drooping eyelids she beheld the scenes of the day mingled with peeps of fairyland. And when at last she was fast asleep I could not say for certain which of her eyelids had closed first, so simultaneous was the downfall of her long dark lashes upon her flushed cheeks. I meant to have asked the Dream-Fairies about it, but before I could do so they whisked out of the window and away with their dreams to a very sleepy little boy who was waiting for them somewhere in the neighbourhood. So you see I am unable to tell you which of the Dream-Fairies won. Maybe neither did, maybe Sweet-One-Darling's sleep that night was dreamless. I have questioned her about it and she will not answer me.

This is all the wonderful tale I had to tell. Maybe it will not seem so wonderful to you, for perhaps you, too, have felt the Dream-Fairies rocking your eyelids down with gentle lullaby music. Perhaps you, too, know all the precious dreams they bring. In that case you will bear witness that my tale, even though it be not wonderful, is strictly true.

Eva's Visit to Fairyland

By Louisa M Alcott

READING TIME: 15 MINUTES

Down among the grass and fragrant clover lay little Eva by the brook-side, watching the bright waves, as they went singing by under the drooping flowers that grew on its banks. As she was wondering where the waters went, she heard a faint, low sound, as of far-off music. She thought it was the wind, but not a leaf was stirring, and soon through the rippling water came a strange little boat.

It was a lily of the valley, whose tall stem formed the mast, while the broad leaves that rose from the roots, and drooped again till they reached the water, were filled with

fairies, who danced to the music of the silver lily-bells above that rang a merry peal, and filled the air with their fragrant breath.

On came the fairy boat till it reached a moss-grown rock, and here it stopped, while the fairies rested beneath the violet leaves, and sang with the dancing waves.

Eva looked with wonder and threw crimson fruit for the little folks to feast upon.

They looked kindly on the child, and, after whispering long among themselves, two little bright-eyed elves flew over the shining water, and, lighting on the clover blossoms, said gently, "Little maiden, many thanks for your kindness, our queen bids us ask if you will go with us to Fairyland, and learn what we can teach you."

"I would go with you, dear fairies," said Eva, "but I cannot sail in your little boat. See! I can hold you in my hand, and could not live among you without harming your tiny kingdom, I am so large."

Then the elves laughed, saying, "You are a good child to fear doing harm to those weaker than yourself. Look in the water and see what we have done."

Eva looked into the brook, and saw a tiny child standing between the elves. "Now I can go with you," said she, "but I can no longer step from the bank to yonder stone, for the brook seems now like a great river, and you have not given me wings like yours."

But the fairies took each a hand, and flew lightly over the stream. The queen and her subjects came to meet her. "Now must we go home," said the queen, "and you shall go with us, little one."

Then there was a great bustle, as they flew about on shining wings, some laying cushions of violet leaves in the boat, others folding the queen's veil and mantle more closely round her, lest the falling dews should chill her.

The cool waves' gentle splashing against the boat, and the sweet chime of the lily-bells, lulled little Eva to sleep, and when she woke it was in Fairyland. A faint, rosy light, as of the setting sun, shone on the white pillars of the queen's palace as they passed in. They led Eva to a bed of pure white leaves, above which drooped the fragrant petals of a crimson rose.

With the sun rose the fairies, and, with Eva, hastened away to the fountain, whose cool waters were soon filled with little forms, as the elves floated in the blue waves among the fair white lilies, or sat on the green moss, smoothing their bright locks, and wearing fresh garlands of dewy flowers. Then they flew away to the gardens, and soon, high up among the tree-tops, or under the broad leaves, sat the elves in little groups, taking their breakfast of fruit and pure fresh dew, while the bright-winged birds came fearlessly among them, pecking the same ripe berries, and dipping their little beaks in the same flower cups.

"Now, little Eva," said they, "you will see that Fairies are not idle, wilful spirits, as mortals believe. Come, we will show you what we do."

They led her to a lovely room, through whose walls of deep green leaves the light stole softly in. Here lay many wounded insects, and creatures, and pale, drooping flowers grew beside urns of healing herbs, from whose fresh leaves came a faint, sweet perfume.

Eva wondered, but silently followed her guide, little Rose-Leaf, who went to the insects – first to a little fly who lay in a flower-leaf cradle.

"Do you suffer much, dear Gauzy-Wing?" asked the Fairy. "I will bind up your poor little leg." So she folded the cool leaves tenderly about the poor fly, bathed his wings, and brought him refreshing drink, while he hummed his thanks, and forgot his pain.

They passed on, and Eva saw beside each bed a fairy, who with gentle hands and loving words soothed the suffering insects.

Then Rose-Leaf led Eva away, saying, "Come now to the Flower Palace, and see the Fairy Court."

Beneath green arches, bright with birds and flowers, went Eva into a lofty hall. The roof of pure white lilies

rested on pillars of green clustering vines, while many-coloured blossoms threw their bright shadows on the walls, as they danced below in the deep green moss.

Suddenly the music grew louder and sweeter, and the fairies knelt, and bowed their heads, as on through the crowd of loving subjects came the queen, while the air was filled with gay voices singing to welcome her.

She placed the child beside her, saying, "Little Eva, you shall see now how the flowers on your great earth bloom so brightly. A band of loving little gardeners go daily forth from Fairyland, to tend and watch them Now, Eglantine, what have you to tell us of your rosy namesakes on the earth?"

From a group of elves, whose rose-wreathed wands showed the flower they loved, came one bearing a tiny urn, and, answering the queen, she said:

"Over hill and valley they are blooming fresh and fair as summer sun and dew can make them and this, the loveliest of their sisters, have I brought to place among the fairy flowers that never pass away." Eglantine laid the urn before the queen, and placed the fragrant rose on the dewy moss beside the throne, while a murmur of approval went through the hall, as each wand waved

to the little fairy who could bring so fair a gift to their
good queen.

Said little Rose-Leaf to Eva, "Come now and see
where we are taught to read the tales written on flower-
leaves, and the sweet language of the birds, and all that
can make a fairy heart wiser and better."

Then into a cheerful place they went, where were
many groups of flowers, among whose leaves sat the
child elves, and learned from their flower-books all that
fairy hands had written there. Some studied how to
watch the tender buds – when to spread them to the
sunlight, and when to shelter them from rain, how to
guard the ripening seeds, and when to lay them in the
warm earth or send them on the summer wind to far off
hills and valleys, where other fairy hands would tend and
cherish them. Others learned to heal the wounded
insects, who, were it not for fairy hands, would die
before half their happy summer life had gone. Eva
nodded to the little ones, as they peeped from among
the leaves at the stranger, and then she listened to the
fairy lessons. Several tiny elves sat on leaves while the
teacher sat among the petals of a flower beside them, and
asked questions that none but fairies would care to know.

"Twinkle, if there lay nine seeds within a flower cup and the wind bore five away, how many would the blossom have?"

"Four," replied the little one.

"Rosebud, if a cowslip opens three leaves in one day and four the next, how many rosy leaves will there be when the whole flower has bloomed?"

"Seven," sang the gay little elf.

"Harebell, if a silkworm spins one yard of fairy cloth in an hour, how many will it spin in a day?"

"Twelve," said the fairy child.

"Primrose, where lies Violet Island?"

"In the Lake of Ripples."

"Lilla, what are the bounds of Rose Land?"

"On the north by Ferndale, south by Sunny Wave River, east by the hill of Morning Clouds, and west by the Evening Star."

"Now, little ones," said the teacher, "you may go to your painting."

Then Eva saw how, on large, white leaves, the fairies learned to imitate the lovely colours, and with tiny brushes to brighten the blush on the anemone's cheek, to deepen the blue of the violet's eye, and add new light to the golden cowslip.

"You have stayed long enough," said the elves at length, "we have many things to show you. Come now and see what is our dearest work."

So Eva said farewell to the child elves, and hastened with little Rose-Leaf to the gates. Here she saw many bands of fairies, folded in dark mantles that mortals might not know them, who, with the child among them, flew away over hill and valley. Some went to the cottages amid the hills, some to the seaside to watch above the humble fisher folks, but little Rose-Leaf and many others went into the noisy city.

Eva wondered within herself what good the tiny elves could do in this great place, but she soon learned, for the fairy band went among the poor and friendless, bringing pleasant dreams to the sick and old, sweet, tender thoughts of love and gentleness to the young, strength to the weak, and patient cheerfulness to the poor and lonely.

Thus to all who needed help or comfort went the faithful fairies, and when at length they turned towards Fairyland, many were the grateful, happy hearts they left behind.

All Fairyland was dressed in flowers, and the soft wind went singing by, laden with their fragrant breath. Sweet music sounded through the air, and troops of elves in their gayest robes hastened to the palace where the feast was spread.

Soon the hall was filled with smiling faces and fair forms, and little Eva, as she stood beside the queen, thought she had never seen a sight so lovely.

The many-coloured shadows of the fairest flowers
played on the pure white walls, and fountains sparkled in
the sunlight, making music as the cool waves rose and
fell, while to and fro, with waving wings and joyous
voices, went the smiling elves, bearing fruit and honey,
or fragrant garlands for each other's hair.

Long they feasted, gaily they sang, and Eva, dancing
merrily among them, longed to be an elf that she might
dwell forever in so fair a home.

At length the music ceased, and the queen said, as she
laid her hand on little Eva's shining hair:

"Dear child, tomorrow we must bear you home,
therefore we will guide you to the brook-side, and there
say farewell till you come again to visit us. Nay, do not
weep, dear Rose-Leaf, you shall watch over little Eva's
flowers, and when she looks at them she will think of
you. Come now and lead her to the fairy garden, and
show her what we think our fairest sight."

With Rose-Leaf by her side, they led her through the
palace, and along green, winding paths, till Eva saw what
seemed a wall of flowers rising before her, while the air
was filled with the most fragrant odours, and the low,
sweet music as of singing blossoms.

"Where have you brought me, and what mean these lovely sounds?" asked Eva.

"Look here, and you shall see," said Rose-Leaf, as she bent aside the vines, "but listen silently or you cannot hear."

Then Eva, looking through the drooping vines, beheld a garden filled with the loveliest flowers. Fair as were all the blossoms she had seen in Fairyland, none were so beautiful as these. The rose glowed with a deeper crimson, the lily's soft leaves were more purely white, the crocus and humble cowslip shone like sunlight, and the violet was blue as the sky that smiled above it.

"How beautiful they are," whispered Eva, "but, dear Rose-Leaf, why do you keep them here, and why call you this your fairest sight?"

"Look again, and I will tell you," answered the fairy.

Eva looked, and saw from every flower a tiny form come forth to welcome the elves, who all, save Rose-Leaf, had flown above the wall, and were now scattering dew upon the flowers' bright leaves and talking gaily with the spirits, who gathered around them, and seemed full of joy that they had come. The child saw that each one wore the colours of the flower that was its home.

Delicate and graceful were the little forms, bright the
silken hair that fell about each lovely face, and Eva heard
the low, sweet murmur of their silvery voices and the
rustle of their wings. She gazed in silent
wonder, forgetting she knew not who they
were, till the fairy said:

"These are the spirits of the flowers,
and this the fairy home where they come
to bloom in fadeless beauty here, when their
earthly life is past. Come now, for you have
seen enough, and we must be away."

On a rosy morning cloud, went
Eva through the sunny sky. The fresh
wind bore them gently on, and soon
they stood again beside the brook,
whose waves danced brightly as
if to welcome them.

"Now, we say farewell,"
said the queen, as they gathered
nearer to the child.

They clung about her
tenderly, and little Rose-Leaf
placed a flower crown on her

head, whispering softly, "When you would come to us again, stand by the brook-side and wave this in the air, and we will gladly take you to our home again.

Farewell, dear Eva. Think of your little Rose-Leaf when among the flowers."

For a long time Eva watched their shining wings, and listened to the music of their voices as they flew singing home, and when at length the last little form had vanished among the clouds, she saw that all around her where the elves had been, the fairest flowers had sprung up, and the lonely brook-side was a blooming garden.

Thus she stood among the waving blossoms, with the fairy garland in her hair, and happy feelings in her heart, better and wiser for her visit to Fairyland.

Betty and the Wood Maiden

By A H Wratislaw

READING TIME: 12 MINUTES

Many fairy stories involve spinning, a skill many girls had to learn to help their mothers weave linen. In this story, Betty takes her goats into the woods to feed every day, and while watching them, she must spin rough flax into thread. She uses a spindle, like a stick, to spin the thread but she is too poor to own a distaff, the tool which holds the raw fibre before it is spun. Her mother then reels the thread off the spindle into skeins (coils) ready for weaving.

*B*etty was a little girl. Her mother was a widow, and had no more of her property left than a dilapidated cottage and two she-goats, but Betty was, nevertheless, always cheerful.

From spring to autumn she pastured the goats in the birch wood. Whenever she went from home, her mother always gave her in a basket a slice of bread and a spindle, with the order, "Let it be full."

As she had no distaff, she used to twine the flax round her head. Betty took the basket and skipped off singing merrily after the goats to the birch wood. When she got there, the goats went after pasture, and Betty sat under a tree, drew the fibres from her head with her left hand, and let down the spindle with her right so that it just hummed over the ground, and therewith she sang till the wood echoed. When the sun indicated midday, she put aside her spindle, called the goats, and after giving them each a morsel of bread that they mightn't stray from her, bounded into the wood for a few strawberries or any other woodland fruit that might happen to be just then in season, that she might have dessert to her bread.

When she had finished her meal, she sprang up, danced and sang. After her dance, she spun again industriously, and at even, when she drove the goats home, her mother never scolded her for bringing back her spindle empty.

Once, when according to custom, exactly at midday, after her scanty dinner, she was getting ready for a dance, all of a sudden – where she came, there she came – a very beautiful maiden stood before her. She had on a white dress as fine as gossamer, golden-coloured hair flowed from her head to her waist, and on her head she wore a garland of woodland flowers. Betty was struck dumb with astonishment. The maiden smiled at her, and said in an attractive voice, "Betty, are you fond of dancing?"

When the maiden spoke so prettily to her, Betty's terror quitted her, and she answered, "Oh, I should like to dance all day long!"

"Come, then, let's dance together. I'll teach you!" So spoke the maiden, tucked her dress up on one side, took Betty by the waist, and began to dance with her. As they circled, such delightful music sounded over their heads, that Betty's heart skipped within her. It was a company of choice musicians that had come together at the beck of the beautiful maiden – nightingales, larks, linnets, goldfinches, greenfinches, thrushes, blackbirds, and a very skilful mockingbird. Betty's cheek flamed, her eyes glittered, she forgot her task and her goats, and only gazed at her partner, who twirled before and round her

with the most charming
movements, and so lightly
that the grass didn't
even bend
beneath her
delicate foot. They
danced from noon till
eve, and Betty's feet
were neither wearied
nor painful. Then the
beautiful maiden
stopped, the music
ceased, and as she came so
she disappeared. Betty
looked about her. The
sun was setting behind the wood. She suddenly
remembered the unspun flax, and saw that her spindle,
which was lying on the grass, was by no means full. She
called the goats, and drove them home. The goats,
hearing no merry song behind them, looked round to see
whether their own shepherdess was really following
them. Her mother, too, wondered, and asked her
daughter whether she was ill, as she didn't sing.

"No, mother dear, I'm not ill, but my throat is dry from singing, and therefore I don't sing," said Betty in excuse, and went to put away the spindle and the unspun flax.

Knowing that her mother was not in the habit of reeling up the yarn at once, she intended to make up the next day what she had neglected to do the first day, and therefore did not say a word to her mother about the beautiful maiden.

The next day Betty again drove the goats as usual to the birch wood, and sang to herself again merrily. On arriving at the birch wood the goats began to pasture, and she sat under the tree and began to spin industriously, The sun indicated midday. Betty went off for strawberries, and after returning began to eat her dinner and chatter with the goats. "Ah, my little goats, I mustn't dance today," sighed she.

"And why mustn't you?" spoke a pleasing voice, and the beautiful maiden stood beside her, as if she had dropped from the clouds.

Betty answered modestly:

"Excuse me, beautiful lady, I can't dance with you, because I should again fail to perform my task of

spinning, and my mother would scold me. Today, before the sun sets, I must make up what I left undone yesterday."

"Only come and dance, and before the sun sets help will be found for you," said the maiden. She tucked up her dress, took Betty round the waist, the musicians sitting on the birch branches struck up, and the two dancers began to whirl.

At last the dancer stopped, the music ceased, the sun was on the verge of setting. Betty clapped her hand on the top of her head, where the unspun flax was twined, and began to cry. The beautiful maiden put her hand on her head, took off the flax, twined it round the stem of a slender birch, seized the spindle, and began to spin. The spindle just swung over the surface of the ground, grew fuller before her eyes, and before the sun set behind the wood all the yarn was spun, as well as that which Betty had not finished the day before. While giving the full spool into the girl's hand the beautiful maiden said: "Reel, and grumble not – remember my words – Reel, and grumble not!" After these words she vanished, as if the ground had sunk in beneath her. Betty was content, and thought on her way, 'If she is so good and kind, I will dance with her again if she comes again.' But her mother gave her no cheerful welcome. Wishing in the course of the day to reel the yarn, she saw that the spindle was not full, and was therefore out of humour.

"What were you doing yesterday that you didn't finish your task?" asked her mother reprovingly.

"Pardon, mother – I danced a little too long," said Betty humbly, and, showing her mother the spindle, added: "Today it is more than full to make up for it." Her mother said no more, but went to milk the goats, and Betty put the spindle away. She wished to tell her mother of her adventure, but bethought herself again, 'No, not unless she comes again, and then I will ask her what kind of person she is, and will tell my mother.'

The third morning, as usual, she drove the goats to the birch wood. The goats began to pasture. Betty sat under the tree, and began to sing and spin. The sun indicated midday. Betty laid her spindle on the grass, gave each of the goats a morsel of bread, collected strawberries, ate her dinner, and while giving the crumbs to the birds, said:

"My little goats, I will dance to you today!" She jumped up, folded her hands, and was just going to see if she could manage to dance as prettily as the beautiful

maiden, when all at once she herself stood before her.

"Let's go together, together!" said she to Betty, seized her round the waist, and at the same moment the music struck up over their heads, and the maidens circled round with flying step. Betty forgot her spindle and her goats, saw nothing but the beautiful maiden, whose body bent in every direction like a willow-wand, and thought of nothing but the delightful music, in tune with which her feet bounded of their own accord. They danced from midday till evening. Then the maiden stopped, and the music ceased.

Betty looked round. The sun was behind the wood. With tears she clasped her hands on the top of her head, and turning in search of the half-empty spindle, lamented about what her mother would say to her.

"Give me your basket," said the beautiful maiden. "I will make up to you for what you have left undone today."

Betty handed her the basket, and the maiden disappeared for a moment, and afterwards handed Betty the basket again, saying, "Not now – look at it at home," and was gone, as if the wind had blown her away.

Betty was afraid to peep into the basket immediately,

but halfway home she couldn't restrain herself. The basket was as light as if there was just nothing in it. She couldn't help looking to see whether the maiden hadn't tricked her. And how frightened she was when she saw that the basket was full – of birch leaves! In anger she threw out two handfuls of leaves, and was going to shake the basket out, but then she bethought herself, 'I will use them as litter for the goats,' and left some leaves in the basket. She was almost afraid to go home.

Her mother was waiting for her on the threshold, full of anxiety. "For heaven's sake, girl! What sort of spool did you bring me home yesterday?" were her first words.

"Why?" asked Betty anxiously.

"When you went out in the morning, I went to reel. I reeled and reeled, and the spool still remained full. One skein, two, three skeins, the spool still full.

"'What evil spirit has spun it?' said I in a temper, and that instant the yarn vanished from the spindle, as if it were spirited away. Tell me what the meaning of this is!"

Then Betty confessed, and began to tell about the beautiful maiden.

"That was a wood-fairy!" cried her mother in astonishment. "About midday and midnight the wood-

ladies hold their dances. Lucky that you are not a boy, or you wouldn't have come out of her arms alive. She would have danced with you as long as there was breath in your body, or have tickled you to death. But they have compassion on girls, and often give them rich presents. It's a pity that you didn't tell me. If I hadn't spoken in a temper, I might have had a room full of yarn."

Then Betty bethought herself of the basket, and it occurred to her that perhaps, after all, there might have been something under those leaves. She took out the spindle and unspun flax from the top, and looked once more, and, "See, mother!" she cried out. Her mother looked and clapped her hands. The birch leaves were turned into gold!

"She ordered me: 'Don't look now, but at home!' but I did not obey."

"Lucky that you didn't empty out the whole basket,"

said her mother. The next morning she went herself to
look at the place where Betty had thrown out the two
handfuls of leaves, but on the road there lay nothing but
fresh birch leaves. But the riches that Betty had brought
home were large enough. Her mother bought a small
estate, and they had many cattle. Betty had handsome
clothes, and was not obliged to pasture goats. But
whatever she had, however cheerful and happy she was,
nothing ever gave her so great delight as the dance with
the wood-lady. She often went to the birch wood. She
hoped for the good fortune of seeing the beautiful
maiden – but she never set eyes on her again.

The Counterpane Fairy

By Katharine Pyle

READING TIME: 15 MINUTES

*T*eddy was all alone, for his mother had been up with him so much the night before that at four o'clock in the afternoon she said that she was going to lie down.

She set a glass of milk on the table beside his bed, and left the door ajar so that he could call Hannah, the cook, if he wanted anything, and then she had gone to her room.

The little boy had always enjoyed being ill, for then he was read aloud to and had lemonade, but this had been a real illness, and though he was better now, the doctor still would not let him have anything but milk and gruel. He

was feeling rather lonely, too, though the fire crackled
cheerfully, and he could hear Hannah singing to herself
in the kitchen below.

He lay staring out of the window at the grey clouds
sweeping across the April sky. He grew lonelier
and lonelier and a lump rose in his
throat. A big tear trickled
down his cheek and dripped
off his chin.

"Oh dear, oh
dear!" said a little
voice just back of the
hill his knees made as
he lay with them
drawn up in bed,
"What a hill to climb!"

Teddy stopped crying and gazed wonderingly at
where the voice came from, and over the top of his knees
appeared a brown peaked hood, a tiny withered face,
a brown cloak, and last of all two small feet in buckled
shoes. It was a little old woman, so weazened and brown
that she looked more like a dried leaf than anything else.

She seated herself on Teddy's knees and gazed at him

solemnly, and she was so light that he felt her weight no more than if she had been a feather.

Teddy lay staring at her for a while, and then he asked, "Who are you?"

"I'm the Counterpane Fairy," said the little figure, in a thin little voice. "I came to you, because you were lonely and sick, and I thought maybe you would like me to show you a story."

"Do you mean tell me a story?" asked Teddy.

"No," said the fairy, "I mean show you a story. It's a game I invented after I joined the Counterpane Fairies. Choose any one of the squares of the counterpane and I will show you how to play it. That's all you have to do – choose a square."

Teddy looked the counterpane over carefully. "I think I'll choose that yellow square," he said, "because it looks so nice and bright."

"Very well," said the Counterpane Fairy. "Look straight at it and don't turn your eyes away until I count seven times seven and then you shall see the story of it."

Teddy fixed his eyes on the square and the fairy began to count. "One – two – three – four," she counted, Teddy heard her voice, thin and clear as the hissing of

the logs on the hearth. "Don't look away from the square," she cried. "Five – six – seven," it seemed to Teddy that the yellow silk square was turning to a mist before his eyes and wrapping everything about him in a golden glow. "Thirteen – fourteen," the fairy counted on and on. "Forty-six – forty-seven – forty-eight – *forty-nine!*"

At the words 'forty-nine', the Counterpane Fairy clapped her hands and Teddy looked about him. He was no longer in a golden mist. He was standing in a wonderful enchanted garden. The sky was like the golden sky at sunset, and the grass was so thickly set with tiny yellow flowers that it looked like a golden carpet. From this garden stretched a long flight of glass steps. They reached up and up and up to a great golden castle with shining domes and turrets.

"Listen!" said the Counterpane Fairy. "In that golden castle there lies an enchanted princess. For more than a hundred years she has been lying there waiting for the hero who is to come and rescue her, and you are the hero who can do it if you will."

With that the fairy led him to a little pool close by, and bade him look in the water. When Teddy looked, he saw himself standing there in the golden garden, and he did not appear as he ever had before. He was tall and strong and beautiful, like a hero.

"Yes," said Teddy, "I will do it."

Without pausing longer, he ran to the glass steps and began to mount them.

Up and up and up he went. Once he turned and waved his hand to the Counterpane Fairy in the golden garden below. She waved her hand, and he heard her voice faint and clear, "Goodbye! Goodbye! Be brave and strong, and beware of that that is little and grey."

Then Teddy turned his face toward the castle, and in a moment he was standing before the great shining gates.

He raised his hand and struck bravely upon the door. There was no answer. Again he struck upon it, and his blow rang through the hall inside. Then he opened the door and went in.

The hall was five-sided, and all of pure gold, as clear and shining as glass. Upon three sides of it were three arched doors – one was of emerald, one was of ruby, and one was of diamond. They were arched, and tall, and wide – fit for a hero to go through. The question was, behind which one lay the enchanted princess?

While Teddy stood there looking at them and wondering, he heard a little thin voice, that seemed to be singing to itself, and this is what it sang:

"In and out and out and in,
  Quick as a flash I weave and spin.
  Some may mistake and some forget,
  But I'll have my spider web finished yet."

When Teddy heard the song, he knew that someone must be awake in the enchanted castle, so he began looking about him.

On the fourth side of the wall there hung a curtain of silvery-grey spider web, and the voice seemed to come from it. The hero went toward it, but he saw nothing, for the spider that was spinning it moved so fast that no eyes could follow it. Presently it paused up in the corner of the web, and then Teddy saw it. It looked very little to have spun all that curtain of silvery web.

"Mistress Spinner! Mistress Spinner!" cried Teddy. "Can you tell me where to find the enchanted princess who lies asleep waiting for me to rescue her?"

The spider sat quite still for a while, and then it said

in a voice as thin as a hair: "You must go through
the emerald door, you must go through the emerald
door. What so fit as the emerald door for the hero who
would do great deeds?"

Teddy did not so much as stay to thank the little grey
spinner, he was in such a hurry to find the princess, but
turning he sprang to the emerald door, flung it open, and
stepped outside.

He found himself standing on the glass steps, and as
his foot touched the topmost one the whole flight closed
up like an umbrella, and in a moment Teddy was sliding
down the smooth glass pane, faster and faster and faster
until he could hardly catch his breath.

The next thing he knew he was standing in the
golden garden, and there was the Counterpane Fairy
beside him looking at him sadly. "You should have
known better than to try the emerald door," she said,
"and now shall we break the story?"

"Oh, no, no!" cried Teddy, and he was still the hero.
"Let me try once more, for it may be I can yet save the
princess."

Then the Counterpane Fairy smiled. "Very well," she
said, "you shall try again. But remember what I told you:

beware of that that is little and grey, and take this with you, for it may be of use." Stooping, she picked up a blade of grass from the ground and handed it to him.

The hero took it wondering, and in his hands it was changed to a sword that shone so brightly that it dazzled his eyes. Then he turned, and there was the long flight of glass steps leading up to the golden castle just as before, so thrusting the magic sword into his belt, he ran nimbly up and up and up, and not until he reached the very topmost step did he turn to wave farewell to the Counterpane Fairy below. She waved her hand to him. "Remember," she called, "beware of what is little and grey."

He opened the door and went into the five-sided golden hall, and there were the three doors just as before, and the spider spinning and singing on the fourth side:

> "*Now the brave hero is wiser indeed,*
> *He may have failed once, but he still may succeed.*
> *Dull are the emeralds, diamonds are bright,*
> *So is his wisdom that shines as the light.*"

"The diamond door!" cried Teddy. "Yes, that is the door that I should have tried. How could I have thought the emerald door was it?" and opening the diamond door he stepped through it.

He hardly had time to see that he was standing at the top of the glass steps, before – *brrrr!* – they had shut up again into a smooth glass hill, and there he was spinning down them so fast that the wind whistled past his ears.

In less time than it takes to tell, he was back again for the third time in the golden garden, with the Counterpane Fairy standing before him, and he was ashamed to raise his eyes.

"So!" said the Counterpane Fairy. "Did you know no better than to open the diamond door?"

"No," said Teddy, "I knew no better."

"Then," said the fairy, "if you can pay no better heed to my warnings than that, the princess must wait for another hero, for you are not the one."

"Let me try but once more," cried Teddy, "for this time I shall surely find her."

"Then you may try once more and for the last time," said the fairy, "but beware of what is little and grey." Stooping she picked from the grass beside her a fallen acorn cup and handed it to him. "Take this with you," she said, "for it may serve you well."

As he took it from her, it was changed in his hand to a goblet of gold set round with precious stones. Turning he ran for the third time up the flight of glass steps. All the time he ran he was wondering what she meant about her warning. She had said, 'Beware of what is little and grey.' What had he seen that was little and grey?

As soon as he reached the great golden hall he walked over to the curtain of spider web. The spider was spinning so fast that it was little more than a grey streak, but presently it stopped up in the corner of the web. As the hero looked at it he saw that it was little and grey. Then it began to sing to him in its little thin voice:

> *"Great hero, wiser than ever before,*
> *Try the red door, try the red door.*
> *Open the door that is ruby, and then*
> *You never need search for the princess again."*

"No, I will not open the ruby door," cried Teddy. "Twice have you sent me back to the golden garden, and now you shall fool me no more."

As he said this he saw that a corner of the web was unfinished, and underneath was something that looked

like a little yellow door. Suddenly he knew that this was
the door he must go through. He pulled at the curtain of
web but it was as strong as steel. Quickly he snatched from
his belt the magic sword, and with one blow the curtain
was cut in two, and fell at his feet.

He heard the spider calling but paid no heed, for he
had opened the door and stooped his head and entered.

Beyond was a great gold courtyard with a fountain
splashing into a golden basin in the middle. But what he
saw first was the princess, who lay stretched out as if
asleep upon a couch all covered with cloth of gold.

He knew she was a princess, because she was so beautiful and because she wore a golden crown.

He stood looking at her without stirring, and at last he whispered, "Princess! Princess! I have come to save you."

Still she did not stir. He bent and touched her, but she lay there in her enchanted sleep, and her eyes did not open. Then Teddy looked about him, and seeing the fountain he drew the magic cup from his bosom and, filling it, sprinkled the hands and face of the princess with the water.

Then her eyes opened and she raised herself upon her elbow and smiled.

"Have you come at last?" she cried.

"Yes," answered Teddy, "I have come."

The princess looked about her. "But what became of the spider?" she said. Then Teddy, too, looked about, and there was the spider running across the floor toward where the princess lay. Quickly he sprang from her side and set his foot upon it. There was a thin squeak and then – there was nothing left of the little grey spinner but a tiny grey smudge on the floor.

Instantly the golden castle was shaken from top to bottom, and there was a sound of many voices shouting outside. The princess rose to her feet and caught the hero by the hand. "You have broken the enchantment," she cried, "and now you shall be the king of the golden castle and reign with me."

"Oh, but I can't," said Teddy, "because, because—"

But the princess drew him out with her through the hall, and there they were at the head of the flight of glass steps. A great host of soldiers and courtiers were running up it. They were dressed in cloth of gold, and they shouted at the sight of Teddy:

"Hail to the hero! Hail to the hero!"

"And all this is yours," said the beautiful princess, turning toward him with—

"So that is the story of the yellow square," said the Counterpane Fairy.

Teddy looked about him. The golden castle was gone, and the stairs, and the shouting courtiers. He was lying in bed with the silk coverlet over his little knees and Hannah was still singing in the kitchen below.

"Did you like it?" asked the fairy.

Teddy heaved a deep sigh. "Oh! Wasn't it beautiful?" he said. Then he lay for a while thinking and smiling. "Wasn't the princess lovely?" he whispered half to himself.

The Counterpane Fairy got up slowly and stiffly, and picked up the staff that she had laid down beside her. "Well, I must be journeying on," she said.

"Oh, no, no!" cried Teddy. "Please don't go yet."

"Yes, I must," said the Counterpane Fairy. "I hear your mother coming."

"But will you come back again?" cried Teddy.

The Counterpane Fairy made no answer. She was walking down the other side of the bed-quilt hill, and Teddy heard her voice, little and thin, dying away in the distance:

"Oh dear, dear, dear! What a hill to go down! What a hill it is! Oh dear, dear, dear!"

Then the door opened and his mother came in. She was looking rested, and she smiled at him lovingly, but the little brown Counterpane Fairy was gone.

Puck of Pook's Hill

By Rudyard Kipling

READING TIME: 20 MINUTES

*T*he children were at the theatre, acting as much as they could remember of *A Midsummer Night's Dream*. Their father had made them a small play out of the big Shakespeare one, and they had rehearsed it with him and with their mother till they could say it by heart.

The theatre lay in a meadow called the Long Slip. A stream, carrying water to a mill two or three fields away, bent round a corner of it, and in the middle of the bend lay an old fairy ring of darkened grass, which was the stage.

They went down after tea on Midsummer Eve, when the

shadows were growing, and took supper with them.

A cuckoo sat on a gate post singing his broken June tune, while a busy kingfisher crossed from the mill stream, to the brook which ran on the other side of the meadow. Everything else was a sort of thick, sleepy stillness smelling of meadow-sweet and dry grass.

Their play went beautifully. Dan remembered all his parts – and Una never forgot a word of Titania. They were both so pleased that they acted it three times over from beginning to end before they sat down in the unthistly centre of the ring to eat eggs and biscuits. This was when they heard a whistle among the alders on the bank, and they jumped.

The bushes parted. In the spot where Dan had stood as Puck they saw a small, brown, broad-shouldered, pointy-eared person with a snub nose, slanting blue eyes, and a grin across his freckled face.

The children looked and gasped. The small thing – no taller than Dan's shoulder – stepped into the ring.

Still the children stared at him – from his dark-blue cap, like a big columbine flower, to his bare, hairy feet. At last he laughed.

"Please don't look like that. What else could you expect?" he said. "What on human earth made you act *A Midsummer Night's Dream* three times, on Midsummer Eve, in the middle of a ring, and under – right under – one of my oldest hills in old England?

"By oak, ash, and thorn! If this had happened a few hundred years ago you'd have had all the people of the hills out like bees in June!"

"We didn't know it was wrong," said Dan.

"Wrong!" The little fellow shook with laughter.

"Indeed, it isn't wrong. You've done something that kings, knights and scholars in old days would have given their crowns and spurs and books to find out. You've broken the hills! It hasn't happened in a thousand years. Unluckily the hills are empty now, and all the people of the hills are gone. I'm the only one left. I'm Puck, the oldest old thing in England, very much at your service – if you care to have anything to do with me."

He looked at the children, and the children looked at him. His eyes were very kind, and there was the beginning of a good smile on his lips.

Una put out her hand. "Don't go," she said. "We like you."

"Have a Bath Oliver biscuit," said Dan, and he passed over the squashy envelope with the eggs.

"By oak, ash and thorn," cried Puck, "I like you too. Sprinkle a plenty salt on the biscuit, Dan, and I'll eat it with you. That'll show you the sort of person I am. Some of us," he went on, with his mouth full, "couldn't abide salt, or horseshoes over a door, or mountain-ash berries, or running water, or cold iron. But I'm Puck!"

He brushed the crumbs carefully from his jacket and shook hands.

"We always said, Dan and I," Una stammered, "that if it ever happened we'd know exactly what to do, but – but now it seems all different somehow."

"She means meeting a fairy," said Dan. "I never believed in 'em."

"The people of the hills have all left. I saw them come into old England and I saw them go. Giants, trolls, kelpies, brownies, goblins, imps, heath-people, hill-watchers, treasure-guards, good people, little people, pishogues, leprechauns, night-riders, pixies, nixies, gnomes, and the rest – gone, all gone! I came into England with oak, ash and thorn, and when oak, ash and thorn are gone I shall go too."

"Then aren't you most awfully old?" said Una.

"Not old – fairly long-lived, as folk say hereabouts. Let me see – my friends used to set my dish of cream for me o' nights when Stonehenge was new."

He stretched himself at length on the dry grass, and the children stretched out beside him. They felt they could not be afraid of him any more than of their particular friend old Hobden the hedger.

"Have you a knife on you?" he said at last.

Dan handed over his big one-bladed outdoor knife,

and Puck began to carve out a piece of turf from the centre of the ring.

"What's that for – magic?" said Una,

"One of my little magics," he answered, and cut another. If you care to take seisin from me, I may be able to show you something out of the common here on human earth. You certainly deserve it."

"What's taking seisin?" said Dan, cautiously.

"It's an old custom the people had when they bought and sold land. They used to cut out a clod and hand it over to the buyer, it didn't really belong to you till the other fellow had actually given you a piece of it – like this." He held out the pieces of turf and turned his eyes on Una.

"I'll do it," she said. Dan followed her example.

"Now are you two lawfully seised and possessed of all old England," began Puck, in a sing-song voice. "By right of oak, ash, and thorn are you free to come and go and look and know where I shall show or best you please. You shall see what you shall see and you shall hear what you shall hear, though it shall have happened three thousand year—"

The children shut their eyes, but nothing happened.

"But there hasn't happened anything at all," said Dan.

"Wait awhile," said Puck. "You don't grow an oak in a year – and old England's older than twenty oaks. Let's sit down again and think. I can do that for a century at a time."

"Ah, but you're a fairy," said Dan.

"Have you ever heard me say that word yet?" said Puck quickly.

"No. You talk about 'the people of the hills', but you never say 'fairies'," said Una. "I was wondering at that. Don't you like it?"

"How would you like to be called 'mortal' or 'human being' all the time?" said Puck. "Or 'son of Adam' or 'daughter of Eve'? That's how I feel about saying – that word that I don't say. Besides, what you call them are made-up things the people of the hills have never heard of – little buzzflies with butterfly wings and gauze petticoats, and shiny stars in their hair, and a wand like a schoolteacher's cane for punishing bad boys and rewarding good ones. I know 'em!"

"We don't mean that sort," said Dan. "We hate 'em too."

"Exactly," said Puck. "Can you wonder that the

people of the hills don't care to be confused with that painty-winged, wand-waving, sugar-and-shake-your-head set of impostors?"

"What made the people of the hills go away?' Una asked.

"Different things. They dropped off, one by one, through the centuries. Most of them were foreigners who couldn't stand our climate. They flitted early."

"How early?" said Dan.

"A couple of thousand years or more. The fact is they began as gods. The Phoenicians brought some over when they came to buy tin, and the Gauls, and the Jutes, and the Danes, and the Frisians, and the Angles brought more when they landed. They always brought their gods with them. England is a bad country for gods. Now, I began as I mean to go on. A bowl of porridge, a dish of milk, and a little quiet fun with the country folk in the lanes was enough for me then, as it is now. I belong here, you see, and I have been mixed up with people all my days. But most of the others insisted on being gods, and having temples, and altars, and priests, and sacrifices of their own."

"People burned in wicker baskets?" said Dan.

"All sorts of sacrifices," said Puck. "'But what was the result? Men don't like being sacrificed at the best of times – they don't even like sacrificing their farm-horses. After a while, men simply left the old things alone, and the roofs of their temples fell in, and the old things had to scuttle out and pick up a living as they could. Some of them took to hanging about trees, and hiding in graves and groaning o' nights. If they groaned loud enough and long enough they might frighten a poor countryman into sacrificing a hen, or leaving a pound of butter for them.

"First they were gods. Then they were people of the hills, and then they flitted to other places because they couldn't get on with the English for one reason or another. There was only one old thing who worked for his living after he came down in the world. He was called Weland, and he was a smith to some gods.

"None the less, when bad times came, he didn't beg or steal. He worked, and I was lucky enough to be able to do him a good turn."

"Tell us about it," said Dan. "I think I like hearing of old things."

They rearranged themselves comfortably, each

chewing a grass stem. Puck propped himself on one strong arm and went on:

"Let's think! I met Weland first on a November afternoon in a sleet storm, on Pevensey Level. I was on Beacon Hill when I saw the pale flame that burning thatch makes, and I went down to look. Some pirates were burning a village on the Levels, and Weland's image – a big, black wooden thing with amber beads round his neck – lay in the bows of a black thirty-two-oar galley that they had just beached.

"When he saw me he began a long chant in his own tongue, telling me how he was going to rule England, and how I should smell the smoke of his altars from

Lincolnshire to the Isle of Wight. I didn't care! I'd seen too many gods charging into old England to be upset about it. I let him sing himself out while his men were burning the village, and then I said (I don't know what put it into my head), 'Smith of the gods,' I said, 'the time comes when I shall meet you plying your trade for hire by the wayside.'"

"What did Weland say?" said Una. "Was he angry?"

"He called me names and rolled his eyes, and I went away to wake up the people inland. But the pirates conquered the country, and for centuries Weland was a most important god. He had temples everywhere – from Lincolnshire to the Isle of Wight. I knew that presently he'd have to come down in the world – like the other old things. I gave him lots of time – I gave him about a thousand years – and at the end of 'em I went into one of his temples near Andover to see how he prospered. There was his altar, and there was his image, and there were his priests, and there were the congregation, and everybody seemed quite happy, except Weland and the priests.

"When the service began a priest rushed out, dragged a man up to the altar, pretended to hit him on the head

with a little gilt axe, and the man fell down and pretended to die. Then everybody shouted: 'A sacrifice to Weland! A sacrifice to Weland!'"

"And the man wasn't really dead?" said Una.

"Not a bit. All as much pretence as a dolls' tea party. I saw poor Weland's face through the smoke. He looked so disgusted I judged it better not to say anything then, and the next time I came to Andover, a few hundred years later, Weland and his temple were gone, and there was a Christian bishop in a church there. None of the people of the hills could tell me anything about him, and I supposed that he had left England."

Puck turned, lay on his other elbow, and thought for a long time.

"Let's see," he said at last. "It must have been some few years later – a year or two before the conquest, I think – that I came back to Pook's Hill here, and one evening I heard old Hobden talking about Weland's Ford. Of course, I pricked up my ears when I heard Weland mentioned, and I scuttled through the woods to the ford just beyond bog wood yonder." He jerked his head westward, where the valley narrows between wooded hills and steep hop-fields.

"Why, that's Willingford Bridge," said Una. "We go there for walks often."

"It was Weland's Ford then, dearie. A road led down to it from the beacon on the top of the hill and all the hillside was thick, thick oak forest, with deer in it. There was no trace of Weland, but presently I saw a fat old farmer riding down from the beacon under the greenwood tree. His horse had cast a shoe in the clay, and when he came to the ford he dismounted, took a penny out of his purse, laid it on a stone, tied the old horse to an oak, and called, 'Smith, Smith, here is work for you!' Then he sat down and went to sleep. You can imagine how I felt when I saw a white-bearded, bent old blacksmith in a leather apron creep out from behind the oak and begin to shoe the horse. It was Weland himself. I was so astonished that I jumped out and said: 'What on human earth are you doing here, Weland?'"

"Poor Weland!" sighed Una.

"He pushed the long hair back from his forehead. Then he said, 'You ought to know. You foretold it, old thing. I'm shoeing horses for hire. I'm not even Weland now,' he said. 'They call me Wayland-Smith.'"

"Poor chap!" said Dan. "What did you say?"

"What could I say? He looked up, with the horse's foot on his lap, and he said, smiling, 'I remember the time when I wouldn't have accepted this old bag of bones as a sacrifice, and now I'm glad enough to shoe him for a penny.

"Isn't there any way for you to get back to Valhalla, or wherever you come from?' I said.

"'I'm afraid not,' he said, rasping away at the hoof. 'You may remember that I was not a gentle god in my day and my time and my power. I shall never be released till some human being truly wishes me well.'

"'Surely,' said I, 'the farmer can't do less than that. You're shoeing the horse all round for him.'

"'Yes,' said he, 'and my nails will hold a shoe from one full moon to the next.'

"But would you believe it, that when that farmer woke and found his horse shod he rode away without one word of thanks? I was so angry that I wheeled his horse right round and walked him back three miles to the beacon, just to teach the old sinner politeness."

"Were you invisible?" said Una.

Puck nodded, gravely. "The farmer thought he was bewitched – well, he was, of course – and began to pray

and shout. I didn't care, and about four o'clock in the morning a young novice came along from the monastery that used to stand on the top of Beacon Hill."

"What's a novice?" said Dan.

"It really means a man who is beginning to be a monk, but in those days people sent their sons to a monastery just the same as a school. This young fellow had been to a monastery in France for a few months every year, and he was finishing his studies in the monastery close to his home here. Hugh was his name, and he had got up to go fishing hereabouts. His people owned all this valley. Hugh heard the farmer shouting, and asked him what in the world he meant. The old man spun him a wonderful tale about fairies and goblins and witches.

"But the novice wasn't a fool. He looked down at the horse's feet, and saw the new shoes fastened as only Weland knew how to fasten 'em.

"'Hm!' said the novice. 'Where did you get your horse shod?'

"The farmer wouldn't tell him at first, because the priests never liked their people to have any dealings with the old things. At

last he confessed that the smith had done it. 'What did you pay him?' said the novice.

"'Penny,' said the farmer, very sulkily.

"'I hope you threw a thank you into the bargain,' the novice replied.

"'No,' said the farmer. 'Wayland-Smith's a heathen.'

"'Heathen or no heathen,' said the novice, 'where you get help there you must give thanks. Come back to the ford and thank the smith, or you'll be sorry.'

"Back the farmer had to go. I led the horse, though no one saw me, and the novice walked beside us, his gown swishing through the shiny dew and his fishing-rod across his shoulders, spear-wise. When we reached the ford again – it was five o'clock and misty still under the oaks – the farmer simply wouldn't say 'Thank you.'

"Then Hugh the novice lost his temper. He just cried, 'Out!' put his arm under the farmer's fat leg, and heaved him from his saddle on to the turf, and before he could rise he caught him by the back of the neck and shook him like a rat till the farmer growled, 'Thank you, Wayland-Smith.'"

"Did Weland see all this?" said Dan.

"Oh yes, and he shouted his old war-cry when the

farmer thudded on to the ground. He was delighted. Then the novice turned to the oak tree and said, 'Ho, Smith of the Gods! I am ashamed of this rude farmer. For all you have done in kindness and charity to him and to others of our people, I thank you and wish you well.' Then he picked up his fishing-rod – it looked more like a tall spear than ever – and tramped off down your valley."

"And what did poor Weland do?" said Una.

"He laughed and he cried with joy, because he had been released at last, and could go away. 'I shall give that novice a gift,' said Weland. 'A gift that shall do him good the wide world over and old England after him. Blow up my fire, old thing, while I get the iron for my last task.' Then he made a sword – a dark-grey, wavy-lined sword – and I blew the fire while he hammered.

"I tell you, Weland was a smith of the gods! He cooled that sword in running water twice, and the third time he cooled it in the evening dew, and he laid it out in the moonlight and said runes (that's charms) over it, and he carved runes of prophecy on the blade. 'old thing,' he said to me, wiping his forehead, 'this is the best blade that Weland ever made. Come to the monastery.'

"We went to the dormitory where the monks slept,

we saw the novice fast asleep in his cot, and Weland put the sword into his hand, and I remember the young fellow gripped it in his sleep. Then Weland strode as far as he dared into the chapel and threw down all his shoeing-tools – his hammers and pincers and rasps – to show that he had done with them for ever. It sounded like suits of armour falling, and the sleepy monks ran in, for they thought the monastery had been attacked by the French. The novice came first of all, waving his new sword and shouting Saxon battle cries. When they saw the shoeing-tools they were very bewildered, till the novice asked leave to speak, and told what he had done to the farmer, and how, he had found the wonderful rune-carved sword in his cot.

"The abbot shook his head at first, and then he laughed and said to the novice: 'Son Hugh, it needed no sign from a heathen god to show me that you will never be a monk. Take your sword, and keep your sword, and go with your sword, and be as gentle as you are strong and courteous.'

"Then they went to bed again, all except the novice, and he sat up in the garth playing with his sword. Then Weland said to me by the stables: 'Farewell, old thing.

You had the right of it. You saw me come to England, and you see me go. Farewell!'

"With that he strode down the hill to the corner of the Great Woods – Woods Corner, you call it now – to the very place where he had first landed – and I heard him moving through the thickets towards Horsebridge for a little, and then he was gone. That was how it happened. I saw it."

Both children drew a long breath.

"But what happened to Hugh the novice?" said Una.

"And the sword?" said Dan.

Puck looked down the meadow that lay all quiet and cool in the shadow of Pook's Hill.

A big white moth flew unsteadily from the alders and flapped round the children's heads, and the least little haze of water-mist rose from the brook.

"Do you really want to know?" Puck said.

"We do," cried the children. "Awfully!"

"Very good, but just now it seems to me that, unless you go back to the house, people will be looking for you. I'll walk with you as far as the gate."

"Will you be here when we come again?" they asked.

"Surely, surely," said Puck. "One minute first, please."

He gave them each three leaves – one of oak, one of ash and one of thorn.

"Bite these," said he." Otherwise you might be talking at home of what you've seen and heard, and – if I know human beings – they'd send for the doctor. Bite!"

They bit hard, and found themselves walking side by side to the lower gate. Their father was leaning over it.

"And how did your play go?" he asked.

"Oh, splendidly" said Dan. "Only afterwards, I think, we went to sleep. It was very hot and quiet. Don't you remember, Una?"

Una shook her head and said nothing.

"I see," said her father. "But why are you chewing leaves at your time of life, daughter? For fun?"

"No. It was for something, but I can't exactly remember," said Una.

My Own Self

By Joseph Jacobs

READING TIME: 6 MINUTES

*I*n a tiny house in the north countrie, far away from any town or village, there lived not long ago, a poor widow all alone with her little son, a six-year-old boy.

The door of the house opened straight on to the hillside and all round about were moorlands and huge stones, and swampy hollows – never a house nor a sign of life wherever you might look – for their nearest neighbours were the 'ferlies' in the glen below, and the 'will-o'-the-wisps' in the long grass along the pathside.

And many a tale she could tell of the 'good folk' calling

to each other in the oak trees, and the twinkling lights hopping on to the very windowsill on dark nights, but in spite of the loneliness she lived on from year to year in the little house, perhaps because she was never asked to pay any rent for it.

But she did not care to sit up late, when the fire burnt low, and no one knew what might be about, so, when they had had their supper she would make up a good fire and go off to bed, so that if anything terrible did happen, she could always hide her head under the bedclothes.

This, however, was far too early to please her little son, so when she called him to bed, he would go on playing beside the fire, as if he did not hear her.

He had always been bad to do with since the day he was born, and his mother did not often care to cross him. Indeed, the more she tried to make him obey her, the less heed he paid to anything she said, so it usually ended by his taking his own way.

But one night, just at the end of winter, the widow could not make up her mind to go off to bed, and leave him playing by the fireside, for the wind was tugging at the door, and rattling the windowpanes, and well she knew that on such a night, fairies and suchlike were

bound to be out and about, and bent on mischief. So she tried to coax the boy into going at once to bed.

The more she begged and scolded, the more he shook his head, and when at last she lost patience and cried that the fairies would surely come and fetch him away, he only laughed and said he wished they would, for he would like one to play with.

At that his mother burst into tears, and went off to bed in despair, certain that after such words something dreadful would happen, while her naughty little son sat on his stool by the fire, not at all put out by her crying.

But he had not long been sitting there alone, when he heard a fluttering sound near him in the chimney and presently down by his side dropped the tiniest wee girl you could think of. She was not a span high, and had hair like spun silver, eyes as green as grass, and cheeks red as June roses. The little boy looked at her with surprise.

"Oh!" said he, "What do they call ye?"

"My own self," she said in a shrill but sweet voice, and she looked at him too. "And what do they call ye?"

"Just my own self too!" he answered cautiously, and with that they began to play together.

She certainly showed him some fine games. She made

animals out of ashes that looked and moved like life, and
trees with leaves waving over tiny houses, with men and
women an inch high in them, who, when she breathed
on them, fell to walking and talking quite properly.

But the fire was getting low, and the light dim, and
presently the little boy stirred the coals with a stick to
make them blaze, when out jumped a red-hot cinder,
and where should it fall, but on the fairy child's tiny foot.

Thereupon she set up such a
squeal that the boy dropped the
stick, and clapped his hands to his
ears but it grew to so
shrill a screech, that
it was like all the
wind in the world
whistling through one
tiny keyhole.

There was a sound in
the chimney again, but this
time the little boy did not wait to
see what it was, but bolted off to bed, where
he hid under the blankets and listened in fear and
trembling to what went on.

A voice came from the chimney speaking sharply:

"Who's there, and what's wrong?" it said.

"It's my own self," sobbed the fairy child, "and my foot's burnt sore. Ooh!"

"Who did it?" said the voice angrily, this time sounding nearer, and the boy, peeping from under the clothes, could see a white face looking out from the chimney-opening.

"Just my own self too!" said the fairy child again.

"Then if ye did it your own self," cried the elf-mother shrilly, "what's the use of making all this fuss about it?"

And with that she stretched out a long thin arm, and caught the creature by its ear, and, shaking it roughly, pulled it after her, out of sight up the chimney.

The little boy lay awake a long time, listening, in case the fairy-mother should come back after all, and next evening after supper, his mother was surprised to find that he was willing to go to bed whenever she liked.

"He's taking a turn for the better at last!" she said to herself, but he was thinking just then that, when next a fairy came to play with him, he might not get off quite so easily as he had done this time.

The Boy Who Wanted More Cheese

By William Elliot Griffis

READING TIME: 10 MINUTES

*K*laas Van Bommel was a Dutch boy, twelve years old, who lived where cows were plentiful. His appetite was always good and his mother declared his stomach had no bottom. His hair was of a colour halfway between a carrot and a sweet potato. It was as thick as reeds in a swamp and was cut level, from under one ear to another.

Klaas stood in a pair of wooden shoes, that made an awful rattle when he ran fast to catch a rabbit, or scuffed

slowly along to school over the brick road of his village.
In summer Klaas was dressed in a rough, blue linen
blouse. In winter he wore woollen breeches as wide as
coffee bags.

Klaas was a farmer's boy. He had rye bread and fresh
milk for breakfast. At dinner time, beside cheese and
bread, he was given a plate heaped with boiled potatoes.
Into these he first plunged a fork and then dipped each
round, white ball into a bowl of hot melted butter. At
supper, he had bread and skim milk, left after the cream
had been taken off, with a saucer, to make butter. Twice
a week the children enjoyed a bowl of soured milk or
curds, with a little brown sugar sprinkled on the top. But
at every meal there was cheese, usually in thin slices,
which the boy thought not thick enough. When Klaas
went to bed he usually fell asleep as soon as his shock of
hair touched the pillow. In summer he slept till the birds
began to sing, at dawn. In winter, when the bed felt
warm he often heard the cows talking, in their way,
before he jumped out of his bag of straw, which served
for a mattress. The Van Bommels were not rich, but
everything was shining clean.

There was always plenty to eat at the Van Bommels'

house. Stacks of rye bread, a yard long and thicker than a man's arm, stood on end in the corner of the cool, stone-lined basement. The loaves of dough were put in the oven once a week. Baking time was a great event at the Van Bommels' and no menfolks were allowed in the kitchen on that day, unless they were called in to help. As for the milk pails and pans, filled or emptied, scrubbed or set in the sun every day to dry, and the cheeses, piled up in the pantry, they seemed sometimes enough to feed a small army.

But Klaas always wanted more cheese. In other ways, he was a good boy, obedient at home, always ready to work on the cow farm, and diligent in school. But at the table he never had enough. Sometimes his father laughed and asked him if he had a well, or a cave, under his jacket.

Klaas had three younger sisters, Trintjé, Anneké and Saartjé – which is Dutch for Kate, Annie and Sally. One summer's evening, after a good scolding, which he deserved well, Klaas moped and, almost crying, went to bed in bad humour. He had teased each one of his sisters to give him her bit of cheese, and this, added to his own slice, made his stomach feel as heavy as lead.

Klaas's bed was up in the garret. When the house was first built, one of the red tiles of the roof had been taken out and another one, made of glass, put in its place. In the morning, this gave Klaas light to put on his clothes. At night, in fair weather, it supplied air to his room.

A gentle breeze was blowing from the pine woods on the sandy slope, not far away. So Klaas climbed up on the stool to sniff the sweet piny odours. He thought he saw lights dancing under the tree. One beam seemed to approach his roof hole. Then it passed to and fro in front of him. It seemed to whisper in his ear, as it moved by. It looked very much as if a hundred fire-flies had united their light into one lamp. Then Klaas thought that the strange beams bore the shape of a lovely girl, but he only laughed at himself at the idea. Pretty soon, however, he thought the whisper became a voice. His eyes twinkled with delight, when the voice gave this invitation:

"There's plenty of cheese. Come with us."

To make sure of it, the sleepy boy now rubbed his eyes and cocked his ears. Again, the light bearer spoke to him:

"Come."

Could it be? He had heard old people tell of the

ladies of the wood, that whispered and warned travellers.
In fact, he himself had often seen the 'fairy ring' in the
pine woods. To this, the flame-lady was inviting him.

Again and again the moving light circled the roof. As
the moon rose higher in the sky, he could hardly see the
moving light that had looked like a lady, but the voice,
no longer a whisper, as at first, was now even plainer:

"There's plenty of cheese.
Come with us."

"I'll see what it is, anyhow," said Klaas, as he drew on his thick woollen stockings and prepared to go downstairs and out, without waking a soul. At the door he stepped into his wooden shoes. Then he sped to the pine woods and towards the fairy ring.

What an odd sight! At first Klaas thought it was a circle of big fireflies. Then he saw clearly that there were dozens of pretty creatures, hardly as large as dolls, but as lively as crickets. They were as full of light as if lamps had wings. Hand in hand, they flitted and danced around the ring of grass, as if this was fun.

Hardly had Klaas got over his first surprise, than all of a sudden he felt himself surrounded by the fairies. Some of the strongest among them had left the main party in the circle and come to him. He felt himself pulled by their dainty fingers. One of them, the loveliest of all, whispered in his ear:

"Come, you must dance with us."

Then a dozen of the pretty creatures murmured in chorus:

"Plenty of cheese here. Plenty of cheese here. Come, come!"

Upon this, the heels of Klaas seemed as light as a feather. In a moment, both hands clasped in those of the fairies, he was dancing in high glee. Klaas had not time to look hard at the fairies, for he was too full of the fun. He danced and danced, all night until the sky in the east began to turn, first grey and then rosy. Then he tumbled down, tired out, and fell asleep. His head lay on the inner curve of the fairy ring, with his feet in the centre.

Klaas felt very happy, for he had no sense of being tired, and he did not know he was asleep. He thought his fairy partners, who had danced with him, were now waiting on him to bring him cheeses. With a golden

knife, they sliced them off and fed him out of their own hands. How good it tasted! He thought now he could, and would, eat all the cheese he had longed for all his life. There was no mother to scold him, or daddy to shake his finger at him. How delightful!

But by and by, he wanted to stop eating and rest a while. His jaws were tired. His stomach seemed to be loaded with cannonballs. He gasped for breath.

But the fairies would not let him stop. Flying out of the sky – from the north, south, east and west – they came, bringing cheeses. These they dropped down around him, until the piles of the round masses threatened first to enclose him as with a wall, and then to overtop him. There were the red balls from Edam, the pink and yellow spheres from Gouda, and the grey loaf-shaped ones from Leyden. Down through the vista of sand, in the pine woods, he looked, and oh, horrors! There were the strongest of the fairies rolling along the huge, round cheeses from Friesland! Any one of these was as big as a cart wheel, and would feed a regiment. The fairies trundled the heavy discs along, as if they were playing with hoops. They shouted hilariously, as, with a pine stick, they beat them forward like boys at play.

Soon the cheeses were heaped so high around him that the boy, as he looked up, felt like a frog in a well. He groaned when he thought the high cheese walls were tottering to fall on him. Then he screamed, but the fairies thought he was making music. They, not being human, do not know how a boy feels.

At last, with a thick slice in one hand and a big hunk in the other, he could eat no more cheese – though the fairies, led by their queen, standing on one side, or hovering over his head, still urged him to take more.

At this moment, while afraid that he would burst, Klaas saw the pile of cheeses, as big as a house, topple over. The heavy mass fell inwards upon him. With a scream of terror, he thought himself crushed as flat as a Friesland cheese.

But he wasn't! Waking up and rubbing his eyes, he saw the red sun rising on the sand dunes. Birds were singing and the cocks were crowing all around him, in chorus, as if saluting him. Just then the village clock chimed out the hour. He felt his clothes. They were wet with dew. He sat up to look around. There were no fairies, but in his mouth was a bunch of grass which he had been chewing hungrily.

Klaas never would tell the story of his night with the fairies, nor has he yet settled the question of whether they left him because the cheese house of his dream had fallen, or because daylight had come.

Mrs Bedonebyasyoudid and Mrs Doasyouwouldbedoneby 180

The Touch of Iron 194

Graciosa and Percinet 205

Whippety Stourie 220

Fairy Helpers

The Phantom Vessel 224

The Story of Wali Dad, the Simple-Hearted 235

Farmer Mybrow and the Fairies 251

Mrs Bedonebyasyoudid and Mrs Doasyouwouldbedoneby

From *The Water Babies* by Charles Kingsley

READING TIME: 15 MINUTES

Tom is a chimney-sweep's boy who has run away from his cruel master. When he tried to wash away his soot in a stream, he fell in and became a water baby. He has been swimming around on his own for some time.

*A*nd now happened to Tom a most wonderful thing, for he had not left the lobster five minutes before he came upon a water baby.

A real live water baby, sitting on the white sand, very

busy about a little point of rock. And when it saw Tom it looked up for a moment, and then cried, "Why, you are not one of us. You are a new baby! Oh, how delightful!"

Tom looked at the baby again, and then he said:

"Well, this is wonderful! I have seen things just like you again and again, but I thought you were shells, or sea creatures. I never took you for water babies like myself."

"Now," said the baby, "come and help me, or I shall not have finished before my brothers and sisters come, and it is time to go home."

"What shall I help you at?"

"At this poor dear little rock. A great clumsy boulder came rolling by in the last storm, and knocked all its head off, and rubbed off all its flowers. And now I must plant it again with seaweeds, coral and anemones, and I will make it the prettiest rock garden on all the shore."

So they worked away at the rock, and planted it, and smoothed the sand down round it, and capital fun they had till the tide began to turn. And then Tom heard all the other babies coming, laughing and singing and shouting and romping, and the noise they made was just like the noise of the ripple. And in they came, dozens and dozens of them, some bigger than Tom and some

smaller, all in the neatest little white bathing dresses, and when they found that he was a new baby, they hugged him and kissed him, and then put him in the middle and danced round him on the sand, and there was no one ever so happy as poor little Tom.

"Now then," they cried all at once, "we must come away home, we must come away home, or the tide will leave us dry. We have mended all the broken seaweed, and put all the rock-pools in order, and planted all the shells again in the sand, and nobody will see where the ugly storm swept in last week."

And this is the reason why the rock-pools are always so neat and clean – because the water babies come inshore after every storm to sweep them out, and comb them down, and put them all to rights again.

Only where men are wasteful and dirty, and let sewers run into the sea instead of putting the stuff upon the fields like thrifty reasonable souls, or throw herrings' heads and dead dog-fish, or any other refuse, into the water, or in any way make a mess upon the clean shore – only there the water babies will not come, sometimes not for hundreds of years (for they cannot abide anything smelly or foul). They leave the sea anemones

and the crabs to clear away everything, till the good
tidy sea has covered up all the dirt in soft mud and
clean sand.

And where is the home of the water babies? In
St Brandan's fairy isle.

Did you never hear of the blessed St Brandan, who
far away, before the setting sun, saw a blue fairy sea, and
golden fairy islands, and he said, "Those are the islands
of the blest." Then he and his friends got into a boat, and
sailed away and away to the westward, and were never
heard of again.

And when St Brandan and the hermits came to that
fairy isle they found it overgrown with cedars and full of
beautiful birds, and he sat down under the cedars and
preached to all the birds in the air. And they liked his
sermons so well that they told the fishes in the sea, and
they came, and St Brandan preached to them. And the
fishes told the water babies, who live in the caves under
the isle, and they came up by hundreds.

He taught the water babies for a great many hundred
years, till his eyes grew too dim to see, and his beard grew
so long that he dared not walk for fear of treading on it,
and then he might have tumbled down. And at last he and

the five hermits fell fast asleep under the cedar-shades, and there they sleep unto this day. But the fairies took to the water babies, and taught them their lessons themselves.

And on still clear summer evenings, when the sun sinks down into the sea, among golden cloud-capes and cloud-islands, and locks and friths of azure sky, the sailors fancy that they see, away to westward, St Brandan's fairy isle.

Now when Tom got there, he found that the isle stood all on pillars, and that its roots were full of caves all curtained and draped with seaweeds, purple and crimson, green and brown, and strewn with soft white sand, on which the water babies sleep every night. But, to keep the place clean and sweet, the crabs picked up all the scraps off the floor and ate them like so many monkeys, while the rocks were covered with ten thousand sea anemones, and corals, who scavenged the water all day long, and kept it nice and pure.

But I wish Tom had given up all his naughty tricks, and left off tormenting dumb animals now that he had plenty of playfellows to amuse him. Instead of that, I am sorry to say, he would meddle with the creatures, all but the water-snakes, for they would stand no nonsense.

So he frightened the crabs, to make them hide in the sand and peep out at him with the tips of their eyes, and put stones into the anemones' mouths, to make them fancy that their dinner was coming.

The other children warned him, and said, "Take care what you are at. Mrs Bedonebyasyoudid is coming." But Tom never listened, being quite riotous with high spirits and good luck, till, one Friday morning early, Mrs Bedonebyasyoudid came indeed.

A very tremendous lady she was, and when the children saw her they all stood in a row, very upright indeed, and smoothed down their bathing dresses, and put their hands behind them, just as if they were going to be examined by the inspector.

And she had on a black bonnet, and a black shawl, and a pair of large green spectacles, and a great hooked nose, hooked so much that the bridge of it stood quite up above her eyebrows, and under her arm she carried a great birch-rod. Indeed, she was so ugly that Tom was

tempted to make faces at her – but did not, for he did not admire the look of the birch-rod under her arm.

And she looked at the children one by one, and seemed very much pleased with them, though she never asked them one question about how they were behaving, and then began giving them all sorts of nice sea-things – sea-cakes, sea-apples, sea-oranges, sea-bullseyes, sea-toffee, and to the very best of all she gave sea-ices, made out of sea-cows' cream, which never melt under water.

And, if you don't quite believe me, then just think – what is more cheap and plentiful than sea-rock? Then why should there not be sea-toffee as well? And every one can find sea-lemons (ready quartered too) if they will look for them at low tide, and sea-grapes too sometimes, hanging in bunches. Now little Tom watched all these sweet things given away, till his mouth watered, and his eyes grew as round as an owl's. For he hoped that his turn would come at last, and so it did. For the lady called him up, and held out her fingers with something in them, and popped it into his mouth – and, lo and behold, it was a nasty cold hard pebble.

"You are a very cruel woman," said he, and began to whimper.

"And you are a very cruel boy, who puts pebbles into the sea anemones' mouths, to take them in, and make them fancy that they had caught a good dinner! As you did to them, so I must do to you."

"Who told you that?" said Tom.

"You did yourself, this very minute."

Tom had never opened his lips, so he was very much taken aback indeed.

"Yes, everyone tells me exactly what they have done wrong, and that without knowing it themselves. So there is no use trying to hide anything from me. Now go, and be a good boy, and I will put no more pebbles in your mouth, if you put none in other creatures.'"

"I did not know there was any harm in it," said Tom.

"Then you know now."

"Well, you are a little hard on a poor lad," said Tom.

"Not at all – I am the best friend you ever had in all your life. But I will tell you, I cannot help punishing people when they do wrong. I like it no more than they do. I am often very, very sorry for them, poor things, but I cannot help it. If I tried not to do it, I should do it all the same. For I work by machinery, just like an engine, and am full of wheels and springs inside, and am wound

up very carefully, so that I cannot help going."

"Was it long ago since they wound you up?" asked Tom. For he thought, the cunning little fellow, 'She will run down some day, or they may forget to wind her up.'

"I was wound up once and for all, so long ago, that I forget all about it."

"You must have been made a long time!" said Tom.

"I never was made, my child, and I shall go forever and ever, for I am as old as Eternity, and yet as young as Time."

And there came over the lady's face a very curious expression – very solemn, and very sad, and yet very, very sweet. And she looked up and away, as if she were gazing through the sea, and through the sky, at something far, far off, and as she did so, there came such a quiet, tender, patient, hopeful smile over her face that Tom thought

for the moment that she did not look ugly at all.

And Tom smiled in her face, she looked so pleasant for the moment. And the strange fairy smiled too, and said:

"Yes. You thought me very ugly just now, did you not?"

Tom hung down his head, and got very red about the ears.

"And I am very ugly. I am the ugliest fairy in the world, and I shall be, till people behave themselves as they ought to do. And then I shall grow as handsome as my sister, who is the loveliest fairy in the world. Her name is Mrs Doasyouwouldbedoneby. So she begins where I end, and I begin where she ends, and those who will not listen to her must listen to me, as you will see."

Poor old Mrs Bedonebyasyoudid! She has a great deal of hard work before her, and had better have been born a washerwoman, and stood over a tub all day. But, you see, people cannot always choose their own profession.

Tom determined to be a very good boy all Saturday, and he was, for he never frightened one crab, nor tickled any live corals, nor put stones into the sea anemones' mouths, to make them fancy they had got a dinner.

And when Sunday morning came, sure enough,
Mrs Doasyouwouldbedoneby came too. Whereat all
the little children began dancing and clapping their
hands and Tom danced too with all his might.

And as for the pretty lady, I cannot tell you what the
colour of her hair was, or, of her eyes. No more could
Tom, for, when anyone looks at her, all they can think of
is that she has the sweetest, kindest, tenderest, funniest,
merriest face they ever saw, or want to see. But Tom saw
that she was a very tall woman, as tall as her sister. But
instead of being gnarly and horny, and scaly, and prickly,
like her, she was the most nice, soft, fat, smooth, pussy,
cuddly, delicious creature who ever nursed a baby, and
she understood babies thoroughly, for she had plenty of
her own, whole rows and regiments of them, and has to
this day. And all her delight was, whenever she had a
spare moment, to play with babies, in which she showed
herself a woman of sense, for babies are the best
company, and the pleasantest playfellows, in the world,
at least, so all the wise people in the world think. And
therefore when the children saw her, they naturally all
caught hold of her, and pulled her till she sat down on a
stone, and climbed into her lap, and clung round her

neck, and caught hold of her hands. And then they all
put their thumbs into their mouths, and began cuddling
and purring like so many kittens, as they ought to have
done. While those who could get nowhere else sat down
on the sand, and cuddled her feet – for no one, you
know, wear shoes in the water. And Tom stood staring at
them, for he could not understand what it was all about.

"And who are you, you little darling?" she said.

"Oh, that is the new baby!" they all cried, pulling
their thumbs out of their mouths, "And he never had any
mother," and they all put their thumbs back again, for
they did not wish to lose any time.

"Then I will be his mother, and he shall have the very
best place, so get out, all of you, this moment."

And she took up two great armfuls of babies – nine
hundred under one arm, and thirteen hundred under
the other – and threw them away, right and left, into the
water. But they did not even take their thumbs out of
their mouths, but came paddling and wriggling back to
her like so many tadpoles, till you could see nothing of
her from head to foot for the swarm of little babies.

But she took Tom in her arms, and laid him in the
softest place of all, and kissed him, and patted him, and

talked to him, tenderly and low, such things as he had never heard before in his life, and Tom looked up into her eyes, and loved her, and loved, till he fell fast asleep from pure love.

And when he woke she was telling the children a story. And what story did she tell them? One story she told them, which begins every Christmas Eve, and yet

never ends at all forever and ever. And, as she went on, the children took their thumbs out of their mouths and listened quite seriously, but not sadly at all, for she never told them anything sad, and Tom listened too, and never grew tired of listening. And he listened so long that he fell fast asleep again, and, when he woke, the lady was nursing him still.

"Don't go away," said little Tom. "This is so nice. I never had any one to cuddle me before."

"Now," said the fairy to Tom, "will you be a good boy for my sake, and torment no more sea beasts till I come back?"

"And you will cuddle me again?" said poor little Tom.

"Of course I will, you little duck. I should like to take you with me and cuddle you all the way, only I must not," and away she went.

So Tom really tried to be a good boy, and tormented no sea beasts after that as long as he lived, and he is quite alive, I assure you, still.

The Touch of Iron

By William Elliot Griffis

READING TIME: 10 MINUTES

Some people believe the fairies were the original inhabitants of ancient lands before humans came and drove them to hide in caves and wild places. Another common belief is that fairies cannot stand the touch of cold iron. This story uses these two ideas to tell its tale. Cymry *is the Welsh word for the inhabitants of Wales.*

Ages ago, before the Cymry rowed in their boats across the sea, there was a race of fairies already in the Land of Honey, as Great Britain was then called.

These ancient fairies, who lived in caves, did not know

how to build houses or to plough the ground. They had no idea that they could get their food out of the earth. As for making bread, pies and goodies, they never heard of such a thing. They did not know how to use fire for melting copper, nor did they know how to get iron from ore to make knives and spears, arrow heads and swords, and armour and helmets.

All they could do was mould clay to make things to cook with. When they baked this soft stuff in the fire, they found they had pots, pans and dishes as hard as stone, though these were easily broken.

To hunt the deer, or fight the wolves and bears, they fashioned clubs of wood. For javelins and arrows, they took hard stone like flint and chipped it to points and sharpened it with edges. This was the time which we now call the Stone Age. When the fairies went to war, their weapons were wholly of wood or stone.

They had not yet learned to weave the wool of the sheep into warm clothing, but they wore the skins of animals. Each one of the caves in which they lived was a boarding house for dogs and pigs, as well as people.

When a young man of one fairy tribe wanted a wife, he sallied out secretly into another neighbourhood.

There he lay in wait for a girl to come along. He then ran away with her, and back to his own daddy's cave.

When the Cymry came into the land, they had iron tools and better weapons of war. Then there were many and long battles and the fairies were beaten many times.

So the fairies hated everything made of iron. Anyone of them, girls or boys, who had picked up iron ornaments, and were found wearing or using iron tools, or buying anything of iron from the cave people's enemies, was looked upon as a rascal, or a villain, or even as a traitor and was driven out of the tribe.

However, some of the daughters of the fairies were so pretty and had such rosy cheeks, and lovely bodies, and beautiful, long hair, that quite often the Cymric youth fell in love with them.

Many of the fairy daughters were captured and became wives of the Cymry and mothers of children. Over time, their descendants helped to make the bright, witty, song-loving Welsh people.

Now the fairies usually like things that are old, and they are very slow to alter the ancient customs to which they have been used, for, in the fairy world, there is no measure of time, nor any clocks, watches, or bells to strike the hours, and no calendars.

The fairies cannot understand why ladies change the fashions so often, and the men their ways of doing things. They wonder why beards are fashionable at one time, then moustaches long or short at another, or smooth faces when razors are cheap. Most fairies like to keep on doing the same thing in the old way. They enjoy being like the mountains, which stand, or the sea, that rolls, or the sun, that rises and sets every day and forever. They never get tired of repeating tomorrow what they did yesterday. They are very different from the people that are always wanting something else.

That is the reason why the fairies did not like iron, or to see men wearing iron hats and clothes, called helmets and armour, when they went to war. They no more wanted to be touched by iron than by filth, or foul disease. They hated knives, stirrups, scythes, swords, pots, pans, kettles, or this metal in any form, whether sheet, barbed wire, lump or pig iron.

Now there was a long, pretty stretch of water, near which lived a handsome lad, who loved nothing better than to go out on moonlight nights and see the fairies dance, or listen to their music. This youth fell in love

with one of these fairies, whose beauty was great beyond description. At last, unable to control his passion, he rushed into the midst of the fairy company, seized the beautiful one, and rushed back to his home, with his prize in his arms. This was in true cave-man fashion.

When the other fairies hurried to rescue her, they found the man's house shut. They dared not touch the door, for it had iron studs and bands, and was bolted with the metal they most abhorred.

The young man immediately began to woo the fairy maid, hoping to win her to be his wife. For a long time she refused, and moped all day and night. While weeping many salt water tears, she declared that she was too homesick to live.

She was a smart fairy, and was sure she could outwit the man, even if he were so strong, and had every sort of iron everywhere in order to keep her as it were in a prison. So, pretending she loved him dearly, she said:

"I will not be your wife, but, if you can find out my name, I shall gladly become your servant."

"Easily won," thought the lover to himself. Yet the game was a harder one to play than he supposed. It was like playing 'Blind Man's Buff', or 'Hunt the Slipper'. Although he made guesses of every name he could think of, he was never 'hot' and got no nearer to the thing sought than if his eyes were bandaged. All the time, he was deeper and deeper in love with the lovely fairy maid.

But one night, on returning home, he saw in a turf bog, a group of fairies sitting on a log. At once, he thought, they might be talking about their lost sister. So he crept up quite near them, and soon found that he had guessed right. After a long discussion, finding themselves

still at a loss as to how to recover her, he heard one of them sigh and say, "Oh, Siwsi, my sister, how can you live with a mortal?"

"Enough," said the young man to himself. "I've got it." Then, crawling away noiselessly, he ran back all the way to his house, and unlocked the door. Once inside the room, he called out his servant's name:

"Siwsi! Siwsi!"

Astonished at hearing her name, she cried out, "What mortal has betrayed me? For, surely no fairy would tell on me? Alas, my fate, my fate!"

But in her own mind, the struggle and the fear were over. She had bravely striven to keep her fairyhood, and in the battle of wits, had lost.

She would not be a wife, but what a wise, superb and faithful servant she made!

Everything prospered under her hand. The house and the farm became models. Not twice, but three times a day, the cows, milked by her, yielded milk unusually rich in cream. In the market, her butter excelled, in quality and price, all others.

In the end, she agreed to become his wife – but only on one condition.

"You must never strike me with iron," she said. "If you do, I'll feel free to leave you, and go back to my relatives in the fairy family."

A hearty laugh from the happy lover greeted this remark, made by the lovely creature, once his servant, but now his betrothed. He thought that the condition was very easy to obey.

So they were married, and no couple in all the land seemed to be happier. Once, twice, the cradle was filled. It rocked with new treasures that had life, and were more dear than farm, or home, or wealth in barns or cattle, cheese and butter. A boy and a girl were theirs. Then the mother's care was unremitting, day and night.

Even though the happy father grew richer every year, and bought farm after farm until he owned five thousand acres, he valued, more than his many possessions, his lovely wife and his two beautiful children.

Yet this very delight and affection made him less careful concerning the promise he had once given to his fairy wife, who still held to the ancient ideas of the fairy family in regard to iron.

One of his finest mares had given birth to a filly,

which, when the day of the great fair came, he
determined to sell at a high price.

So with a halter on his arm, he went out to catch her.
But she was a lively creature, so frisky that it was much
like his first attempt to win his fairy bride. The lively and
frolicsome beast scampered here and there, grazing as
she stopped, as if she were determined to put off her
capture as long as possible.

So, calling to his wife, the two of them together
tried their skill to catch the filly. This time, leaving the
halter in the house, the man took bit and bridle, and
the two managed to get the pretty creature into a
corner, but, when they had almost captured her, away
she dashed again.

By this time, the man was so vexed that he lost his
temper, and he who does that, usually loses the game,
while he who controls the wrath within, wins. Mad as a
flaming fire, he lost his brains also and threw the bit and
bridle and the whole harness as far as he could, after the
fleeting animal.

Alas! Alas! The wife had started to run after the filly
and the iron bit struck her on the cheek. It did not hurt,
but he had broken his vow.

Now came the surprise of his life. It was as if, at one moment, a flash of lightning had made all things bright, and then in another second was inky darkness. He saw this lovely wife, one moment active and fleet as a deer. In another, in the twinkling of an eye, nothing was there. She had vanished. After this, there was a lonely home, empty of its light and cheer.

But by living with human beings, a new idea and form of life had transformed this fairy, and a new spell was laid on her. Mother-love had been awakened in her heart. Henceforth, though the law of the fairy world would not allow her to touch again the realm of earth,

she, having once been wife and parent, could not forget the babies born of her body. So, making a grass raft, a floating island, she came up at night. And often, while these three mortals lived, this fairy mother would spend hours tenderly talking to her husband and her two children, who were now big boy and girl, as they stood on the lake shore.

Even today, good people sometimes see a little island floating on the lake, and point it out as the place where the fairy mother used to come and talk with her dear ones.

Graciosa and Percinet

By Dinah Maria Mulock Craik

READING TIME: 15 MINUTES

*O*nce upon a time there lived a king and queen, who had an only daughter named Graciosa. She was all her mother's joy. At the same court was an elderly young lady named Duchess Grognon, who was the very opposite of Graciosa. Her hair was fiery red, her face fat and spotty, and she had but one eye. Her mouth was so big that you might have thought she could eat you up, only she had no teeth to do it with. She was also humpbacked and lame. Of course she could not help her ugliness, and nobody would have disliked her for that, if she had not been of such an

unpleasant temper that she hated everything sweet and beautiful, and especially Graciosa. She had also a very good opinion of herself, and when any one praised the princess, would say angrily, "That is a lie! My little finger is worth her whole body."

In course of time the queen fell sick and died, and her daughter was almost broken-hearted. So was her husband for a year, and then he began to comfort himself by hunting. One day, after a long chase, he came to a strange castle, which happened to be that of the Duchess Grognon. She, informed of his approach, went out to meet him, and received him most respectfully. As he was very hot with hunting, she took him into the coolest place in the palace, which was a vaulted cave, most elegantly furnished, where there were two hundred barrels arranged in long rows.

"Madam, are these all yours?" inquired the king.

"Yes, sire, but I shall be most happy if you will taste their contents. Which wine do you prefer?" and she ran over a long list, out of which his majesty made his choice.

Grognon took a little hammer, and struck – *toc toc* – on the cask, from which there rolled out a handful of silver money. "Nay, what is this?" said she, smiling, and passed on to the next, from which, when she tapped it, out poured a stream of gold coins. "I never saw the like – what nonsense!" and she tried the third, out of which came a heap of pearls and diamonds, so that the floor of the cave was strewn with them.

"Sire," she exclaimed, "someone has robbed me of my good wine, and put this rubbish in its place."

"Rubbish, madam! Why, such rubbish would buy my whole kingdom."

"It is yours, sire," replied the duchess, "if you will make me your queen."

The king, who was a great lover of money, replied eagerly, "Certainly, madam, I'll marry you tomorrow if you will."

Grognon, highly delighted, made but one other condition – that she should have the Princess Graciosa entirely in her own power, just as if she had been her real mother, to which the foolish king consented.

When the king returned home, Graciosa ran out with joy to welcome her father, and asked him if he had had good sport in his hunting.

"Yes, my child," said he, "for I have taken a dove alive."

"Oh, give it me, and I will nourish and cherish it," cried the princess.

"That is impossible, for it is the Duchess Grognon, whom I have promised to marry."

"She a dove! She is rather a hawk," sighed the princess in despair, but her father bade her hold her tongue, and promise to love her stepmother.

The obedient princess went to her apartment, where her nurse soon found out the sorrow in her face, and its cause.

"My child," said the good old woman, "Promise me to do your best to please your father, and to make yourself agreeable to the stepmother he has chosen for you. She may not be so bad after, all."

And the nurse gave so much good advice, that Graciosa began to smile, and dressed herself in her best attire – a green robe embroidered with gold – while her fair, loose-falling hair was adorned, according to the fashion of the day, with a coronet of jasmine, of which the leaves were made of large emeralds.

Grognon, on her part, made the best of herself that was possible. She put on a high-heeled shoe to appear less lame, she padded her shoulders and put in a false eye, then dressed herself in a hooped petticoat of violet satin trimmed with blue, and an upper gown of yellow with green ribands. In this costume, she wished to enter the city on horseback, as she understood queens were in the habit of doing.

Meantime, Graciosa waited in fear the moment of her arrival, and, to pass the time away, she went all alone into a little wood, where she sobbed and wept in secret, until suddenly there appeared before her a young page, whom she had never seen before.

"Who are you?" she inquired, "and when did his majesty take you into his service?"

"Princess," said the page, bowing, "I am Percinet, a prince in my own country. I have loved you long, and seen you often, for I have the fairy gift of making myself invisible. I might longer have concealed myself from you, but for your present sorrow, in which, however, I hope to be of both comfort and assistance – a page and yet a prince, and your faithful love."

At these words, at once tender and respectful, the princess, who had long heard of the fairy prince Percinet, felt so happy that she feared Grognon no more. They talked a little while together, and then returned to the palace, where the page assisted her to mount her horse, on which she looked so beautiful, that all the new queen's splendours faded into nothing in comparison, and not one of the courtiers had eyes for any except Graciosa.

Soon after, the king, who knew that his wife's weak point was her vanity, gave a tournament, at which he ordered the six bravest knights of the court to proclaim that Queen Grognon was the fairest lady alive. No knight ventured to dispute this fact, until there appeared one who carried a little box adorned with diamonds, and proclaimed aloud that Grognon was the ugliest woman in the universe, and that the most beautiful was she whose portrait was in the box. He opened it, and behold the image of the Princess Graciosa!

The princess, who sat behind her stepmother, felt sure that the unknown knight was Percinet, but she dared say nothing. The contest was fixed for next day, but in the meantime, Grognon, wild with anger, commanded Graciosa to be taken in the middle of the night to a forest a hundred leagues distant, full of wolves, lions, tigers and bears.

Graciosa, in solitude and darkness, groped through the forest, sometimes falling against the trunks of trees,

sometimes tearing herself with bushes and briers. At last,
overcome with fear and grief, she sank on the ground,
sobbing out, "Percinet, Percinet, have you forsaken me?"

When she spoke, a bright light dazzled her eyes, the
midnight forest was changed into glittering alleys, at the
end of which appeared a palace of crystal, shining like
the sun. She knew it was the doing of the fairy prince
who loved her, and felt a joy mingled with fear. She
turned to fly, but saw him standing before her, more
handsome and charming than ever.

"Princess," said he, "why are you afraid of me? This
is the palace of the fairy queen my mother, and the

princesses my sisters, who will take care of you, and love you tenderly. Enter this chariot, and I will convey you there."

Graciosa entered, and passing through many a lovely forest glade, where it was clear daylight, and shepherds and shepherdesses were dancing to merry music, they reached the palace, where the queen and her two daughters received the forlorn princess with great kindness, and led her through many rooms of rock-crystal, glittering with jewels.

She spent eight days in his palace – days full of every enjoyment – and Percinet tried all the arguments he could think of to induce her to marry him, and remain there forever. But the good and gentle Graciosa remembered her father who was once so kind to her, and she preferred rather to suffer than to be wanting in duty. She entreated Percinet to use his fairy power to send her home again, and meantime to tell her what had become of her father.

"Come with me into the great tower there, and you shall see for yourself."

Thereupon he took her to the top of a tower, prodigiously high, put her little finger to his lips, and her

foot upon his foot. Then he bade her look, and she saw
as in a play upon the stage, the king and Grognon sitting
together on their throne. The latter was telling how
Graciosa had hanged herself in a cave.

"She will not be much loss, sire, and as, when dead,
she was far too frightful for you to look at, I have given
orders to bury her at once."

The sight of her father's grief quite overcame
Graciosa. "Oh, Percinet!" she cried, "my father believes
me dead. If you love me, take me home."

The prince consented, though very sorrowfully,
saying that she was as cruel to him as Grognon was to
her, and mounted with her in his chariot, drawn by four
white stags. As they quitted the courtyard, they heard
a great noise, and Graciosa saw the palace all falling to
pieces with a great crash.

"What is this?" she cried, terrified.

"Princess, my palace, which you forsake, is among the
things which are dead and gone. You will enter it no
more till after your burial."

"Prince, you are angry with me," said Graciosa
sorrowfully, only she knew well that she suffered quite
as much as he did in thus departing and quitting him.

Arrived in her father's presence, she had great
difficulty in persuading him that she was not a ghost,
until the coffin was taken up, and Grognon's trickery
discovered But even then, the king was so weak a man,
that the queen soon made him believe he had been
cheated, that the princess was really dead, and that this
was a false Graciosa. Without more ado, he abandoned
his daughter to her stepmother's will.

Grognon, transported with joy, dragged her to a dark
prison, took away her clothes, made her dress in rags,
feed on bread and water, and sleep upon straw. Forlorn
and hopeless, Graciosa dared not now call upon
Percinet. She doubted if he still loved her enough to
come to her aid.

Meantime, Grognon had sent for a fairy, who was
scarcely less cruel than herself. "I have here," said she,
"a little wretch of a girl for whom I wish to find all sorts
of difficult tasks. Pray assist me in giving her a new one
every day."

The fairy promised to think of it, and soon brought a
skein as thick as four persons, yet composed of thread so
fine, that it broke if you only blew upon it, and so
tangled that it had neither beginning nor end. Grognon,

delighted, sent for her poor prisoner.

"There, miss, teach your clumsy fingers to unwind this skein, and if you break a single thread I will flay you alive. Begin when you like, but you must finish at sunset, or it will be the worse for you." Then she sent her to her miserable cell, and treble-locked the door.

Graciosa stood dismayed, turning the skein over and over, and breaking hundreds of threads each time. "Ah! Percinet," she cried in despair, "come and help me, or at least receive my last farewell."

Immediately Percinet stood beside her, having entered the cell as easily as if he carried the key in his pocket. "Behold me, princess, ready to serve you, even though you forsook me." He touched the skein with his wand, and it untangled itself, and wound itself up in perfect order. "Do you wish anything more, madam?" asked he coldly.

"Percinet, Percinet, do not reproach me. I am only too unhappy."

"It is your own fault. Come with me, and make us both happy." But she said nothing, and the fairy prince disappeared.

At sunset, Grognon eagerly came to the prison door with her three keys, and found Graciosa smiling and fair, her task all done. There was no complaint to make, yet Grognon exclaimed that the skein was dirty, and boxed the princess's ears till her rosy cheeks turned yellow and blue. Then she left her, and overwhelmed the fairy with reproaches.

"Find me, by tomorrow, something absolutely impossible for her to do."

The fairy brought a great basket full of feathers, plucked from every kind of bird – nightingales, canaries, linnets, larks, doves, thrushes, peacocks, ostriches, pheasants, partridges, magpies, eagles – in fact, if I told them all over, I should never come to an end – and all these feathers were so mixed up together, that they could not be distinguished.

"See," said the fairy, "even one of ourselves would find it difficult to separate these, and arrange them as belonging to each sort of bird. Command your prisoner to do it. She is sure to fail."

Grognon jumped for joy, sent for the princess, and ordered her to take her task, and finish it, as before, by set of sun.

Graciosa tried patiently, but she could see no difference in the feathers. She threw them all back again into the basket, and began to weep bitterly. "Let me die," said she, "for death only will end my sorrows. Percinet loves me no longer – if he did, he would already be here."

"Here I am, my princess," cried a voice from under the basket, and the fairy prince appeared. He gave three taps with his wand – the feathers flew by millions out of the basket, and arranged themselves in little heaps, each belonging to a different bird.

"What do I not owe you?" cried Graciosa.

"Love me!" answered the prince, tenderly, and said no more.

When Grognon arrived, she found the task done.

If a fairy could be strangled, Grognon certainly would have done it in her rage. At last, she resolved to ask help no more, but to work her own wicked will upon Graciosa.

She caused to be dug a large hole in the garden, and taking the princess there, showed her the stone which covered it.

"Underneath this stone lies a great treasure. Lift it up, and you will see."

Graciosa obeyed, and while she was standing at the edge of the pit, Grognon pushed her in, and let the stone fall down again upon her, burying her alive. After this, there seemed no more hope for the poor princess.

"Oh Percinet," cried she, "you are avenged. Why did I not return your love, and marry you? Still, death will be less bitter, if only you regret me a little."

While she spoke, she saw through the blank darkness a glimmer of light. It came through a little door. She remembered what Percinet had said – that she would never return to the fairy palace, until after she was buried. Perhaps this final cruelty of Grognon would be the end of her sorrows. So she took courage, crept through the little door. She came out into a beautiful garden, with long alleys, fruit trees, and flowerbeds. Well she knew it, and well she knew the glitter of the rock-crystal walls. And there, at the palace gate, stood Percinet, and the queen, his mother, and the princesses, his sisters. "Welcome, Graciosa!" cried they all, and Graciosa, after all her sufferings, wept for joy.

The marriage was celebrated with great splendour,

and all the fairies, for a thousand leagues round, attended it. Some came in chariots drawn by dragons, or swans, or peacocks. Some were mounted upon floating clouds, or globes of fire. Among the rest, appeared the very fairy who had assisted Grognon to torment Graciosa. When she discovered that Grognon's poor prisoner was now Prince Percinet's bride, she was overwhelmed with remorse.

"But I will make amends for all the evil that I have done," said the fairy, and, refusing to stay for the wedding dinner, she remounted her chariot, drawn by two terrible serpents, and flew to the palace of Graciosa's father. There, before either king, or courtiers, or ladies-in-waiting could stop her – even had they wished to do it, which remains doubtful – she came behind the wicked Grognon, and twisted her neck, just as a cook does a fowl. So Grognon died and was buried, and nobody was particularly sorry for the same.

Whippety Stourie

Anon

READING TIME: 4 MINUTES

*T*here was once a gentleman that lived in a very grand house, and he married a young lady that had been delicately brought up. In her husband's house she found everything that was fine – fine tables and chairs, fine looking-glasses, and fine curtains, but then her husband expected her to be able to spin twelve skeins of thread every day, besides attending to her house, and, to tell the truth, the lady could not spin a bit. This made her husband cross with her, and, before a month had passed, she found herself very unhappy.

One day the husband went away upon a journey, after telling her that he expected her, before his return, to have not only learned to spin, but to have spun a hundred skeins of thread. Quite downcast, she took a walk along the hillside, till she came to a big flat stone, and there she sat down and cried. By and by she heard a strain of fine music, coming as it were from underneath the stone, and, on turning it up, she saw a cave below, where there were sitting six wee ladies in green gowns, each one of them spinning on a little wheel, and singing:

> *"Little knows my dame at hame*
> *That Whippety Stourie is my name."*

The lady walked into the cave, and was kindly asked by the wee bodies to take a chair and sit down, while they still continued their spinning. She observed that each one's mouth was twisted away to one side, but she did not venture to guess the reason. They asked why she looked so unhappy, and she told them that she was expected by her husband to be a good spinner, when the plain truth was that she could not spin at all, and found herself quite unable for it, having been so delicately

brought up. Neither was there any need for it, as her husband was a rich man.

"Oh, is that all?" said the little wifies, speaking out of their cheeks alike.

"Yes, and is it not a very good all too?" said the lady, her heart like to burst with distress.

"We could easily quit ye of that trouble," said the wee women. "Just ask us all to dinner for the day when your husband is to come back. We'll then let you see how we'll manage him."

So the lady asked them all to dine with herself and her husband, on the day when he was to come back.

When the good man came home, he found the house so occupied with preparations for dinner, that he had no time to ask his wife about her thread, and, before ever he had once spoken to her on the subject, the company was announced at the hall door. The six fairy ladies all came in a coach-and-six, and were as fine as princesses, but still wore their gowns of green. The gentleman was very polite, and showed them up the stairs with a pair of wax

candles in his hand. And so they all sat down to dinner, and conversation went on very pleasantly, till at length the husband, becoming familiar with them, said:

"Ladies, if it be not an uncivil question, I should like to know how it happens that all your mouths are turned away to one side?"

"Oh," said each one at once, "it's with our constant spin-spin-spinning."

"Is that the case?" cried the gentleman. "Then, John, Tam, and Dick, fie, go haste and burn every rock, and reel, and spinning-wheel in the house, for I'll not have my wife to spoil her bonnie face with spin-spin-spinning."

And so the lady lived happily with her good man all the rest of her days.

The Phantom Vessel

By Norman Hinsdale Pitman

READING TIME: 12 MINUTES

Once a ship loaded with pleasure seekers was sailing from North China to Shanghai. High winds and stormy weather had delayed her, and she was still one week from port when a great plague broke out on board. This plague was of the worst kind. It attacked passengers and sailors alike until there were so few left to sail the vessel that it seemed as if she would soon be left to the mercy of winds and waves.

On all sides lay the dead, and the groans of the dying were most terrible to hear. Of that great company of travellers only one, a little boy named Ying-lo, had escaped.

At last the few sailors, who had been trying hard to save their ship, were obliged to lie down upon the deck, a prey to the dreadful sickness, and soon they too were dead.

Ying-lo now found himself alone on the sea. For some reason – he did not know why – the gods or the sea fairies had spared him, but as he looked about in terror at the friends and loved ones who had died, he almost wished that he might join them.

The sails flapped about like great broken wings, while the giant waves dashed higher above the deck, washing many of the bodies overboard and wetting the little boy to the skin. Shivering with cold, he gave himself up for lost and prayed to the gods, whom his mother had often told him about, to take him from this dreadful ship and let him escape the fatal illness.

As he lay there praying, he heard a slight noise in the rigging just above his head. Looking up, he saw a ball of fire running along a yardarm near the top of the mast. The sight was so strange that he forgot his prayer and stared with open-mouthed wonder. To his astonishment, the ball grew brighter and brighter, and then suddenly began slipping down the mast, all the time increasing in

size. Nearer and nearer came the fireball. At last, when it reached the deck, to Ying-lo's surprise, something very, very strange happened. Before he had time to feel alarmed, the light vanished, and a funny little man stood in front of him peering anxiously into the child's frightened face.

"Yes, you are the lad I'm looking for," he said at last, speaking in a piping voice that almost made Ying-lo smile. "You are Ying-lo, and you are the only one left of this wretched company."

Although he saw that the old man meant him no harm, the child could say nothing, but waited in silence, wondering what would happen next.

By this time the vessel was tossing and pitching so violently that it seemed every minute as if it would upset and go down beneath the foaming waves, never to rise again. Not many miles distant on the right, some jagged rocks stuck out of the water, lifting their cruel heads as if waiting for the helpless ship.

The newcomer walked slowly towards the mast and tapped on it three times with an iron staff he had been using as a cane. Immediately the sails spread, the vessel righted itself and began to glide over the sea so fast that

the gulls were soon left far behind, while the threatening rocks upon which the ship had been so nearly dashed seemed like specks in the distance.

"Do you remember me?" said the stranger, suddenly turning and coming up to Ying-lo, but his voice was lost in the whistling of the wind, and the boy knew only by the moving of his lips that the old man was talking. The greybeard bent over until his mouth was at Ying-lo's ear: "Did you ever see me before?"

With a puzzled look, at first the child shook his head. Then as he gazed more closely there seemed to be something that he recognized about the wrinkled face. "Yes, I think so, but I don't know when."

With a tap of his staff the fairy stopped the blowing of the wind, and then spoke once more to his small companion:

"One year ago I passed through your village. I was dressed in rags, and was begging my way along the street, trying to find someone who would feel sorry for me. Alas! No one answered my cry for mercy. Not a crust was thrown into my bowl. All the people were deaf, and fierce dogs drove me from door to door. Finally when I was almost dying of hunger, I began to feel that here was a village without one good person in it. Just then you saw my suffering, ran into the house, and brought me out food. Your heartless mother saw you doing this and beat you cruelly. Do you remember now, my child?"

"Yes, I remember," he answered sadly, "and that mother is now lying dead. Alas! All, all are dead, my father and my brothers also. Not one is left of my family."

"Little did you know, my boy, to whom you were giving food that day. You took me for a lowly beggar, but, behold, it was not a poor man that you fed, for I am Iron Staff. You must have heard of me when they were telling of the fairies in the Western Heaven, and of their adventures here on earth."

"Yes, yes," answered Ying-lo, trembling half with fear and half with joy, "indeed I have heard of you many, many times, and all the people love you for your kind deeds of mercy."

"Alas! They did not show their love, my little one. Surely you know that if any one wishes to reward the fairies for their mercies, he must begin to do deeds of the same kind himself. No one but you in all your village had pity on me in my rags."

Ying-lo listened in wonder to Iron Staff, and when he had finished, the boy's face was glowing with the love of which the fairy had spoken. "My poor, poor father and mother!" he cried, "they knew nothing of these beautiful things you are telling me. They were brought up in poverty. As they were knocked about in childhood by those around them, so they learned to beat others who begged them for help. Is it strange that they did not have hearts full of pity for you when you looked like a beggar?"

"But what about you, my boy? You were not deaf when I asked you. Have you not been whipped and punished all your life? How then did you learn to look with love at those in tears?"

The child could not answer these questions, but only looked sorrowfully at Iron Staff. "Oh, can you not, good fairy, restore my parents and brothers, and give them another chance to be good and useful people?"

"Listen, Ying-lo, it is impossible unless you do two things first," he answered, stroking his beard gravely and leaning heavily upon his staff.

"What are they? What must I do to save my family? Anything you ask of me will not be too much to pay for your kindness."

"First you must tell me of some good deed done by these people for whose lives you are asking. Name only one, for that will be enough, but it is against our rules to help those who have done nothing."

Ying-lo was silent, and for a moment his face was clouded. "Yes, I know," he said, brightening. "Last year when the foreigner rode through our village and fell sick in front of our house, they cared for him."

"How long?" asked the other sharply.

"Until he died the next week."

"And what did they do with the mule he was riding, his bed, and the money in his bag? Did they try to restore them to his people?"

"No, they said they'd keep them to pay for the trouble." Ying-lo's face turned scarlet.

"But try again, dear boy! Is there not one little deed of goodness that was not selfish? Think once more."

For a long time Ying-lo did not reply. At length he spoke in a low voice, "I think of one, but I fear it amounts to nothing."

"No good, my child, is too small to be counted when the gods are weighing a man's heart."

"Last spring the birds were eating in my father's garden. My mother wanted to buy poison from the shop to destroy them, but my father said no, that the little things must live, and he for one was not in favour of killing them."

"At last, Ying-lo, you have named a real deed of mercy, and as he spared the tiny birds from poison, so shall his life and the lives of your mother and brothers be restored from the deadly plague.

"But remember there is one other thing that depends on you."

Ying-lo's eyes glistened gratfully. "Then if it rests with me, and I can do it, you have my promise."

"Very well, Ying-lo. What I require is that you carry

out to the letter my instructions. Now it is time for me to keep my promise to you."

So saying, Iron Staff called on Ying-lo to point out the members of his family, and, approaching them one by one, with the end of his iron stick he touched their foreheads. In an instant each, without a word, arose. Looking round and recognizing Ying-lo, they stood back, frightened at seeing him with the fairy. When the last had risen to his feet, Iron Staff beckoned all of them to listen. This they did willingly, too much terrified to speak, for they saw on all sides signs of the plague that had swept over the vessel, and they remembered the frightful agony they had suffered in dying. Each knew that he had been lifted by some magic power from darkness into light.

"My friends," began the fairy, "little did you think when less than a year ago you drove me from your door that soon you yourselves would be in need of mercy. As you look back through your wicked lives can you think of any reason why you deserved this rescue? No, there is no memory of goodness in your black hearts. Well, I shall tell you – it is this little boy, this Ying-lo, who many times has felt the weight of your wicked hands and

has hidden in terror at your coming. To him alone you owe my help."

"If at any time you treat him badly and do not heed his wishes – mark you well my words – by the power of this magic staff which I shall place in his hands, he may enter at once into the land of the fairies, leaving you to die in your wickedness. This I command him to do, and he has promised to obey my slightest wish.

"This plague took you off suddenly and ended your wicked lives. Ying-lo has raised you from its grasp and his power can lift you from the bed of sin. No other hand than his can bear the rod which I am leaving. If one of you but touch it, instantly he will fall dead upon the ground.

"And now, my child, the time has come for me to leave you. First, however, I must show you what you are now able to do. Around you lie the corpses of sailors and passengers. Tap three times upon the mast and wish that they shall come to life," So saying he handed Ying-lo the iron staff.

Although the magic rod was heavy, the child lifted it as if it were a fairy's wand. Then, stepping forward to the mast, he rapped three times as he had been commanded.

233

Immediately on all sides arose the bodies, once more full of life and strength.

"Now command the ship to take you back to your home port, for such sinful creatures as these are in no way fit to make a journey among strangers. They must first return and free their homes of sin."

Again rapping on the mast, the child willed the great vessel to take its homeward course. No sooner had he moved the staff than the boat swung round and started on the return journey. Swifter than a flash of lightning it flew, for it had become a fairy vessel. Before the sailors and the travellers could recover from their surprise, land was sighted and they saw that they were entering the harbour.

Just as the ship was darting toward the shore the fairy suddenly changed into a ball of fire which rolled along the deck and ascended the spars. As it reached the top of the rigging it floated off into the sky, and all on board watched it until it vanished.

With a cry of thanksgiving, Ying-lo flung his arms about his parents and descended with them to the shore.

The Story of Wali Dad, the Simple-Hearted

By Andrew Lang

READING TIME: 20 MINUTES

In India, a fairy is called a Peri *or* Pari, *and often appears to give help to the virtuous.*

*O*nce upon a time there lived a poor old man whose name was Wali Dad Gunjay, or Wali Dad the Bald. He had no relations, but lived all by himself in a little mud hut some distance from any town, and made his living by cutting grass in the jungle, and selling it as fodder for horses. He only earned by this five halfpence a day, but he was a simple

old man, and needed so little out of it, that he saved up
one halfpenny daily, and spent the rest upon such food
and clothing as he required.

In this way he lived for many years until, one night,
he thought that he would count the money he had
hidden away in the great earthen pot under the floor of
his hut. So he set to work, and with much trouble he
pulled the bag out on to the floor, and sat gazing in
astonishment at the heap of coins which tumbled out
of it. What should he do with them all? But he never
thought of spending the money on himself, because he
was content to pass the rest of his days as he had been
doing for ever so long, and he really had no desire for
any greater comfort or luxury.

At last he threw all the money into an old sack,
which he pushed under his bed, and then, rolled in his
ragged old blanket, he went off to sleep.

Early next morning he staggered off with his
sack of money to the shop of a jeweller whom
he knew in the town, and bargained with him
for a beautiful gold bracelet. With this
carefully wrapped up in his cotton waistband
he went to the house of a rich friend, who

was a travelling merchant, and used to wander about
with his camels and merchandise through many
countries. Wali Dad was lucky enough to find him at
home, so he sat down, and after a little talk he asked the
merchant who was the most virtuous and beautiful lady
he had ever met with. The merchant replied that the
princess of Khaistan was renowned everywhere as well
for the beauty of her person as for the kindness and
generosity of her disposition.

"Then," said Wali Dad, "next time you go that way,
give her this little bracelet, with the respectful
compliments of one who admires virtue far more than
he desires wealth."

With that he pulled the bracelet from his waistband,
and handed it to his friend. The merchant was naturally
much astonished, but said nothing, and made no
objection to carrying out his friend's plan.

Time passed by, and at length the merchant arrived
in the course of his travels at the capital of Khaistan. As
soon as he had opportunity he presented himself at the
palace, and sent in the bracelet, neatly packed in a little
perfumed box provided by himself, giving at the same
time the message entrusted to him by Wali Dad.

The princess could not think who could have
bestowed this present on her, but she told her servant to
tell the merchant that if he would return, after he had
finished his business in the city, she would give him her
reply. In a few days, therefore, the merchant came back,
and received from the princess a return present in the
shape of a camel-load of rich silks, besides a present of
money for himself. With these he set out on his journey.

Some months later he got home again from his
journeyings, and proceeded to take Wali Dad the
princess's present. Great was the perplexity of the good
man to find a camel-load of silks at his door! What was
he to do with these costly things? But, presently, after
much thought, he begged the merchant to consider
whether he did not know of some young prince to
whom such treasures might be useful.

"Of course," cried the merchant, greatly amused,
"from Delhi to Baghdad, and from Constantinople to
Lucknow, I know them all, and there lives none worthier
than the gallant and wealthy young prince of Nekabad."

"Very well, then, take the silks to him, with the
blessing of an old man," said Wali Dad, much relieved to
be rid of them.

So, the next time that the merchant journeyed that way he carried the silks with him, and in due course arrived at Nekabad, and sought an audience of the prince. When he was shown into his presence he produced the beautiful gift of silks that Wali Dad had sent, and begged the young man to accept them as a humble tribute to his worth and greatness. The prince was much touched by the generosity of the giver, and ordered, as a return present, twelve of the finest breed of horses for which his country was famous to be delivered over to the merchant, to whom also, before he took his leave, he gave a reward for his services.

As before, the merchant at last arrived at home, and next day, he set out for Wali Dad's house with the twelve horses. When the old man saw them coming in the distance he said to himself:

"Here's luck! A troop of horses coming! They are sure to want quantities of grass, and I shall sell all I have without having to drag it to market." Thereupon he rushed off and cut grass as fast he could. When he got back, with as much grass as he could possibly carry, he was greatly discomfited to find that the horses were all for himself. At first he could not think what to do with

them, but, after a little, a brilliant idea struck him! He gave two to the merchant, and begged him to take the rest to the princess of Khaistan, who was clearly the fittest person to possess such beautiful animals.

The merchant departed, laughing. But, true to his old friend's request, he took the horses with him on his next journey, and eventually presented them safely to the princess. This time the princess sent for the merchant, and questioned him about the giver.

Now, the merchant was usually a most honest man, but he did not quite like to describe Wali Dad in his true light as an old man whose income was five halfpence a day, and who had hardly clothes to cover him. So he told her that his friend had heard stories of her beauty and goodness, and had longed to lay the best he had at her feet. The princess then took her father into her confidence, and begged him to advise her what courtesy she might return to one who persisted in making her such presents.

"Well," said the king, "you cannot refuse them, so the best thing you can do is to send this unknown friend at once a present so magnificent that he is not likely to be able to send you anything better, and so will be ashamed

to send anything at all!" Then he ordered that, in place of each of the ten horses, two mules laden with silver should be returned by her.

Thus, in a few hours, the merchant found himself in charge of a splendid caravan, and he had to hire a number of armed men to defend it on the road against robbers, and he was glad indeed to find himself back again in Wali Dad's hut.

"Well, now," cried Wali Dad, as he viewed all the wealth laid at his door, "I can well repay that kind prince for his magnificent present of horses, but to be sure you have been put to great expenses! Still, if you will accept six mules and their loads, and will take the rest straight to Nekabad, I shall thank you heartily."

The merchant felt handsomely repaid for his trouble, and wondered greatly how the matter would turn out. So he made no difficulty about it, and as soon as he could get things ready, he set out for Nekabad with this new and princely gift.

This time the prince, too, was embarrassed, and questioned the merchant closely. The merchant felt that

his credit was at stake, and whilst inwardly determining that he would not carry the joke any further, could not help describing Wali Dad in such glowing terms that the old man would never have known himself had he heard them. The prince, like the king of Khaistan, determined that he would send in return a gift that would be truly royal, and which would perhaps prevent the unknown giver sending him anything more. So he made up a caravan of twenty splendid horses covered in gold embroidered cloths, with fine morocco saddles and silver bridles and stirrups, also twenty camels of the best breed, which had the speed of racehorses, and could swing along at a trot all day without getting tired, and, lastly, twenty elephants, with magnificent silver howdahs and coverings of silk embroidered with pearls. To take care of these animals the merchant hired a little army of men, and the troop made a great show as they travelled along.

When Wali Dad from a distance saw the cloud of dust which the caravan made, and the glitter of its appointments, he said to himself:

"By Allah! Here's a grand crowd coming! Elephants, too! Grass will be selling well today!" And with that he hurried off to the jungle and cut grass as fast as he could.

As soon as he got back he found the caravan had
stopped at his door, and the merchant was waiting, a
little anxiously, to tell him the news and to congratulate
him upon his riches.

"Riches!" cried Wali Dad, "what has an old man like
me with one foot in the grave to do with riches? That
beautiful young princess, now! She'd be the one to enjoy
all these fine things! Do you take for yourself two horses,
two camels, and two elephants, with all their trappings,
and present the rest to her."

The merchant at first objected to these remarks, and
pointed out to Wali Dad that he was beginning to feel
these embassies a little awkward. Of course he was
himself richly repaid, so far as expenses went, but still he
did not like going so often, and he was getting nervous.
At length, however he consented to go once more, but
he promised himself never to embark on another such
enterprise. So, after a few days' rest, the caravan started
off once more for Khaistan.

The moment the king of Khaistan saw the gorgeous
train of men and beasts entering his palace courtyard, he
was so amazed that he hurried down in person to inquire
about it, and became dumb when he heard that these

also were a present from the princely Wali Dad, and were for the princess, his daughter.

He went hastily off to her apartments, and said to her, "I tell you what it is, my dear, this man wants to marry you – that is the meaning of all these presents! There is nothing for it but that we go and pay him a visit in person. He must be a man of immense wealth, and as he is so devoted to you, perhaps you might do worse than marry him!"

The princess agreed with all that her father said, and orders were issued for vast numbers of elephants and camels, and gorgeous tents and flags, and litters for the ladies, and horses for the men, to be prepared without delay, as the king and princess were going to pay a visit to the great and munificent prince Wali Dad. The merchant, the king declared, was to guide the party.

The feelings of the poor merchant in this sore dilemma can hardly be imagined. Willingly would he have run away, but he was treated with so much hospitality as Wali Dad's representative, that he hardly got an instant's real peace, and never any opportunity of slipping away. On the seventh day they all started, amidst thunderous salutes from the ramparts of the city,

and much dust, and cheering, and blaring of trumpets.

At last they were only one day's march from Wali Dad's little mud home. Here a great encampment was made, and the merchant was sent on to tell Wali Dad that the king and princess of Khaistan had arrived and were seeking an interview. When the merchant arrived he found the poor old man eating his evening meal of onions and dry bread, and when he told him of all that had happened he had not the heart to proceed to load him with the reproaches which rose to his tongue. For Wali Dad was overwhelmed with grief and shame for himself, for his friend, and for the name and honour of the princess, and he wept and plucked at his beard, and groaned most piteously. With tears he begged the merchant to detain them for one day by any kind of excuse he could think of, and to come in the morning to discuss what they should do.

As soon as the merchant was gone Wali Dad made up his mind that there was only one honourable way out of the shame and distress that he had created by his foolishness, and that was – to kill himself. So, without stopping to ask any one's advice, he went off in the middle of the night to a place where the river wound

along at the base of steep rocky cliffs of great height, and
determined to throw himself down and put an end to his
life. When he got to the place he drew back a few paces,
took a little run, and at the very edge of that dreadful
black gulf he stopped short! He could not do it!

From below, unseen in the blackness of the deep
night shadows, the water roared and boiled round the
jagged rocks – he could picture the place as he knew it,
only ten times more pitiless and forbidding in the
visionless darkness. An owl laughed – *Hoo! Hoo!* –
almost in his face, as he peered over the edge of the gulf,
and the old man threw himself back in a perspiration of
horror. He was afraid! He drew back shuddering, and
covering his face in his hands he wept aloud.

Presently he was aware of a gentle radiance that shed
itself before him. Surely morning was not already
coming to hasten and reveal his disgrace! He took his
hands from before his face, and saw before him two
lovely beings whom his instinct told him were not
mortal, but were Peris from Paradise.

"Why do you weep, old man?" said one, in a voice as
clear and musical as that of the bulbul bird.

"I came here to die," said Wali Dad. And as they

questioned him, he confessed all his story.

Then the first stepped forward
and laid a hand upon his shoulder,
and Wali Dad began to feel that
something strange – what, he did
not know – was happening to him.
His old cotton rags of clothes
were changed to beautiful linen
and embroidered cloth. On his
hard, bare feet were warm, soft
shoes, and on his head a great
jewelled turban. Round his neck
there lay a heavy golden chain,
and the little old bent sickle, which
he cut grass with, and which hung in
his waistband, had turned into a gorgeous
scimitar, whose ivory hilt gleamed in the pale light like
snow in moonlight.

As he stood wondering, like a man in a dream, the
other peri waved her hand and bade him turn and see,
and before him a noble gateway stood open. And up an
avenue of giant trees the peris led him, dumb with
amazement. At the end of the avenue, on the very spot

where his hut had stood, a gorgeous palace appeared, ablaze with innumerable lights. Its great porticoes and verandahs were occupied by hurrying servants, and guards paced to and fro and saluted him respectfully as he drew near, along mossy walks and through sweeping grassy lawns where fountains were playing and flowers scented the air. Wali Dad stood stunned and helpless.

"Fear not," said one of the peris. "Go to your house, and learn that God rewards the simple-hearted."

With these words they both disappeared and left him. He walked on, thinking still that he must be dreaming. Very soon he retired to rest in a splendid room, far grander than anything he had ever dreamed of.

When morning dawned he woke, and found that the palace, and himself, and his servants were all real, and that he was not dreaming after all!

If Wali Dad was dumbfounded, the merchant, who was ushered into his presence soon after sunrise, was much more so. He told Wali Dad that he had not slept all night, and by the first streak of daylight had started to seek out his friend. And what a search he had had! A great stretch of wild jungle country had, in the night, been changed into parks and gardens, and if it had not

been for some of Wali Dad's new servants, who found
him and brought him to the palace, he would have fled
away under the impression that his trouble had sent him
crazy, and that all he saw was only imagination.

Then Wali Dad told the merchant all that had
happened. By his advice he sent an invitation to the king
and princess of Khaistan to come and be his guests,
together with all their retinue and servants, down to the
very humblest in the camp.

For three nights and days a great feast was held in
honour of the royal guests. Every evening the king and
his nobles were served on golden plates and from golden
cups, and the smaller people on silver plates and from
silver cups, and each evening each guest was requested to
keep the places and cups that they had used as a
remembrance of the occasion. Never had anything so
splendid been seen. Besides the great dinners, there
were sports and hunting, and dances, and amusements
of all sorts.

On the fourth day the king of Khaistan took his host
aside, and asked him whether it was true, as he had
suspected, that he wished to marry his daughter. But
Wali Dad, after thanking him very much for the

compliment, said that he had never dreamed of so great an honour, and that he was far too old and ugly for so fair a lady, but he begged the king to stay with him until he could send for the Prince of Nekabad, who was a most excellent, brave, and honourable young man, and would surely be delighted to try to win the hand of the beautiful princess.

To this the king agreed, and Wali Dad sent the merchant to Nekabad, with a number of attendants, and with such handsome presents that the prince came at once, fell head over ears in love with the princess, and married her at Wali Dad's palace amidst a fresh outburst of rejoicings.

And now the King of Khaistan and the Prince and Princess of Nekabad, each went back to their own country, and Wali Dad lived to a good old age, befriending all who were in trouble and preserving, in his prosperity, the simple-hearted and generous nature that he had when he was only Wali Dad Gunjay, the grass cutter.

Farmer Mybrow
and the Fairies

By William H Barker

READING TIME: 4 MINUTES

$\mathcal{F}$armer Mybrow was one day looking about for a suitable piece of land to convert into a field. He wished to grow corn and yams. He discovered a fine spot, close to a great forest – which was the home of some fairies. He set to work at once to prepare the field.

Having sharpened his great knife, he began to cut down the bushes. No sooner had he touched one than he heard a voice say, "Who is there, cutting down the bushes?"

Mybrow was too much astonished to answer. The question was repeated. This time the farmer realized that it must be one of the fairies, and so replied, "I am Mybrow, come to prepare a field."

Fortunately for him the fairies were in great good humour. He heard one say, "Let us all help Farmer Mybrow to cut down the bushes." The rest agreed. To Mybrow's great delight, the bushes were all rapidly cut down with very little trouble on his part. He returned home, exceedingly well pleased with his day's work, having resolved to keep the field a secret even from his wife.

Early in January, when it was time to burn the dry bush, he set off to his field, one afternoon, with the means of making a fire. Hoping to have the fairies' assistance once more, he intentionally struck the trunk of a tree as he passed. Immediately came the question, "Who is there, striking the stumps?"

He promptly replied, "I am Mybrow, come to burn down the bush." Accordingly, the dried bushes were all burned down, and the field left clear in less time that it takes to tell it.

Next day the same thing happened. Mybrow came to

chop up the stumps for
firewood and clear the field
for digging. In a very short
time his faggots and
firewood were piled ready,
while the field was bare.

So it went on. The field
was divided into two parts
– one for maize and one for
yams. In all the preparations
– digging, sowing, planting –
the fairies gave great
assistance. Still, the
farmer had managed to
keep the whereabouts of
his field a secret from his
wife and neighbours.

The soil having been so
carefully prepared, the
crops promised
exceedingly well. Mybrow visited them from time to
time, and congratulated himself on the splendid harvest
he would have.

One day, while maize and yams were still in their green and milky state, Mybrow's wife came to him. She wished to know where his field lay, that she might go and fetch some of the firewood from it. At first he refused to tell her. Being very persistent, however, she finally succeeded in obtaining the information – but on one condition. She must not answer any question that should be asked her. This she readily promised, and set off for the field.

When she arrived there she was utterly amazed at the wealth of the corn and yam. She had never seen such magnificent crops. The maize looked most tempting – being still in the milky state – so she plucked an ear. While doing so she heard a voice say, "Who is there, breaking the corn?"

"Who dares ask me such a question?" she replied angrily – quite forgetting her husband's command. Going to the field of yams she plucked one of them also.

"Who is there, picking the yams?" came the question again.

"It is I, Mybrow's wife. This is my husband's field and I have a right to pick." Out came the fairies.

"Let us all help Mybrow's wife to pluck her corn and

yams," said they. Before the frightened woman could say a word, the fairies had all set to work with a will, and the corn and yams lay useless on the ground. Being all green and unripe, the harvest was now utterly spoiled. The farmer's wife wept bitterly, but to no purpose. She returned slowly home, not knowing what to say to her husband about such a terrible catastrophe. She decided to keep silence about the matter.

Accordingly, next day the poor man set off gleefully to his field to see how his fine crops were going on. His anger and dismay may be imagined when he saw his field a complete ruin. All his work and foresight had been absolutely ruined through his wife's forgetfulness of her promise.

Paddy Corcoran's Wife 258

The Fairy Cure 261

Master and Man 267

A French Puck 279

The Fairy Fluffikins 283

Iktomi and the Ducks 288

Iktomi and the Muskrat 294

Magic and Mischief

Adventures of a Brownie 299

The Fairies and the Envious Neighbour 310

Drak, the Fairy 313

The Hillman and the Housewife 322

Paddy Corcoran's Wife

By William Carleton

READING TIME: 3 MINUTES

Paddy Corcoran's wife was for several years afflicted with a kind of complaint which nobody could properly understand. She was sick, and she was not sick, she was well, and she was not well, she was as ladies wish to be who love their lords, and she was not as such ladies wish to be. In fact nobody could tell what the matter with her was. The poor woman was delicate beyond belief, and had no appetite at all.

Well, as we have said, she lay a bedridden invalid for long enough, trying doctors of all sorts and sizes, and all without a farthing's benefit, until, at the long run, poor Paddy was nearly brought to despair.

The seventh year was on the point of closing, when, one harvest day, as she lay bemoaning her hard condition, on her bed beyond the kitchen fire, a little woman, dressed in a neat red cloak, came in, and sitting down by the hearth, said:

"Well, Kitty Corcoran, you've had a long lie of it there on the broad of yer back for seven years, and you're just as far from being cured as ever."

"Ay" said the other, "in truth that's what I was this minute thinking of, and a sorrowful thought it's to me."

"It's yer own fault, then," says the little woman, "and, indeed, for that matter, it's yer fault that ever you were there at all."

"Ah, how is that?" asked Kitty, "sure I wouldn't be here if I could help it? Do you think it's a comfort or a pleasure to me to be sick and bedridden?"

"No," said the other, "I do not – but I'll tell you the truth – for the last seven years you have been annoying us. I am one of the good people, and as I have a regard for you, I'm come to let you know the reason why you've been sick so long as you are. For all the time you've been

ill, if you'll take the trouble to remember, your children
have thrown out yer dirty water after dusk and before
sunrise, at the very time we're passing yer door, which we
pass twice a day. Now, if you avoid this
and throw it out in a different place,
at a different time, the complaint
you have will leave you, so will
the gnawing at the heart, and
you'll be as well as ever you
were. If you don't follow this
advice, why, remain as you are,
and all the art of man can't cure
you." She then bade her goodbye,
and disappeared.

Kitty, who was glad to be cured
on such easy terms, immediately
complied with the injunction of the fairy, and the result
was, that the next day she found herself in as good health
as ever she enjoyed during her life.

The Fairy Cure

By Patrick Kennedy

READING TIME: 7 MINUTES

For nearly a year, Nora's daughter, Judy, had been confined to her bed by a sore leg, which neither she, nor the neighbouring doctor, could 'make any hand of.'

Now Nora's mother was a midwife, and one night she was summoned by a dark rider to help with a lady about to have a child. She was whisked away and brought to the door of a magnificent palace. In the hall she was surprised to see an old neighbour, who had long been spirited away from the haunts of his youth and manhood. He at once took an opportunity, when the

dark man was not observing him, to warn Nora that if
she ever wanted to return home, she must take no
refreshment of any kind while under the roof of the fairy
castle, and refuse money or any other reward in any
form. The only exception he made was in favour of cures
for diseases inflicted by evil spirits or by fairies.

She found the lady of the castle in a bed with pillows
and quilts of silk, and in a short time (for Nora was a
handy woman) there was a beautiful little girl lying on
the breast of the delighted mother. All the fine ladies
that were scattered through the large room now
gathered round, and congratulated their queen, and paid
many compliments to the lucky-handed Nora. "I am so
pleased with you," said the lady, "that I shall be glad to
see you take as much gold, and silver, and jewels, out of
the next room, as you can carry."

Nora stepped in out of curiosity and saw piles of gold
and silver coins, and baskets of diamonds and pearls,
lying about on every side, but she remembered her
caution, and came out empty-handed.

"I'm much obliged to you, my lady," said she, "but if I
took them guineas, and crowns, and jewels home, no
one would ever call on me again to help his wife, and I'd

be sitting and doing nothing but drinking tea, an' I'd be
dead before a year'd be gone by."

"Oh dear!" said the lady, "What an odd person you
are! At any rate, sit down at that table, and help yourself
to food and drink."

"Oh, ma'am, is it them jellies, an' custards, an' pastry
you'd like to see me at? Lord love you! I would'n know
the way to me mouth with the likes of them."

"Alas! Alas! Is there any way in which I can show you
how grateful I am for your help and your skill?"

"Indeed is there, ma'am. My girl, Jude, is lying under a
sore leg for a twelvemonth, an' I'm sure that the lord or
yourself can make her as sound as a bell if you only say
the word."

"Ask me anything but that, and you shall have it."

"Oh, lady, dear, that's giving me everything but the
thing I want."

"You don't know the offence your daughter gave to
us, I am sure, or you would not ask me to cure her."

"Judy offend you, ma'am! Oh, it's impossible!"

"Not at all, and this is the way it happened. You
know that all the fairy court enjoy their lives in the night
only, and we frequently go through the country, and

hold our feasts where the kitchen, and especially the hearth, is swept up clean. About a twelvemonth ago, myself and my ladies were passing your cabin, and one of the company liked the appearance of the neat thatch, and the whitewashed walls, and the clean pavement outside the door, so much, that she persuaded us all to go in. We found the cheerful fire shining, the well swept hearth and floor, and the clean pewter and delft plates on the dresser, and the white table. We were so well pleased, that we sat down on the hearth, and laid our tea tray, and began to drink our tea as comfortably as could be. You know we can be any size we please, and there was a score of us settled before the fire.

"We were vexed enough when we saw your daughter come up out of your bedroom, and make towards the fire. Her feet, I acknowledge, were white and clean, but one of them would cover two or three of us, the size we were that night. On she came stalking, and just as I was raising my cup of tea to my lips, down came the soft flat sole on it, and spilled the tea all over me. I was very much annoyed, and I caught the thing that came next to my hand, and hurled it at her. It was the tea pot, and the point of the spout is in her leg from that night till now."

"Oh, lady! How can you hold spite to the poor girl, that knew no more of you being there, nor of offending you, that she did of the night she was born?"

"Well, well, now that is all past and gone. Take this ointment, and rub it where you will see the purple mark, and I hope that your thoughts of me may be pleasant."

Just then, a messenger came to say that the lord was at the hail door waiting for Nora, for the cockerels would be soon crowing. So she took leave of the lady, and mounted behind the dark man. The horse's back seemed as hard and as thin as a hazel stick, but it bore her safely to her home. She was in a sleepy state all the time she was returning, but at last she woke up, and found herself standing by her own door. She got into bed as fast as she could, and when she woke next

morning, she fancied it was all a dream. She put her hand in her pocket, and there, for a certainty, was the box of ointment. She stripped the clothes off her daughter's leg, rubbed some of the stuff on it, and in a few seconds she saw the skin bursting, and a tiny spout of a tea-pot working itself out.

Poor Judy awoke and wondered at the ease she felt in her leg. I warrant she was rejoiced at the story her mother told her. She soon received health and strength, and never neglected to leave her kitchen spotless when she was going to bed. She took good care never to let her feet stray after bedtime, for fear of giving offence to her unseen visitors.

Master and Man

By T Crofton Croker

READING TIME: 12 MINUTES

*People are often superstitious about calling fairies by that name.
Instead they use descriptions such as 'the good people,' or 'the
men of peace'. They didn't really think that fairies were good or
peaceful, but they hoped that these names would make fairies
leave them alone. In this story, 'the good people' are actually the
worst of company, and they can be scared off by mentioning the
name of God.*

Billy Mac Daniel was once as likely a young man as
ever emptied a glass, or handled a cudgel. More is the
pity that, through the means of his thinking, and

fearing, and caring for nothing, Billy Mac Daniel fell into bad company, for surely 'the good people' are the worst of all company anyone could come across.

It so happened that Billy was going home one clear frosty night not long after Christmas. The moon was round and bright, but although it was as fine a night as heart could wish for, he felt pinched with cold.

"By my word," chattered Billy, "a drop of good liquor would be no bad thing to keep a man's soul from freezing in him, and I wish I had a full measure of the best."

"Never wish it twice, Billy," said a little man in a three-cornered hat, bound all about with gold lace, and with great silver buckles in his shoes, and he held out a glass as big as himself, filled with as good liquor as ever eye looked on or lip tasted.

"Success, my little fellow," said Billy Mac Daniel, nothing daunted, though well he knew the little man to

belong to 'the good people'. "Here's your health, anyway, and thank you kindly, no matter who pays for the drink," and he took the glass and drained it to the very bottom without ever taking a second breath to it.

"Success," said the little man, "and you're heartily welcome, Billy, but don't think to cheat me as you have done others – out with your purse and pay me like a gentleman."

"I am to pay you?" said Billy, "Could I not just take you up and put you in my pocket as easily as a blackberry?"

"Billy Mac Daniel," said the little man, getting very angry, "you shall be my servant for seven years and a day, and that is the way I will be paid, so make ready to follow me."

When Billy heard this he began to be very sorry for having used such bold words towards the little man, and he felt himself, yet could not tell how, obliged to follow the little man the live-long night about the country, up and down, and over hedge and ditch, and through bog and brake, without any rest.

When morning began to dawn the little man turned round to him and said, "You may now go home, Billy,

but on your peril don't fail to meet me in the fort-field tonight, or if you do it may be the worse for you in the long run. If I find you a good servant, you will find me an indulgent master."

Home went Billy Mac Daniel, and though he was tired and weary enough, never a wink of sleep could he get for thinking of the little man, but he was afraid not to do his bidding, so up he got in the evening, and away he went to the Fort-field. He was not long there before the little man came towards him and said, "Billy, I want to go a long journey tonight, so saddle one of my horses, and you may saddle another for yourself, as you are to go along with me."

"If I may be so bold, sir," said Billy, "I would ask which is the way to your stable, for never a thing do I see except the old thorn tree in the corner of the field, and the stream running at the bottom of the hill."

"Ask no questions, Billy," said the little man, "but go over to that bit of a bog, and bring me two of the strongest rushes you can find."

Billy did accordingly, wondering what the little man would be at, and he picked two of the stoutest rushes he could find, and brought them back to his master.

"Get up, Billy," said the little man, taking one of the rushes from him and striding across it.

"Where shall I get up, please your honour?" said Billy.

"Why, upon horseback, like me, to be sure," said the little man.

"Is it after making a fool of me you'd be," said Billy, "bidding me get a horseback upon that bit of rush?"

"Up! Up! And no words," said the little man, looking very angry, "the best horse you ever rode was but a fool to it." So Billy, thinking all this was in joke, and fearing to vex his master, straddled across the rush.

"Borram! Borram! Borram!" cried the little man three times (which, in English, means 'become big'), and Billy did the same after him. Presently the rushes swelled up into fine horses, and away they went at full speed, but Billy, who had put the rush between his legs, without much minding how he did it, found himself sitting on horseback the wrong way, which was rather awkward, with his face to the horse's tail, and so quickly had his steed started off with him that he had no power to turn round, and there was therefore nothing for it but to hold on by the tail.

At last they came to their journey's end, and stopped at the gate of a fine house. "Now, Billy," said the little man, "do as you see me do, and follow me close."

The little man then said some queer kind of words, out of which Billy could make no meaning, but he contrived to say them after him for all that, and in they both went through the keyhole of the door, and through one keyhole after another, until they got into the wine cellar, which was well stored with all kinds of wine.

The little man fell to drinking as hard as he could, and Billy did the same. "The best of masters are you surely," said Billy to him, "no matter who is the next. Well pleased will I be with your service if you continue to give me plenty to drink."

"I have made no bargain with you," said the little man, "and will make none, but up and follow me." Away they went, through key hole after key hole, and each mounting upon the rush which he left at the hall door, scampered off, kicking the clouds before them like snowballs, as soon as the words, 'Borram, Borram, Borram', had passed their lips.

When they came back to the fort-field the little man dismissed Billy, bidding him to be there the next night at the same hour. Thus did they go on, night after night, shaping their course one night here, and another night there, sometimes north, and sometimes east, and sometimes south, until there was not a gentleman's wine cellar in all Ireland they had not visited, and could tell the flavour of every wine in it as well, ay, better than the butler himself.

One night when Billy Mac Daniel met the little man as usual in the Fort-field, and was going to the bog to fetch the horses for their journey, his master said to him, "Billy, I shall want another horse tonight, for maybe we may bring back more company than we take." So Billy, who now knew better than to question any order given to him by his master, brought a third rush, much wondering who it might be that would travel back in their company, and whether he was about to have a fellow-servant.

'If I have,' thought Billy, 'he shall go and fetch the horses from the bog every night, for I don't see why I am not, every inch of me, as good a gentleman as my master.'

Well, away they went, Billy leading the third horse, and never stopped until they came to a snug farmer's house, in the county Limerick. Within the house there

was a great deal of noise and the little man stopped outside for some time to listen, then turning round all of a sudden, said, "Billy, I will be a thousand years old tomorrow!"

"God bless us, sir," said Billy, "will you?"

"Don't say these words again, Billy," said the little old man, "or you will be my ruin for ever. Now Billy, as I will be a thousand years in the world tomorrow, I think it is full time for me to get married."

"I think so too, without any kind of doubt at all," said Billy, "if ever you mean to marry."

"And to that purpose," said the little man, "have I come all the way to Carrigogunniel, for in this house, this very night, is young Darby Riley going to be married to Bridget Rooney, and as she is a tall and comely girl, and has come of decent people, I think of marrying her myself, and taking her off with me."

"And what will Darby Riley say to that?" said Billy.

"Silence!" said the little man, putting on a mighty severe look, "I did not bring you here with me to ask questions," and without holding further argument, he began saying the queer words which had the power of passing him through the keyhole as free as air, and which

Billy thought himself mighty clever to be able to say after him.

In they both went. For the better viewing the company, the little man perched himself up as nimbly as a cock sparrow upon one of the big beams which went across the house over all their heads, and Billy did the same upon another facing him, but not being much accustomed to roosting in such a place, his legs hung down as untidy as may be.

There they were, both master and man, looking down upon the fun that was going forward, and under them were the priest and piper, and the father of Darby Riley, with Darby's two brothers and his uncle's son, and there were both the father and the mother of Bridget Rooney, and proud enough the old couple were that night of their daughter, as good right they had, and her four sisters, with brand new ribbons in their caps, and her three brothers all looking as clean and as clever as any three boys in Munster, and plenty was there to eat and drink on the table for every one of them, if they had been double the number.

Now it happened, just as Mrs Rooney had helped his reverence to the first cut of the pig's head which was

placed before her,
beautifully bolstered up with
white savoys, that the bride gave a
sneeze, which made everyone at table start,
but not a soul said 'God bless us'. All thinking that
the priest would have done so, as he ought if he had

done his duty, no one wished to take the word out of his mouth, which, unfortunately, was preoccupied with pig's head and greens. And after a moment's pause the fun and merriment of the bridal feast went on without the blessing.

"Ha!" exclaimed the little man, throwing one leg from under him with a joyous flourish, and his eye twinkled with a strange light, whilst his eyebrows became elevated into the curvature of gothic arches. "Ha!" said he, leering down at the bride, and then up at Billy, "I have half of her now, surely. Let her sneeze but twice more, and she is mine, in spite of priest, mass-book, and Darby Riley."

Again the fair Bridget sneezed, but it was so gently, and she blushed so much that few except the little man took, or seemed to take, any notice, and no one thought of saying 'God bless us'.

Billy all this time could not help thinking what a terrible thing it was for a nice young girl of nineteen, with large blue eyes, transparent skin, and dimpled checks, suffused with health and joy, to be obliged to marry an ugly little bit of a man, who was a thousand years old, barring a day.

At this critical moment the bride gave a third sneeze, and Billy roared out with all his might, "God bless you!"

No sooner was it uttered than the little man, his face glowing with rage and disappointment, sprung from the beam on which he had perched himself, and shrieking out in the shrill voice of a cracked bagpipe, "I discharge you from my service, Billy Mac Daniel – take that for your wages," and gave poor Billy a most furious kick in the back, which sent his unfortunate servant sprawling upon his face and hands right in the middle of the dinner table.

If Billy was astonished, how much more so was every one of the company into which he was thrown with so little ceremony. But when they heard his story, Father Cooney laid down his knife and fork, and married the young couple out of hand with all speed, and Billy Mac Daniel danced the Rinka at their wedding.

A French Puck

By Paul Sébillot

READING TIME: 4 MINUTES

*A*mong the mountain pastures and valleys that lie
in the centre of France there dwelt a mischievous kind of
spirit (whom we will call Puck), whose delight it was to
play tricks on everybody, and particularly on the
shepherds. They never knew when they were safe from
him, as he could change himself into a man, woman or
child, a stick, a goat or a ploughshare. Indeed, there was
only one thing whose shape he could not take, and that
was a needle. At least, he could transform himself into
a needle, but he never was able to imitate the hole, so

every woman would have found him out at once, and this he knew.

Puck was careful not always to play his tricks in the same place, but visited one village after another, so that everyone trembled lest he should be the next victim.

One day he was told of a young couple who were going to the nearest town to buy all that they needed for setting up house. Quite certain that they would forget something which they could not do without, Puck waited patiently till they were jogging along in their cart on their return journey, and changed himself into a fly in order to overhear their conversation. For a long time it was very dull – all about their wedding day next month, and who were to be invited. This led the bride to her dress, and she gave a scream.

"Oh how could I be so stupid! I have forgotten to buy the coloured reels of cotton to match my clothes!"

"Dear, dear!" exclaimed the young man. "That is unlucky, and didn't you tell me that the dressmaker was coming in tomorrow?"

"Yes, I did," and then she gave another little scream, which had quite a different sound from the first. "Look!"

The bridegroom looked, and on one side of the road

he saw a large ball of thread of all colours – of all the colours, that is, of the dresses that were tied on to the back of the cart.

"Well, that is a wonderful piece of good fortune," cried he, as he sprang out to get it. "One would think a fairy had put it there on purpose."

"Perhaps she has," laughed the girl, and as she spoke she seemed to hear an echo of her laughter coming from the horse, but of course that was nonsense.

The dressmaker was delighted with the thread that was given her. It matched the clothes so perfectly, and never tied itself in knots, or broke perpetually, as most thread did. She finished her work much quicker than she expected and the bride said she was to be sure to come to the church and see her in her wedding dress.

There was a great crowd assembled to witness the ceremony, for the young people were immense favourites in the neighbourhood, and their parents were very rich. The doors were open, and the bride could be seen from afar, walking under the chestnut avenue.

"What a beautiful girl!" exclaimed the men.
"What a lovely dress!" whispered the women. But just
as she entered the church and took the hand of the
bridegroom, who was waiting for her, a loud noise
was heard.

Crick! Crack! Crick! Crack! And the wedding
garments fell to the ground, to the great confusion
of the wearer.

Not that the ceremony was put off for a little thing
like that! Cloaks were instantly offered to the young
bride, but she was so upset that she could hardly keep
from tears. One of the guests, more curious than the rest,
stayed behind to examine the dress, to find out the cause
of the disaster.

"The thread must have been rotten," she said to
herself. "I will see if I can break it." But search as she
would she could find none. The thread had vanished!

The Fairy Fluffikins

By Michael Fairless

READING TIME: 4 MINUTES

The Fairy Fluffikins lived in a warm woolly nest in a hole down an old oak tree. She was the sweetest, funniest little fairy you ever saw. She wore a little, soft dress, and on her head a little woolly cap. Fairy Fluffikins had red hair and the brightest, naughtiest, sharpest brown eyes imaginable.

What a life she led the animals! Fairy Fluffikins was a sad tease. She would creep into the nests where the fat baby dormice were asleep in bed while mamma dormouse nodded over her knitting and papa smoked

his little acorn pipe, and she would tickle the babies till they screamed with laughter.

One night she had fine fun. She found a little dead mouse in a field, and an idea struck her. She hunted about till she found a piece of long, strong grass, and then she took the little mouse, tied the piece of grass round its tail, and ran away with it to the big tree where the ancient owl lived. There was a little hole at the bottom of the tree and into it Fairy Fluffikins crept, leaving the mouse outside in the moonlight. Presently she heard a gruff voice in the tree saying:

"I smell mouse, I smell mouse." Then there was a swoop of wings, and Fairy Fluffikins promptly drew the mouse into the little hole and stuffed its tail into her mouth so that she might not be heard laughing, and the gruff voice said angrily:

"Where's that mouse gone? I smelt mouse, I know I smelt mouse!"

She grew tired of this game after a few times, so she left the mouse in the hole and crept away to a new one. She really was a naughty fairy. She blew on the buttercups so that they thought the morning breeze had come to wake them up, and opened their cups in a great

hurry. She buzzed outside the clover and made it talk in its sleep, so that it said in a cross, sleepy voice:

"Go away, you stupid busy bee, and don't wake me up in the middle of the night."

She pulled the tail of the nightingale who was singing to his lady love in the hawthorn bush, and he lost his place in his song.

Next she took to tormenting the squirrels. She used to find their stores of nuts and carry them away and fill the holes with pebbles, and this, when you are a hard-working squirrel with a large family to support, is very trying to the temper. Then she would tie acorns to their tails, and she would clap her hands to frighten them, and pull the baby-squirrels' ears, till at last they offered a reward to anyone who could catch Fairy Fluffikins and bring her to be punished.

No one caught Fairy Fluffikins – but she caught herself, as you shall hear.

She was poking about round a haystack one night, trying to find something naughty to do, when she came upon a sweet little house with pretty wire walls and a wooden door standing invitingly open. In hopped Fluffikins, thinking she was going to have some new kind of fun. There was a little white thing dangling from the roof, and she laid hold of it. Immediately there was a bang, the wooden door slammed, and Fluffikins was caught.

How she cried and stamped and pushed at the door, and promised to be a good fairy and a great many other things! But all to no purpose, the door was tight shut, and Fluffikins was not like some fortunate fairies who can get out of anywhere.

There she remained, and in the morning one of the labourers found her, and, thinking she was some kind of dormouse, he carried her home to his little girl, and if you call on Mary Ann Smith you will see Fairy Fluffikins there still in a little cage. There is no one to tease and no mischief to get into, so if there is a miserable little fairy anywhere it is Fairy Fluffikins, and I'm not sure it doesn't serve her quite right.

Iktomi and the Ducks

By Zitkala-sa

READING TIME: 5 MINUTES

*I*ktomi is a spider fairy. He wears brown deerskin leggings with long soft fringes on either side, and tiny beaded moccasins on his feet. His long black hair is parted in the middle and wrapped with red, red bands. He even paints his funny face with red and yellow, and draws big black rings around his eyes. He wears a deerskin jacket, with bright coloured beads sewed tightly on it. Iktomi dresses like a real Dakota brave.

Iktomi is a wily fellow. He prefers to spread a snare rather than to earn the smallest thing with honest hunting. Why, he laughs outright with wide open mouth when some simple folk are caught in a trap, sure and fast.

Thus Iktomi lives alone in a cone-shaped wigwam upon the plain. One day he sat hungry within his teepee. Suddenly he rushed out, dragging after him his blanket. Quickly spreading it on the ground, he tore up dry tall grass with both his hands and tossed it fast into the blanket.

Tying all the four corners together in a knot, he threw the light bundle of grass over his shoulder.

Snatching up a slender willow stick with his free left hand, he started off with a leap. Soon he came to the edge of the great level land. On the hilltop he paused for breath. With a thin palm shading his eyes from the western sun, he peered far away into the lowlands.

"Ah ha!" grunted he, satisfied with what he saw.

A group of wild ducks were dancing and feasting in the marshes. With wings outspread, tip to tip, they moved up and down in a large circle. Within the ring, around a small drum, sat the chosen singers, nodding their heads and blinking their eyes.

They sang in unison a merry dance-song, and beat a lively tattoo on the drum.

Following a winding footpath soon came a bent figure of a Dakota brave. He bore on his back a very large bundle. With a willow cane he propped himself up as he staggered along beneath his burden.

"Ho! Who is there?" called out a curious old duck, still bobbing up and down in the circular dance.

"Ho, Iktomi! Old fellow, pray tell us what you carry in your blanket. Do not hurry off! Stop! Halt!" urged one of the singers.

"My friends, I must not spoil your dance. Oh, you would not care to see if you only knew what is in my blanket. Sing on! Dance on! I must not show you what I carry on my back," answered Iktomi. Now all the ducks crowded about Iktomi.

"We must see what you carry! We must know what is in your blanket!" they shouted in both his ears. Some even brushed their wings against the mysterious bundle.

Nudging himself again, wily Iktomi said, "My friends, it is only a pack of songs I carry in my blanket."

"Oh, then let us hear your songs!" cried the curious ducks.

At length Iktomi consented to sing his songs, and with great delight all the ducks flapped their wings and

cried together, "Hoye! Hoye!"

Iktomi, with great care, laid down his bundle on the ground.

"I will build first a round straw house, for I never sing my songs in the open air," said he.

Quickly he bent green willow sticks, planting both ends of each pole into the earth. These he covered thick with reeds and grasses. Soon the straw hut was ready. One by one the fat ducks waddled in through a small opening, which was the only entrance way.

In a strange low voice Iktomi began his queer old tunes. All the ducks sat round-eyed in a circle about the mysterious singer. It was dim in that straw hut, for Iktomi had not forgotten to cover up the small entrance way.

All of a sudden his song burst into full voice. These were the words he sang:

"*Istokmus wacipo, tuwayatunwanpi kinhan ista nisasapi kta.*"

This means: 'With eyes closed you must dance. He who dares to open his eyes, forever red eyes shall have.'

Up rose the circle of seated ducks and holding their wings close against their sides began to dance to the rhythm of Iktomi's song and drum.

With eyes closed they did dance! Iktomi ceased to beat his drum. He began to sing louder and faster. He seemed to be moving about in the center of the ring. No duck dared blink a wink. Each one shut his eyes very tight and danced even harder.

At length one of the dancers could close his eyes no longer! It was a Skiska who peeped the least tiny blink at Iktomi within the center of the circle.

"Oh! Oh!" squawked he in awful terror! "Run! Fly! Iktomi is twisting your heads and breaking your necks! Run out and fly! Fly!" he cried.

Hereupon the ducks opened their eyes. There beside

Iktomi's bundle of songs lay half of their crowd – flat on their backs.

Out they flew through the opening Skiska had made as he rushed forth with his alarm.

But as they soared high into the blue sky they cried to one another, "Oh! Your eyes are red-red!"

"And yours are red-red!" For the warning words had proven true.

"Ah ha!" laughed Iktomi, untying the four corners of his blanket, "I shall sit no more hungry within my dwelling." Homeward he trudged along with nice fat ducks in his blanket. He left the little straw hut for the rains and winds to pull down.

Iktomi and the Muskrat

By Zitkala-sa

READING TIME: 5 MINUTES

*B*eside a white lake, beneath a large grown willow tree, sat Iktomi the fairy on the bare ground. With ankles crossed together around a pot of soup, Iktomi bent over some delicious boiled fish.

Fast he dipped his black horn spoon into the soup, for he was ravenous. Iktomi had no regular meal times. Often when he was hungry he went without food.

"How, how, my friend!" said a voice out of the wild rice.

Iktomi started. He almost choked with his soup. He

peered through the long reeds from where he sat with
his long horn spoon in mid-air.

"How, my friend!" said the voice again, this time
close at his side. Iktomi turned and there stood a
dripping muskrat who had just come out of the lake.

"Oh, it is my friend who startled me. I wondered
if among the wild rice some spirit voice was talking.
How, how, my friend!" said Iktomi. The muskrat
stood smiling. On his lips hung a ready 'Yes, my
friend,' for when Iktomi would ask, 'My friend, will
you sit down beside me and share my food?'

That was the custom of the plains people. Yet
Iktomi sat silent. He hummed an old song and beat
gently on the pot with his buffalo-horn spoon. The
muskrat began to feel awkward before such lack of
hospitality and wished himself under water.

After many heart throbs Iktomi stopped
drumming with his spoon, and looking upward into
the muskrat's face, he said, "My friend, let us run a
race to see who shall win this pot of fish. If I win,
I shall not need to share it with you. If you win, you
shall have half of it." Springing to his feet, Iktomi
began at once to tighten the belt about his waist.

"My friend Iktomi, I cannot run a race with you! I am not a swift runner, and you are nimble as a deer," answered the hungry muskrat.

For a moment Iktomi stood with a hand on his long protruding chin. The muskrat looked out of the corners of his eyes without moving his head. He watched the wily Iktomi concocting a plot.

"I shall carry a large stone on my back. That will slacken my usual speed, and the race will be a fair one."

Saying this he laid a firm hand upon the muskrat's shoulder and started off along the edge of the lake. When they reached the opposite side Iktomi pried about in search of a heavy stone.

He found one half buried in the shallow water. Pulling it out upon dry land, he wrapped it in his blanket.

"Now, my friend, you shall run on the left side of the lake, I on the other. The race is for the boiled fish in yonder kettle!" said Iktomi.

The muskrat helped to lift the heavy stone upon Iktomi's back. Then they parted. Each took a narrow path through the tall reeds fringing the shore. Iktomi

found his load a heavy one. Perspiration hung like beads
on his brow. His chest heaved hard and fast.

He looked across the lake to see how far the muskrat
had gone, but nowhere did he see any sign of him.
"Well, he is running low under the wild rice!" said he.
Yet as he scanned the tall grasses on the lake shore, he
saw not one stir as if to make way for the runner.

"Ah, has he gone so fast ahead that the disturbed grasses in his trail have quieted again?" exclaimed Iktomi. With that thought he quickly dropped the heavy stone. "No more of this!" said he, patting his chest with both hands.

Off with a springing bound, he ran swiftly towards the goal. Tufts of reeds and grass fell flat under his feet. Hardly had they raised their heads when Iktomi was many paces gone.

Soon he reached the heap of cold ashes. Iktomi halted stiff as if he had struck an invisible cliff. His black eyes showed a ring of white about them as he stared at the empty ground. There was no pot of boiled fish! There was no muskrat in sight!

"Oh, if only I had shared my food like a real Dakota, I would not have lost it all! Why did I not remember the muskrat would run through the water? He swims faster than I could ever run! That is what he has done. He has laughed at me for carrying a weight on my back while he shot hither like an arrow!"

"Ha! Ha! Ha!" laughed the muskrat. "Next time, say to a visiting friend, 'Be seated beside me, my friend. Let me share with you my food.'"

Adventures of a Brownie

By Dinah Maria Mulock Craik

READING TIME: 12 MINUTES

*T*here once was a little brownie who lived – where do you think he lived? – in a coal cellar.

Now a coal cellar may seem a most curious place to choose to live, but then a brownie is a curious creature – a fairy, and yet not one of that sort of fairies who fly about on gossamer wings, and dance in the moonlight, and so on. He never dances, and as to wings, what use would they be to him in a coal cellar? He is a sober, stay-at-home household elf – nothing much to look at, even if you did see him, which you are not likely to do – only a little old man, about a foot high, all dressed in brown, with a brown face and hands, and a brown peaked cap, just the colour of a brown mouse. And like a mouse he hides in corners – especially kitchen corners – and only comes out after dark when nobody is about, and so sometimes people call him Mr Nobody.

I said you were not likely to see him. I never did, and never knew anybody that did, but still, if you were to go into Devonshire, you would hear many funny stories about brownies in general, and so I may as well tell you the adventures of this particular brownie, who belonged to a family there, a family he had followed from house to house, most faithfully, for years and years.

A good many people had heard him – or supposed they had – when there were noises about the house which must have come from a mouse or a rat – or a brownie. But nobody had ever seen him, except the children, the three boys and three girls who declared he often came to play with them when they were alone, and was the nicest companion in the world, though he was such an old man – hundreds of years old! He was full of fun and mischief and up to all sorts of tricks, but he never did anybody any harm unless they deserved it.

Brownie was supposed to live in the darkest corner
of the cellar, which was never allowed to be disturbed.
Why he had chosen it nobody knew, and how he lived
there, nobody knew either, nor what he lived upon.
Except that, ever since the family could remember,
there had always been a bowl of milk put behind the
coal cellar door for the brownie's supper. Perhaps he
drank it – perhaps he didn't. Anyhow, the bowl was
always found empty next morning.

The old cook, who had lived all her life in the family,
had never once forgotten to give brownie his supper,
but at last she died, and a young cook came in her stead,
who was very apt to forget everything. She was also both
careless and lazy, and disliked taking the trouble to put
a bowl of milk in the same place every night for
Mr Nobody. She didn't believe in brownies, she said,
she had never seen one, and seeing's believing. So she
laughed at the other servants, who looked very grave,
and put the bowl of milk in its place as often as they
could, without saying much about it.

But once, when Brownie woke up, at his usual hour
for rising – ten o'clock at night – and looked round in
search of his supper, which was in fact his breakfast, he

found nothing there. At first he could not imagine such neglect, and went smelling and smelling about for his bowl of milk – it was not always placed in the same corner now – but in vain.

"This will never do," said he, and being extremely hungry, began running about the coal cellar to see what he could find. His eyes were as useful in the dark as in the light, but there was nothing to be seen – not even a potato paring, or a dry crust, or a well-gnawed bone, such as Tiny the terrier sometimes brought into the coal cellar and left on the floor – nothing, in short, but heaps of coals and coal dust, and even a brownie cannot eat that, you know.

"Can't stand this, quite impossible!" said the brownie, tightening his belt to make his poor little inside feel less empty. "What's to be done? Since nobody brings my supper, I must go and fetch it."

So Brownie put his head out of his coal cellar door, which, to his surprise, he found open. The old cook used to lock it every night, but the young cook had left the keys dangling in the lock.

"Hurrah, here's luck!" cried Brownie, tossing his cap up in the air, and bounding right through the scullery into the kitchen. It was quite empty, but there was the remains of an excellent supper spread on the table – enough for half a dozen people – left still.

Would you like to know what there was? Devonshire cream, of course, and part of a large dish of junket, which is something like curds and whey. Lots of bread and butter and cheese, and half an apple pudding. Also a great jug of cider and another of milk, and several half-full glasses, and no end of dirty plates, knives and forks.

"Whew!" said Brownie, "Here's a chance! What a supper I'll get now!"

And he jumped on to a chair and thence to the table, but so quietly that the large black cat with four white paws, called Muff because she was so fat and soft and her fur so long, who sat dozing in front of the fire, just opened one eye and went to sleep again. She had tried to get her nose into the milk jug, but it was too small, and the junket dish was too deep for her to reach, except with one paw. Oh, what a supper he did eat!

First one thing and then another, and then trying everything all over again. And oh, what a lot he drank! First milk and then cider, and then mixed the two together in a way that would have disagreed with anybody except a brownie. He must have had a most extraordinary capacity for eating and drinking, since, after he had nearly cleared the table, he was just as lively as ever, and began jumping about on the table as if he had had no supper at all.

Now his jumping was a little awkward, for there happened to be a clean white tablecloth. As this was only Monday, it had had no time to get dirty – untidy as the cook was. And you know Brownie lived in a coal cellar, and his feet were black with running about in coal dust. So wherever he trod, he left the impression behind, until at last the whole tablecloth was covered with black marks.

Not that he minded this. In fact, he took great pains to make the cloth as dirty as possible, and then laughing loudly – 'Ho, ho, ho!' – leaped on to the hearth, and began teasing the cat, squeaking like a mouse, or chirping like a cricket, or buzzing like a fly.

Well, the cook came downstairs rather earlier than

usual, for she remembered she had to clear off the remains of supper, but lo and behold, there was nothing left to clear! Every bit of food was eaten up – the cheese looked as if a dozen mice had been nibbling at it, and nibbled it down to the very rind, the milk and cider were all drunk – and mice don't care for milk and cider, you know. As for the apple pudding, it had vanished altogether, and the dish was licked as clean as if Boxer the yard-dog had been at it, in his hungriest mood.

"And my white tablecloth – oh, my clean white tablecloth! What can have been done to it?" cried she in amazement. For it was all over little black footmarks, just the size of a baby's foot – only babies don't wear shoes with nails in them, and don't run about and climb on kitchen tables after all the family have gone to bed.

Cook was a little frightened, but her fright changed to anger when she saw the large black cat stretched comfortably on the hearth. Poor Muff had crept there for a little snooze after brownie went away.

"You nasty cat! I see it all now, it's you that have eaten up all the supper, it's you that have been on my clean tablecloth with your dirty paws."

They were white paws, and as clean as possible,

but Cook never thought of that, any more than she did of the fact that cats don't usually drink cider or eat apple pudding.

"I'll teach you to come stealing food in this way, take that – and that – and that!"

Cook got hold of a broom and beat poor Pussy till the creature ran mewing away. Next night, Cook thought she would make all safe and sure, so, instead of letting the cat sleep by the fire, she shut her up in the chilly coal cellar, locked the door, put the key in her pocket, and went off to bed, leaving the supper as before.

When Brownie woke up and looked out of his hole, there was as usual no supper for him, and the cellar door was shut. He peered about, to try and find some cranny under the door to creep out at, but there was none. And he felt so hungry that he could almost have eaten the cat, who kept walking to and fro in a melancholy manner – only she was alive, and he couldn't well eat her alive. Besides he knew she was old, and had an idea she might be tough, so he merely said, politely, "How do you do, Mrs Pussy," to which she answered nothing – of course.

Something must be done, and luckily brownies can do things which nobody else can do. So he thought he would change himself into a mouse, and gnaw a hole through the door. But then he suddenly remembered the cat, who, though he had decided not to eat her, might take this opportunity of eating him. So he thought it advisable to wait till she was fast asleep, which did not happen for a good while. At length, quite tired with walking about, Pussy turned round on her tail six times, curled down in a corner, and fell fast asleep.

Immediately Brownie changed himself into the smallest mouse possible, and, taking care not to make the least noise, gnawed a hole in the door, and squeezed himself through – immediately turning into his proper shape again, for fear of accidents.

The kitchen fire was at its last glimmer, but it showed a better supper than even last night, for the cook had had friends with her, a brother and two cousins, and they had been exceedingly merry. The food they had left behind was enough for three brownies at least, but this one managed to eat it all up. Only once, in trying to cut a great slice of beef, he let the carving knife and fork fall with such a clatter, that Tiny the terrier, who was tied up at the foot of the stairs, began to bark furiously. However, he brought her her puppy, which had been left in a basket in a corner of the kitchen, and so succeeded in quieting her.

After that he enjoyed himself amazingly, and made more marks than ever on the white table-cloth.

When Cook came downstairs and saw that the same thing had happened again – that the supper was all eaten, and the table-cloth blacker than ever with the extraordinary footmarks, she was greatly puzzled. Who could have done it all? Not the cat, who came mewing out of the coal cellar the minute she unlocked the door. Possibly a rat – but then would a rat have come within reach of Tiny?

"It must have been Tiny herself, or her puppy," which just came rolling out of its basket over Cook's feet. "You little wretch! You and your mother are the greatest nuisance imaginable. I'll punish you!"

And quite forgetting that Tiny had been safely tied up all night, and that her poor little puppy was so fat and helpless it could scarcely stand on its legs – to say nothing of jumping on chairs and tables – she gave them both such a thrashing that they ran howling together out of the kitchen door, where the kind little kitchen maid took them up in her arms.

"You ought to have beaten the Brownie, if you could catch him," said she in a whisper. "He'll do it again and again, you'll see, for he can't bear an untidy kitchen. You'd better do as poor Old Cook did, and clear the supper things away, and put the odds and ends safe in the larder. Also," she added mysteriously, "if I were you, I'd put a bowl of milk behind the coal cellar door."

"Nonsense!" answered Young Cook, and flounced away. But afterwards she thought better of it, and did as she was advised, grumbling all the time, but doing it.

Next morning, the milk was gone! Perhaps Brownie had drunk it up. Anyhow nobody could say that he hadn't. As for the supper, Cook having safely laid it on the shelves of the larder, nobody touched it. And the tablecloth, which was wrapped up tidily and put in the dresser drawer, came out as clean as ever, with not a single black footmark upon it. No mischief being done, the cat and the dog both escaped beating, and Brownie played no more tricks with anybody – till the next time.

The Fairies and the Envious Neighbour

By Algernon Freeman-Mitford

READING TIME: 2 MINUTES

*O*nce upon a time there was a certain man, who, being overtaken by darkness among the mountains, was driven to seek shelter in the trunk of a hollow tree. In the middle of the night, a large company of fairies assembled at the place, and the man, peeping out from his hiding place, was frightened out of his wits. After a while, however, the fairies began to feast and drink wine, and to amuse themselves by singing and dancing, until at last the man, caught by the infection of the fun, forgot all

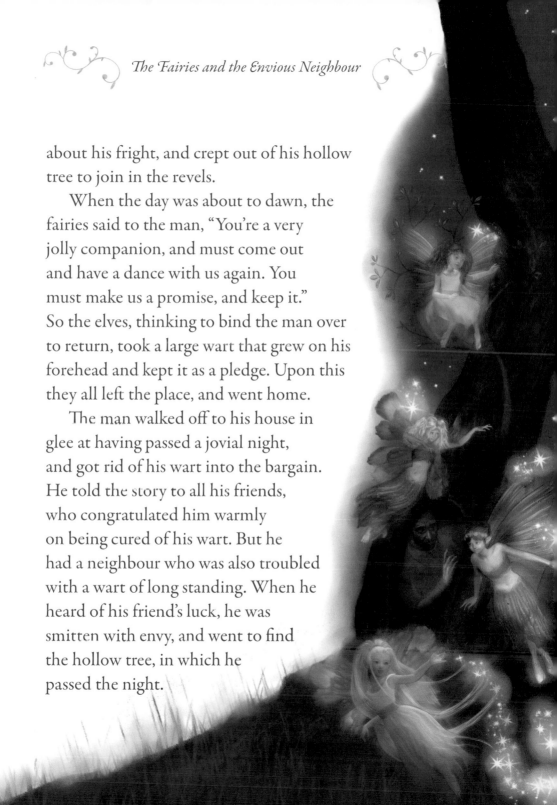

about his fright, and crept out of his hollow
tree to join in the revels.

When the day was about to dawn, the
fairies said to the man, "You're a very
jolly companion, and must come out
and have a dance with us again. You
must make us a promise, and keep it."
So the elves, thinking to bind the man over
to return, took a large wart that grew on his
forehead and kept it as a pledge. Upon this
they all left the place, and went home.

The man walked off to his house in
glee at having passed a jovial night,
and got rid of his wart into the bargain.
He told the story to all his friends,
who congratulated him warmly
on being cured of his wart. But he
had a neighbour who was also troubled
with a wart of long standing. When he
heard of his friend's luck, he was
smitten with envy, and went to find
the hollow tree, in which he
passed the night.

Towards midnight the elves came, as he had expected, and began feasting and drinking, with songs and dances as before. As soon as he saw this, he came out of his hollow tree, and began dancing and singing as his neighbour had done. The elves, mistaking him for their former boon-companion, were delighted to see him, and said:

"You're a good fellow to recollect your promise, and we'll give you back your pledge," so one of the elves, pulling the pawned wart out of his pocket, stuck it onto the man's forehead, on the top of the other wart which he already bad. And the envious neighbour went home weeping, with two warts instead of one. This is a good lesson to people who cannot see the good luck of others, without coveting it for themselves.

Drak, the Fairy

By Kate Douglas Wiggin

READING TIME: 8 MINUTES

*I*n the last century there lived in the little town of Gaillac, in Languedoc, a young merchant named Michael, who, having arrived at an age when he wished to settle down in life, sought a wife. Providing she was sweet-tempered, witty, rich, beautiful, and of good family, he was not particular about the rest. Unhappily, he could not see in Gaillac one who appeared worthy of his choice. At length he was told of a young lady with good qualities and a dowry of twenty thousand crowns. This sum was exactly that required by Michael to

establish himself in business, so he instantly fell in love
with the young lady of Lavaur. He obtained an
introduction to the family, who liked his appearance,
and gave him a good reception. But the young heiress
had many suitors, from whom she hesitated to make a
definite choice. After several discussions it was decided
by her parents that the suitors should be brought
together at a ball, and after having compared them a
choice should be made.

On the appointed day Michael set out for Lavaur.
His case was packed with his finest clothes – an apple-
green coat, a lavender waistcoat, breeches of black velvet,
silk stockings with silver trees, buckled shoes, powder
box to powder his hair, and a satin ribbon for his pigtail.
His horse was harnessed with gay trappings.

Furthermore, the prudent traveller, not having a
pistol to put in his holsters, had slipped in a little bottle
of wine and several slices of almond cake, in order to
have something at hand to keep his courage up. For in
reality, now that the day had come he was in a very
anxious state, and when he saw in the distance the
church of Lavaur he felt quite taken aback. He slackened
the pace of his horse, then dismounted, and in order

to reflect upon what he should do at the ball he entered a little wood and sat down on the turf. He drew from his holsters, to keep him company, the almond cake and the bottle, the latter he placed between his knees, so that without thinking of it he varied his reflections by sips of wine and mouthfuls of cake.

The sun having disappeared from the horizon he was about to pursue his journey, when he heard a sound behind him among the leaves, as of a multitude of little footsteps trampling the grass in tune to the music of a flute and cymbals. Astonished, he turned around, and by the light of the first stars, he perceived a troop of fairies, who were running, headed by the king, Tambourinet. In their rear, turning over and over like a wheel, was the buffoon of the little people – Drak, the fairy.

The fairies surrounded the traveller, and gave him a thousand welcomes and good wishes. Michael, who had drunk too freely not to be brave, began to crumble and throw his cake to them as one would to the birds. Each one had his crumb with the exception of Drak, who arrived when everyone had finished. King Tambourinet next asked what was in the bottle, and the fairies passed it from hand to hand till it reached the buffoon, who, finding it empty, threw it away.

Michael burst out laughing.

"That is justice, my little man," said he to the fairy. "For those who arrive late, there remains nothing but regret."

"I will make you remember what you have just said," cried Drak in anger.

"And how?" asked the traveller. "Do you think, now, you are big enough to revenge yourself?"

Drak disappeared without answering, and Michael, after taking leave of Tambourinet, mounted his horse.

He had not gone a hundred paces, when the saddle turned and threw him roughly to the ground. He arose a little stunned, rebuckled the straps, and mounted again. A little farther on, as he was going over a bridge, the right stirrup bent slightly, and he found himself thrown in the middle of the river. He got out again in a very bad humour, and fell the third time over the pebbles in the road, hurting himself so much that he could hardly proceed. He began to think that if he persisted in riding in the saddle he would be unable to present himself at all to the family of the young lady, so he decided to ride his horse barebacked, and take the saddle upon his shoulder. In this manner, he made his entry into Lavaur amid the laughter of the people who were sitting at their doors.

At length he reached the inn, where he alighted, and asked for a room in which to change his travelling clothes. Having obtained a chamber, he proceeded with much care to open his suitcase and lay out carefully on the bed the articles for his toilet.

His first consideration was whether he should powder his hair white or yellow. Having decided it should be white, he seized his swans-down powder puff, and commenced the operation on the right side. But at the moment when he had finished that side he saw that an invisible hand had powdered the other side yellow, so that his head had the appearance of a half-peeled lemon. Michael, stupefied, stretched out his hand toward the reel on which the ribbon for his pigtail was wound. The reel escaped from his fingers and fell to the ground.

Michael went to pick it up, but it seemed to roll before him. Twenty times he was about to seize it, and twenty times his impatient hands missed it. One would have said he looked like a kitten playing with a reel. At length, seeing that time was going, he lost patience and resigned himself to wearing his old ribbon.

He now hastened to put on his morocco shoes. He buckled the right, then having finished the left, he stopped to admire them, but as he did so the right buckle fell to the ground. He replaced it, but no sooner had he done so than the left followed suit. Furious, he finished by putting on his travelling boots, and was about to put on his velvet breeches, when, immediately he approached the bed, the breeches began of their own accord to walk about the room.

Michael, petrified, stood mute, with his arm extended, contemplating with a frightened air this incongruous dance. But you may guess how he looked when he saw the vest, coat, and hat join the breeches and form a sort of counterfeit of himself, which commenced to walk about and copy his movements.

Pale with fear he drew back to the window, but at this moment the Michaelesque figure turned toward him, and he saw under the cocked hat the grimacing face of Drak, the fairy.

Michael uttered a cry. "It is you, you villain, is it? I'll make you repent of your insolence if you don't instantly give me back my clothes."

So saying, he rushed to take them, but the fairy, turning sharply around, ran to the other side of the room. Michael was beside himself with anger and impatience, and rushed again towards the fairy, who this time passed between his legs and rushed out on to the staircase. Michael pursued him angrily up four flights of stairs till they arrived at the garret, where the fairy dodged round and round, and then skipped out of the window. Michael, exasperated, took the same route. The malicious fairy led him from roof to roof, dragging the velvet breeches, the vest, and coat in all the gutters, to Michael's despair.

The young gallant sat down upon the roof with a cry of despairs, but rising immediately, said with resolution:

"Well, I'll go to the ball in my travelling dress."

"Hark!" interrupted the fairy.

The sound of a bell rang out from a neighbouring steeple. Midnight struck! Michael counted the twelve strokes, and could not restrain a cry. It was the hour designated by the parents when they would proclaim their daughter's choice for a husband. He wrung his hands in despair.

"Unhappy man that I am!" he cried. "When I arrive all will be over, she and her parents will laugh at me."

"And that would be justice, my big man," replied Drak. "For you have said yourself, 'For those who arrive late, there remains nothing but regret.' This time will serve you, I hope, as a lesson and prevent you another time from laughing at the feeble, for from henceforth you will know that the smallest are big enough to avenge themselves."

The Hillman
and the Housewife

By Juliana Horatia Gatty Ewing

READING TIME: 3 MINUTES

*In this story from Ireland, the fairy is called the hillman,
because it was believed that fairies lived inside hills. Fairies in
stories often reward humans who treat them fairly, but they can
be quick to punish anyone who is greedy or tries to trick them.
'Tinkers' are Irish travellers who often earned money by
travelling from village to village mending old pots and pans.*

*I*t is well known that the good people cannot stand
mean ways. Now, there once lived a housewife who had

a sharp eye to her own good in this world, and gave only of what she had no use, for the good of her soul.

One day a hillman knocked at her door.

"Can you lend us a saucepan, good mother?" said he. "There's a wedding in the hill, and all the pots are in use."

"Is he to have one?" asked the servant girl.

"Ay, to be sure," said the housewife.

But when the maid was taking a saucepan from the shelf, she pinched her arm and whispered sharply, "Not that, stupid, get the old one out of the cupboard. It leaks, and the hillmen are so neat and such nimble workers that they are sure to mend it before they send it home. So one does a good turn to the good people and saves sixpence from the tinker."

The maid fetched the saucepan, which had been laid by till the tinker's next visit, and gave it to the hillman, who thanked her and went away.

The saucepan was soon returned neatly mended and ready for use. At supper time the maid filled the pan with milk and set it on the fire for the children's supper, but in a few minutes the milk was so burnt and smoked that no one could touch it, and even the pigs would not drink the wash into which it was thrown.

"You good-for-nothing!" cried the housewife to the maid, as she this time filled the pan herself. "You would ruin the richest, with your careless ways, there's a whole quart of good milk spoilt at once."

"And that's two pence," cried a voice from the chimney, a queer whining voice like some old body who was always grumbling over something. The housewife had not left the saucepan for two minutes when the milk boiled over, and it was all burnt and smoked as before.

"The pan must be dirty," cried the housewife in a rage, "and there are two full quarts of milk as good as thrown to the dogs."

"And that's four pence," said the voice in the chimney.

After a long scrubbing the saucepan was once more filled and set on the fire, but it was not the least use, the milk was burnt and smoked again, and the housewife burst into tears at the waste, crying out, "Never before did such a thing happen to me since I kept house! Three quarts of milk burnt for one meal!"

"And that's six pence," cried the voice from the chimney. "You didn't save the tinker after all." With which the hillman himself came tumbling down the chimney, and went off laughing through the door. But from that time the saucepan was as good as any other.

A Boy that Visited Fairyland 328

Murdoch's Rath 338

Billy Beg, Tom Beg and the Fairies 349

The Fairy Cow 355

Fairy Ointment 361

Bruno's Revenge 366

Visitors to Fairyland

The Fiddler in the Fairy Ring 386

The Fairy Wife 396

The Treasure Stone of the Fairies 404

Guleesh 413

A Boy that Visited Fairyland

By William Elliot Griffis

READING TIME: 10 MINUTES

Many are the places in Wales where the ground is lumpy and humpy with burial mounds. Among these the sheep graze, the donkeys bray, and the cows chew the cud.

Here the ground is strewn with the ruins of Welsh strongholds, of old Roman camps, and of chapels and monasteries, showing that many different races of men have come and gone, while the birds still fly and the flowers bloom.

Centuries ago, the good monks of St David had a school where lads were taught Latin and good manners. One of their pupils was a boy named Elidyr. He was such a poor scholar and he so hated books and loved play, that in his case punishments were almost of daily occurrence. Still he made no improvement. One day, though he was only twelve years old, the boy started on a long run into the country. The further he got, the happier he felt – at least for one day.

At night, tired out, he crept into a cave. When he woke up in the morning, he thought it was glorious to be as free as the wild asses. So like them, he quenched his thirst at the brook. But when, towards noon, he could find nothing to eat, and his stomach seemed to enlarge with very emptiness, his hunger grew every minute. Then he thought that a bit of oat cake, a leek, or a bowl of oatmeal might suit a king.

He dared not go out far and pick berries, for by this time he saw that people were out searching for him. He did not feel yet like going back to books, rods and scoldings, but the day seemed as long as a week. He was glad when the sunset and darkness came. His bed was no softer in the cave. When daylight came, the question in his mind was still whether to stay and starve, or to go home and get two thrashings – one from his daddy, and another from the monks. Finally, he came to a stern resolve. He started out, ready to face two whippings, rather than one death by starvation.

But he did not have to go home yet, for at the cave's mouth, he met two elves, who delivered a most welcome message. "Come with us to a land full of fun, play, and good things to eat."

All at once, his hunger left him. All fear, or desire to go home, or to risk either schooling or a thrashing, passed away also.

Into a dark passage all three went, but they soon came out into a beautiful country, where birds sang and flowers bloomed! All around could be heard the shouts of little folks at play. Never did things look so lovely.

Soon, in front of the broad path along which they were travelling, there rose up before him a glorious palace. It had a splendid gateway, and the silver-topped towers seemed to touch the blue sky.

"What building is this?" asked the lad of his guides.

They made answer that it was the palace of the king of Fairyland. Then they led him into the throne room,

where sat in golden splendour, a king of august figure and of majestic presence, who was clad in resplendent robes. He was surrounded by courtiers in rich apparel, and all about him was magnificence, such as this boy, Elidyr, had never even read about or dreamed.

Yet everything was so small that it looked like Toy Land, and he felt like a giant among them, even though many of the little men around him were old enough to have whiskers on their cheeks and beards on their chins.

The king spoke kindly to Elidyr, asking him who he was, and whence he had come.

While talking thus the prince, the king's only son appeared. He was dressed in white velvet and gold, and had a long feather in his cap. In the pleasantest way, he took Elidyr's hand and said:

"Glad to see you. Come and let us play together."

That was just what Elidyr liked to hear. They played with golden balls, and rode little horses with silver saddles and bridles, but these pretty animals were no larger than small dogs, or greyhounds.

No meat was ever seen on the table, but plenty of milk. They never told a lie, nor used bad language. They often talked about mortal men, but usually to despise them. To the elves, human beings were never satisfied, or long happy, even when they got what they wanted.

Everything in this part of Fairyland was lovely, but it was always cloudy. No sun, star or moon was ever seen, yet the little men did not seem to mind it and enjoyed themselves every day. There was no end of play, and that suited Elidyr.

Yet by and by, he got tired even of games and play, and grew very homesick. He wanted to see his mother.

So he asked the king to let him visit his old home. He promised solemnly to come back, after a few hours. His majesty gave his permission, but charged him not to take with him anything whatever from Fairyland, and to go with only the clothes on his back.

The same two elves who had brought him into Fairyland, were chosen to conduct him back. When they had led him again through the underground passage into the sunlight, they made him invisible until he arrived at his mother's cottage. She was overjoyed to find that no wolf had torn him to pieces, or wild bull had pushed him over a precipice. She asked him many questions, and he told her all he had seen, felt, or known.

When he rose up to go, she begged him to stay longer, but he said he must keep his word. So he made his mother agree not to tell – not even to his father – as to where he was, or what he was doing. Then he made off and reported again to his playmates in Fairyland.

The king was so pleased at the lad's promptness in returning, and keeping his word, and telling the truth, that he allowed him to go see his mother as often as he wanted to do so. He even gave orders releasing the two little men from constantly guarding him and told them to let the lad go alone, and whenever he liked, for he always kept his word.

Many times did Elidyr visit his mother. By one road or another, he made his way, keeping himself invisible all the time, until he got inside her cottage. One day, in telling his mother of the fun he had in Fairyland, he spoke of the heavy yellow balls, with which he and the king's sons played, and how these rolled around.

Before leaving home, this boy had never seen gold, and did not know what it was, but his mother guessed that the yellow balls were made of the precious metal. So she begged him to bring one of them back to her.

This, Elidyr thought, would not be right, but after much argument, his parents being poor, and she telling him that out of hundreds in the king's palace, one single ball would not be missed, he decided to please her.

One day, when he supposed no one was looking, Elidyr picked up one of the yellow balls and

started off through the passageway homeward.

But no sooner was he back on the earth, and in the sunlight again, than he heard footsteps behind him. Then he knew that he had been discovered.

He glanced over his shoulder and there were the two little men, who had formerly been his guards. They scowled at him as if they were mad enough to bite off the heads of nails. Then they rushed after him, and there began a race to the cottage.

But the boy had legs twice as long as the little men, and got to the cottage door first. He now thought himself safe, but pushing open the door, he stumbled over the copper threshold, and the ball rolled out of his hand, across the floor of hardened clay, even to the nearly white-washed border, which ran about the edges of the room. It stopped at the feet of his mother, whose eyes opened wide at the sight of the ball of shining gold.

As he lay sprawling on the floor, and before he could pick himself up, one of the little men leaped over him, rushed into the room, and, from under his mother's petticoats, picked up the ball.

They spat at the boy and shouted, 'traitor,' 'rascal,' 'thief,' 'false mortal,' 'fox,' 'rat,' 'wolf,' and other bad names. Then they turned and sped away.

Now Elidyr, though he had been a mischievous boy, often wilful, lazy, and never liking his books, had always loved the truth. He was very sad because he had broken his word of honour. So, almost mad with grief and shame, and from an accusing conscience, he went back to find the cave in which he had slept. He would return to the king of the fairies, and ask his pardon, even if his majesty never allowed him to visit Fairyland again.

But though he often searched, and spent whole days in trying to find the opening in the hills, he could never discover it.

So, fully penitent, and resolving to live right, and become what his father wanted him to be, he went back to the monastery. There he plied his tasks so diligently that he excelled in all learning. In time, he became one of the most famous scholars in Welsh history. When he died, he asked to be buried, not in the monk's cemetery, but with his father and mother, in the churchyard. He made request that no name, record, or epitaph, be chiselled on his tomb, but only these words:

WE CAN DO NOTHING AGAINST THE TRUTH,
BUT ONLY FOR THE TRUTH.

Murdoch's Rath

By Juliana Horatia Gatty Ewing

READING TIME: 12 MINUTES

A rath is an ancient hillfort, which looks like a grassy mound on top of a high bank. They are scattered all over Ireland and fairies are believed to live inside them.

There was not a nicer boy in all Ireland than Pat, and clever at his trade too, if only he'd had one.

But from his cradle he learnt nothing (small blame to him with no one to teach him!), so when he grew old enough to make his own decisions, he earned his living by running errands for his neighbours. Pat could always be trusted to make the best of a bad bargain, and bring

Murdoch's Rath

back all the change, for he was the soul of honesty and good nature.

It's no wonder then that he was beloved by everyone, and got as much work as he could do, and if the pay had but fitted the work, he'd have been mighty comfortable. But as it was, what he got wouldn't have kept him in shoe leather, if it wasn't for the fact that he made ends meet by wearing his shoes in his pocket, except when he was in the town and obliged to look genteel for the credit of the place he came from.

Well, all was going on as peacefully as could be, till one market day, when business (or it may have been pleasure) detained him till the end of the evening, and by nightfall, when he began to make the journey home, he never bethought him to leave off his shoes, but tramped on just as if shoe leather were made to be knocked to bits on the king's highway.

And this was what he was saying:

"A dozen hanks of grey yarn for Mistress Murphy. Three gross of bright buttons for the tailor. Half an ounce of throat drops for Father Andrew, and an ounce of snuff for his housekeeper," and so on. For these were what he went to the town to fetch, and he was afraid one of the lot might have slipped his memory.

Now everybody knows there are two ways home from the town – the highway, and the way by Murdoch's Rath.

Murdoch's Rath was a pleasant enough spot in the daytime, but not many cared to go by it when the sun was down. And in all the years Pat was going backwards and forwards, he never once came home except by the high road till this unlucky evening, when, just at the place where the two roads part, he got, as one may say, into a sort of confusion. How far he walked he never could tell, before all of a sudden the moon shone out as bright as day, and Pat found himself in Murdoch's Rath. And this was the smallest part of the wonder, for the Rath was full of fairies.

When Pat got in they were dancing round and round till his feet tingled to look at them, being a good dancer himself. As he sat on the side of the Rath, and snapped his fingers to mark the time, the dancing stopped, and a little man came up, in a black hat and a green coat, with white stockings, and red shoes on his feet.

"Won't you take a turn with us, Pat?" said he, bowing till he nearly touched the ground. And, indeed, he had

not far to go, for he was barely two feet high.

"Don't say it twice, sir," said Pat. "I will be proud to foot the floor with ye," and before you could look round, there was Pat in the circle dancing away for bare life.

At first his feet felt like feathers for lightness, and it seemed as if he could have gone on forever. But at last he grew tired, and would have liked to stop, but the fairies would not, and so they danced on and on. Pat tried to think of something good to say, that he might free himself from the spell, but all he could think of was:

'A dozen hanks of grey yarn for Mistress Murphy. Three gross of bright buttons for the tailor. Half an ounce of throat drops for Father Andrew, and an ounce of snuff for his housekeeper,' and so on.

And it seemed to Pat that the moon was on the one side of the Rath when they began to dance, and on the other side when they left off, but he could not be sure after all that going round. One thing was plain enough. He danced every bit of leather off the soles of his feet, and they were blistered so that he could hardly stand, but all the little folk did was to stand and hold their sides with laughing at him.

At last the one who spoke before stepped up to him.

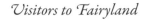

"Don't break your heart about it, Pat," said he, "I'll lend you my own shoes till the morning, for you seem to be a good natured boy."

Well, Pat looked at the fairy man's shoes, which were the size of a baby's, and he looked at his own feet, but not wishing to be uncivil, "Thank ye kindly, sir," said he. "And if your honour'll be good enough to put them on for me, maybe you won't spoil the shape." For he thought to himself, 'Small blame to me if the little gentleman can't get them to fit.'

With that he sat down on the side of the Rath, and the fairy man put on the shoes for him. As soon as they touched Pat's feet they became altogether a convenient size, and fitted him like wax. And, more than that, when he stood up, he didn't feel his blisters at all.

"Bring 'em back to the Rath at sunrise, Pat, my boy," said the little man. And as Pat was climbing over the ditch, "Look round, Pat," said he. And when Pat looked round, there were jewels and pearls lying at the roots of the bushes on the ditch, as thick as peas.

"Will you help yourself, or take what's given ye, Pat?" said the fairy man.

"Did I ever learn manners?" said Pat. "Would you have me help myself before company? I'll take what your honour pleases to give me, and be thankful."

The fairy man picked a lot of yellow blossoms from the bushes, and filled Pat's pockets.

"Keep 'em for love, Pat, me darling" said he.

Pat would have liked some of the jewels, but he put the blossoms by for love.

"Good evening to your honour," said he.

"And where are you going, Pat, dear?" said the fairy man.

"I'm going home," said Pat. And if the fairy man didn't know where that was, small blame to him.

"Just let me dust them shoes for ye, Pat," said the fairy man. And as Pat lifted up each foot he breathed on it, and dusted it with the tail of his green coat.

"Home!" said he, and when he let go, Pat was at his own doorstep before he could look round, and his parcels safe and sound with him.

Next morning he was up with the sun, and carried the fairy man's shoes back to the Rath. As he came up, the little man looked over the ditch.

"The top of the morning to your honour," said Pat, "here's your shoes."

"You're an honest boy, Pat," said the little gentleman. "It's inconvenienced I am without them, for I have only the one pair. Have you looked at the yellow flowers this morning?" he said.

"I have not, sir," said Pat, "I'd be loth to deceive you. I came off as soon as I was up."

"Be sure to look when you get back, Pat," said the fairy man, "and good luck to ye."

With which he disappeared, and Pat went home. He looked for the blossoms, as the fairy man told him, and there's not a word of truth in this tale if they weren't all pure gold pieces.

Well, now Pat was so rich, he went to the shoemaker to order another pair of brogues, and being a kindly, gossiping boy, the shoemaker soon learnt the whole

story of the fairy man and the Rath. And this so stirred up the shoemaker's greed that he resolved to go the very next night himself, to see if he could not dance with the fairies, and have like luck.

He found his way to the Rath, and sure enough the fairies were dancing, and asked him to join. He danced the soles off his brogues, as Pat did, and the fairy man lent him his shoes, and sent him home in a twinkling.

As he was going over the ditch, he looked round, and saw the roots of the bushes glowing with precious stones as if they had been glow worms.

"Will you help yourself, or take what's given ye?" said the fairy man.

"I'll help myself, if you please," said the cobbler, for he thought, 'If I can't get more than Pat brought home, my fingers must all be thumbs.'

So he drove his hand into the bushes, and if he didn't get plenty, it wasn't for want of grasping.

When he got up in the morning, he went straight to the jewels. But not a stone of the lot was more precious than roadside pebbles. "I ought not to look till I come from the Rath," said he. "It's best to do like Pat."

But he made up his mind not to return the fairy

man's shoes. "Who knows the virtue that's in them?" he said. So he made a small pair of red leather shoes, as like them as could be, and he blacked the others upon his feet, that the fairies might not know them, and at sunrise he went to the Rath.

The fairy man was looking over the ditch as before.

"Good morning to you," said he.

"The top of the morning to you, sir," said the cobbler. "Here's your shoes." And he handed him the pair that he had made, with a face as grave as a judge.

The fairy man looked at them, but he said nothing, though he did not put them on. "Have you looked at the things you got last night?" said he.

"I'll not deceive you, sir," said the cobbler. "I came off as soon as I was up. Not a peep I took at them."

"Be sure to look when you get back," said the fairy man. And just as the cobbler was getting over the ditch to go home, he said, "If my eyes don't deceive me," said he, "there's a little dirt on your left shoe. Let me dust it with the tail of my coat."

'That means home in a twinkling,' thought the cobbler, and he held up his foot.

The fairy man dusted it, and muttered something the

cobbler did not hear. "It's the dirty pastures that you've come through," said he, "for the other shoe's as bad."

So the cobbler held up his right foot, and the fairy man rubbed that with the tail of his green coat.

When all was done the cobbler's feet seemed to tingle, and then to itch, and then to smart, and then to burn. And at last he began to dance, and he danced all round the Rath (the fairy man laughing and holding his sides), and then round and round again. And he danced till he cried out with weariness, and tried to shake the shoes off. But they stuck fast, and the fairies drove him over the ditch, and through the bushes, and he danced away. Where he danced to, I cannot tell you. Whether he ever got rid of the fairy shoes, I do not know. The jewels never were more than wayside pebbles, and they were swept out when his cabin was cleaned, which was not too soon, you may be sure.

All this happened long ago, but there are those who say that the covetous cobbler dances still, between sunset and sunrise, round Murdoch's Rath.

Billy Beg, Tom Beg, and the Fairies

By Sophia Morrison

READING TIME: 6 MINUTES

Not far from Dalby, Billy Beg and Tom Beg, two humpback cobblers, lived together on a lonely croft. Billy Beg was sharper and cleverer than Tom Beg, who was always at his command. One day Billy Beg gave Tom a staff, and said, "Tom Beg, go to the mountain and fetch home the white sheep."

Tom Beg took the staff and went to the mountain, but he could not find the white sheep. At last, when he was far from home, and dusk was coming on, he began to think that he had best go back. The night was fine, and stars and a small crescent moon were in the sky. Tom was hastening home, and had almost reached Glen Rushen, when a grey mist gathered, and he lost his way. But it was not long before the mist cleared, and Tom Beg found himself in a green glen such as he had never seen before, though he thought he knew every glen within five miles of him. He was marvelling and wondering where he could be, when he heard a faraway sound drawing nearer to him.

"Aw," said he to himself, "there's more than myself afoot on the mountains tonight, I'll have company."

The sound grew louder. First, it was like the humming of bees, then like the rushing of Glen Meay waterfall, and last it was like the marching and the murmur of a crowd. It was the fairies. All of a sudden the glen was full of fine horses and of little people riding on them, with the lights on their red caps shining like the stars above and making the night as bright as day. There was the blowing of horns, the waving of flags, the playing of music, and the barking of many little dogs. Tom Beg thought that he had never seen anything so splendid as all he saw there. In the midst of the drilling and dancing and singing one of them spied Tom, and then Tom saw coming towards him the grandest little man he had ever set eyes upon, dressed in gold and silver silk, shining like a raven's wing.

"It is a bad time you have chosen to come this way," said the little man, who was the king.

"But it is not here that I'm wishing to be," said Tom.

Then said the king, "Are you one of us tonight, Tom?"

"I am surely," said Tom.

"Then," said the king, "it will be your duty to take the password. You must stand at the foot of the glen, and as each regiment goes by, you must take the password – it is: 'Monday, Tuesday, Wednesday, Thursday, Friday, Saturday.'"

"I'll do that with a heart and a half," said Tom.

At daybreak the fiddlers took up their fiddles, the fairy army set itself in order, the fiddlers played before them out of the glen, and sweet that music was. Each regiment gave the password to Tom as it went by, "Monday, Tuesday, Wednesday, Thursday, Friday, Saturday."

Last of all came the king, and he, too, gave it, "Monday, Tuesday, Wednesday, Thursday, Friday, Saturday."

Then he called to one of his men, "Take the hump from this fellow's back," and before the words were out of his mouth the hump was whisked off Tom Beg's back and thrown into the hedge.

How proud now was Tom, who so found himself the

straightest man in the Isle of Man! He went down the mountain and came home early in the morning with light heart and eager step. Billy Beg wondered greatly when he saw Tom Beg so straight and strong, and when Tom Beg had rested and refreshed himself he told his story about how he had met the fairies who came every night to Glen Rushen to drill.

The next night Billy Beg set off along the mountain road and came at last to the green glen. About midnight he heard the trampling of horses, the lashing of whips, the barking of dogs, and a great hullabaloo, and, behold, the fairies and their king, their dogs and their horses, all at drill in the glen as Tom Beg had said.

When they saw the humpback they all stopped, and one came forward and very crossly asked his business.

"I am one of yourselves for the night, and should be glad to do you some service," said Billy Beg.

So he was set to take the password, 'Monday, Tuesday, Wednesday, Thursday, Friday, Saturday.' And at daybreak the King said, "It's time for us to be off," and up came regiment after regiment giving Billy Beg the password, "Monday, Tuesday, Wednesday, Thursday, Friday, Saturday."

Last of all came the king with his men. and gave the password also, "Monday, Tuesday, Wednesday, Thursday, Friday, Saturday."

"And *Sunday*," said Billy Beg, thinking himself clever. Then there was a great outcry.

"Get the hump that was taken off that fellow's back last night and put it on this man's back," said the king, with flashing eyes, pointing to the hump that lay under the hedge.

Before the words were well out of his mouth the hump was clapped onto Billy Beg's back.

"Now," said the king, "be off, and if ever I find you here again, I will clap another hump on to your front!"

And they all marched away with one great shout, and left poor Billy Beg standing where they had found him, with a hump growing on each shoulder. And he came home next day dragging one foot after another, with a wizened face as cross as two sticks, with his two humps on his back, and if they are not off they are there still.

The Fairy Cow

By Jeremiah Curtin

READING TIME: 7 MINUTES

*I*n the parish of Drummor lived a farmer, whose name was Tom Connors. He had a nice bit of land and four cows. He was a fine, strong, honest man, and had a wife and five children.

Connors had one cow which was better than the other three, and she went by the name of Cooby. On one corner of Connors' farm there was a fairy fort, and the cow Cooby used to go into the fort, but Connors always drove her out, and told his wife and boys to keep her away from the fort, "For," said he, "there isn't much luck for any cow or calf that is fond of going into these fairy forts."

One morning when Connors went to drive his cows home to be milked he found Cooby in the field with her legs broken. He ran home that minute for a knife and killed and skinned the cow for the family to eat.

What of the meat himself and family didn't eat fresh he salted, and now and then of a Sunday evening or a holiday they had a meal of it with cabbage, and it lasted a long time.

One morning after Tom was gone to the bog to cut turf his wife went out to milk their remaining cows, and what should she see but a cow walking into the fort, and she the living image of Cooby. Soon the cow came out, and with her a girl with a pail and stool.

"Oh, then," said Mrs Connors, "I'd swear that is Cooby, only that we are after eating the most of her. She has the white spots on her back and the horns growing into her eyes."

The girl milked the cow, and then cow and girl disappeared. The following day Tom went again to cut turf, his wife went to milk, and again she saw the cow go into the fort, and the girl come out with a pail and a

stool and begin to milk it. 'God knows 'tis the very cow, and sure why shouldn't I know Cooby with the three white spots and the bent horns,' thought Mrs Connors, and she watched the cow and girl till the milking was over and thought, 'I'll tell Tom tonight, and he may do what he likes, but I'll have nothing to do with fort or fairies myself.'

When Connors came home in the evening, the first words his wife said were:

"Wisha then, Tom, I have the news for you tonight."

"And what news is it?" asked Tom.

"You remember Cooby?"

"Why shouldn't I remember Cooby, after eating most of her?"

"Indeed then, Tom, I saw Cooby today, inside in the fort with a girl milking her."

"But what is the use in telling me the like of that,"

said Tom, "when we haven't but two or three bits of her left inside the tub?"

"But it was Cooby I saw today."

"Well, I'll go in the morning, and if it's our Cooby I'll bring her home with me," said Tom, "Even if all the devils in the fort are before me."

Early in the morning Tom started across his land, and never stopped till he came to the fort, and there, sure enough, he saw the cow walking in through the gap to the fort, and he knew her that minute.

"'Tis my cow Cooby," said Connors, "and I'll have her. I'd like to see the man who would keep her from me."

That minute the girl came out with her pail and stool and was going up to Cooby.

"Stop where you are – don't milk that cow!" cried Connors, and springing toward the cow he caught her by the horn.

"Let the cow go," said Tom, "this is my cow. It's a year that she's from me now. Go to your master and tell him to come out to me."

The girl went inside the fort and disappeared, but soon a fine-looking young man came and spoke to

Connors. "What are you doing here, my man," asked he, "and why did you stop my servant from milking the cow?"

"She is my cow," said Tom, "and by that same token I'll keep her, and that's why I stopped the girl from milking her."

"How could she be your cow? Haven't I this cow a long time, and aren't you after eating your own cow?"

"I don't care what cow I'm after eating," said Tom. "I'll have this cow, for she is my Cooby."

They argued and argued. Tom declared that he'd take the cow home. "And if you try to prevent me," said he to the man, "I'll tear the fort to pieces or take her with me."

"Indeed, then, you'll not tear the fort."

Tom got so vexed that he made as though to fight the man. The man ran and Tom after him into the fort. When Tom was inside he forgot all about fighting. He saw many people dancing and enjoying themselves, and he thought, 'Why shouldn't I do the like myself?' With that he made up to a fine-looking girl, and, taking her out to dance, told the piper to strike up a hornpipe.

Tom danced till he was tired. He offered two pence to the piper, but not a penny would the piper take from him.

The young man came up and said, "Well, you are a brave man and courageous, and for the future we'll be good friends. You can take the cow."

"I will not take her, you may keep her and welcome, for you are all very good people."

"Well," said the young man, "the cow is yours, and it's why I took her because there were many children in the fort without nurses, but the children are reared now, and you may take the cow. I put an old stray horse in place of her and made him look like your own beast, and it's an old horse you've been eating all the year. From this day forwards you'll grow rich and have luck. We'll not trouble you, but help you."

Tom took the cow and drove her home. From that day forwards Tom Connors' cows had two calves apiece and his mare had two foals and his sheep two lambs every year, and every acre of the land he had gave him as much crop in one year as another man got from an acre in seven. At last Connors was a very rich man – and why not, when the fairies were with him?

Fairy Ointment

By Joseph Jacobs

READING TIME: 5 MINUTES

$\mathcal{D}$ame Goody was a nurse that looked after sick people, and minded babies. One night she was woke up at midnight, and when she went downstairs, she saw a strange, little old fellow, who asked her to come to his wife who was too ill to mind her baby. Dame Goody didn't like the look of the old fellow, but business is business, so she popped on her things, and went down to him. And when she got down to him, he whisked her up on to a large coal-black horse with fiery eyes, that stood at the door, and soon they were going at a rare pace, Dame Goody holding on to the old fellow like grim death.

They rode and they rode, till at last they stopped before a cottage door. So they got down and went in and found the good woman in bed with the children playing about, and the babe, a fine bouncing boy, beside her.

Dame Goody took the babe, which was as fine a baby boy as you'd wish to see. The mother, when she handed the baby to Dame Goody to mind, gave her a box of ointment, and told her to stroke the baby's eyes with it as soon as it opened them.

After a while it began to open its eyes. Dame Goody saw that it had eyes just like its father. So she took the box of ointment and stroked its two eyelids with it. But she couldn't help wondering what it was for, as she had never seen such a thing done before. So she looked to see if the others were looking, and, when they were not noticing, she stroked her own right eyelid with the ointment.

No sooner had she done so, than everything seemed changed about her. The cottage became elegantly furnished. The mother in the bed was a beautiful lady,

dressed up in white silk. The little baby was still more beautiful than before, and its clothes were made of a sort of silvery gauze.

Its little brothers and sisters around the bed were flat-nosed imps with pointed ears, who made faces at one another, and scratched their heads. In fact, they were up to all kinds of mischief, and Dame Goody knew that she had got into a house of fairies. But she said nothing to nobody, and as soon as the lady was well enough to mind the baby, she asked the old fellow to take her back home. So he came round to the door with the coal-black horse with eyes of fire, and off they went as fast as before till they came to Dame Goody's cottage, where the strange fellow lifted her down and left her, thanking her civilly enough, and paying her more than she had ever been paid before for such service.

Now next day happened to be market day, and as Dame Goody had been away from home, she wanted many things in the house, and trudged off to get them at the market. As she was buying the things she wanted, who should she see but the strange fellow who had taken her on the coal-black horse. And what do you think he was doing? Why he went about from stall to stall taking things from each – here some fruit, and there some eggs, and so on – and no one seemed to take any notice.

Now Dame Goody did not think it her business to interfere, but she thought she ought not to let so good a customer pass without speaking. So she went up to him, bobbed a curtsey and said:

"Good day, sir, I hope your good lady and the little one are as well as—"

But she couldn't finish what she was saying, for the funny old fellow started back in surprise, and he said to her, "What! Do you see me today?"

"See you," said she, "why, of course I do, as plain as the sun in the skies, and what's more," said she, "I see you are busy, too, into the bargain."

"Ah, you see too much," said he, "now, pray, with which eye do you see all this?"

"With the right eye to be sure," said she, as proud as can be to find him out.

"The ointment! The ointment!" cried the old fairy thief. "Take that for meddling with what don't concern you – you shall see me no more." And with that he struck her on the right eye, and she couldn't see him anymore, and, what was worse, she was blind on the right side from that hour till the day of her death.

Bruno's Revenge

From *Sylvie and Bruno* by Lewis Carroll

READING TIME: 20 MINUTES

What is the best time for seeing Fairies? I believe
I can tell you all about that.

The first rule is, that it must be a very hot day, and
you must be just a little sleepy, but not too sleepy to keep
your eyes open, mind. Well, and you ought to feel a
little, what one may call 'fairyish' – the Scotch call it
'eerie,' and perhaps that's a prettier word. If you don't
know what it means, I'm afraid I can hardly explain it –
you must wait till you meet a fairy, then you'll know.
And the last rule is, that the crickets should not be

chirping. I can't stop to explain that – you must take it on trust for the present.

So, if all these things happen together, you have a good chance of seeing a fairy – or at least a much better chance than if they didn't.

The first thing I noticed, as I went lazily along through an open place in the wood, was a large beetle lying struggling on its back, and I went down upon one knee to help the poor thing to its feet again. I was just reaching out a little stick to turn the beetle over, when I saw a sight that made me draw back hastily and hold my breath, for fear of making any noise and frightening the little creature away.

Not that she looked as if she would be easily frightened – she seemed so good and gentle that I'm sure she would never expect that anyone could wish to hurt her. She was only a few inches high, and was dressed in green, so that you really would hardly have noticed her among the long grass, and she was so delicate and graceful that she quite seemed to belong to the place, almost as if she were one of the flowers. I may tell you, besides, that she had no wings (I don't believe in fairies with wings), and that she had quantities of long brown hair and large earnest brown eyes, and then I shall have done all I can to give you an idea of her.

Sylvie (I found out her name afterwards) had knelt down, just as I was doing, to help the beetle, but it needed more than a little stick for her to get it on its legs again, it was as much as she could do, with both arms, to roll the heavy thing over, and all the while she was talking to it, half scolding and half comforting, "There, there! You needn't cry so much about it. And how did you come to tumble over? But I can see well enough how it was – I needn't ask you that – walking over sand pits with your chin in the air, as usual. You should look." The beetle murmured something that sounded like "I did look," and Sylvie went on again.

"But I know you didn't! You never do! You always walk with your chin up. Well, let's see how many legs are broken this time. Why, none of them, I declare! And what's the good of having six legs, my dear, if you can

only kick them all about in the air when you tumble? Legs are meant to walk with, you know. Now don't begin putting out your wings yet, I've more to say. Go to the frog that lives behind that buttercup – and tell him he's to give you some of that salve I left with him yesterday. And you'd better get him to rub it in for you. He's got rather cold hands, but you mustn't mind that."

I think the beetle must have shuddered at this idea, for Sylvie went on in a graver tone. "Now you needn't pretend to be so particular as all that. Suppose you could get nobody but a toad to do it, how would you like that?"

There was a little pause, and then Sylvie added "Now you may go. Be a good beetle, and don't keep your chin in the air."

And then began one of those performances of humming, and whizzing, and restless banging about, such as a beetle indulges in when it has decided on flying, but hasn't quite made up its mind which way to go. At last, in one of its awkward zigzags, it managed to fly right into my face, and, by the time I had recovered from the shock, the little fairy was gone.

I looked about in all directions for the little creature,

but there was no trace of her – and my 'eerie' feeling was quite gone off, and the crickets were chirping again merrily – so I knew she was really gone.

And now I've got time to tell you the rule about the crickets. They always stop chirping when a fairy goes by – because a fairy's a kind of queen over them, I suppose (at all events it's a much grander thing than a cricket) so whenever you're walking out, and the crickets suddenly leave off chirping, you may be sure that they see a fairy.

I walked on sadly enough, you may be sure. However, I comforted myself with thinking 'It's been a very wonderful afternoon, so far. I'll just go quietly on and look about me, and I shouldn't wonder if I were to come across another Fairy somewhere.'

And so I did, indeed, I very nearly walked over him, without seeing him, which would have been dreadful, always supposing that fairies can be walked over (my own belief is that they are something of the nature of will-o'-the-wisps, and there's no walking over them).

Think of any pretty little boy you know, with rosy cheeks, large dark eyes, and tangled brown hair, and then fancy him made small enough to go comfortably into a coffee cup, and you'll have a very fair idea of him.

"What's your name, little one?" I began, in as soft a voice as I could manage.

I felt it quite necessary to know his name, so, as he didn't answer my question,

I asked it again a little louder. "What's your name, my little man?"

"What's oors?" he said, without looking up.

I told him my name quite gently, for he was much too small to be angry with.

"Duke of Anything?" he asked, just looking at me for a moment, and then going on with his work.

"Not duke at all," I said.

"Oo're big enough to be two dukes," said the little creature. "I suppose oo're Sir Something, then?"

"No," I said, feeling more and more ashamed. "I haven't got any title."

The fairy seemed to think that in that case I really wasn't worth the trouble of talking to, for he quietly went on digging, and tearing the flowers to pieces.

After a few minutes I tried again. "Please tell me what your name is."

"Bruno," the little fellow answered, very readily. "Why didn't oo say 'please' before, anyway?"

'That's something like what we used to be taught in the nursery,' I thought to myself, looking back through the long years (about a hundred of them, since you ask the question), to the time when I was a little child. And here an idea came into my head, and I asked him, "Aren't you one of the fairies that teach children to be good?"

"Well, we have to do that sometimes," said Bruno, "and a dreadful bother it is." As he said this, he tore a heartsease in two, and trampled on the pieces.

"What are you doing there, Bruno?" I said.

"Spoiling Sylvie's garden," was all the answer Bruno would give at first. But, as he went on tearing up the flowers, he muttered to himself. "The nasty cross thing wouldn't let me go and play this morning, said I must finish my lessons first – lessons, indeed! I'll vex her finely, though!"

"Oh, Bruno, you shouldn't do that!" I cried. "Don't you know that's revenge? And revenge is a wicked, cruel, dangerous thing!"

"River-edge?" said Bruno. "What a funny word! I suppose oo call it cruel and dangerous 'cause, if oo wented too far and tumbleded in, oo'd get drownded."

"No, not river-edge," I explained, "revenge" (saying the word very slowly). But I couldn't help thinking that Bruno's explanation did very well for either word.

"Oh!" said Bruno, opening his eyes very wide, but without trying to repeat the word.

"Come! Try and pronounce it, Bruno!" I said, cheerfully. "Re-venge, re-venge."

But Bruno only tossed his little head, and said he couldn't, that his mouth wasn't the right shape for words of that kind.

"Well, never mind, my little man!" I said. "Shall I help you with that job?"

"Yes, please," Bruno said, quite pacified. "Only I wiss I could think of somefin to vex her more. Oo don't know how hard it is to make her angry!"

"Now listen to me, Bruno, and I'll teach you quite a splendid kind of revenge!"

"Somefin that'll vex her finely?" he asked with gleaming eyes.

"Something that will vex her finely. First, we'll get up all the weeds in her garden. See, there are a good many at this end quite hiding the flowers."

"But that won't vex her!" said Bruno.

"After that," I said, without noticing the remark, "we'll water this highest bed – up here. You see it's getting quite dry and dusty."

Bruno looked at me inquisitively, but he said nothing this time.

"Then after that," I went on, "the walks want sweeping a bit, and I think you might cut down that tall nettle – it's so close to the garden that it's quite in the way—"

"What is oo talking about?" Bruno impatiently interrupted me. "All that won't vex her a bit!"

"Won't it?" I said, innocently. "Then, after that, suppose we put in some of these coloured pebbles – just to mark the divisions between the different kinds of flowers, you know. That'll have a very pretty effect."

Bruno turned round and had another good stare at me. At last there came an odd little twinkle into his eyes,

and he said, with quite a new meaning in his voice, "That'll do nicely. Let's put 'em in rows – all the red together, and all the blue together. "

"That'll do capitally," I said, "and then – what kind of flowers does Sylvie like best?"

Bruno had to put his thumb in his mouth and considered a little before he could answer. "Violets," he said, at last.

"There's a beautiful bed of violets by the brook."

"Oh, let's fetch 'em!" cried Bruno, giving a little skip into the air. "Here! Catch hold of my hand, and I'll help oo along. The grass is rather thick down that way."

I couldn't help laughing at his having so entirely forgotten what a big creature he was talking to. "No, not yet, Bruno," I said, "we must consider what's the right thing to do first. You see we've got quite a business before us."

"Yes, let's consider," said Bruno, putting his thumb into his mouth again, and sitting down upon a dead mouse.

"What do you keep that mouse for?" I said. "You should either bury it, or else throw it into the brook."

"Why, it's to measure with!" cried Bruno. "How ever

would oo do a garden without one? We make each bed three mouses and a half long, and two mouses wide."

I stopped him, as he was dragging it off by the tail to show me how it was used, for I was half afraid the 'eerie' feeling might go off before we had finished the garden, and in that case I should see no more of him or Sylvie. "I think the best way will be for you to weed the beds, while I sort out these pebbles, ready to mark the walks with."

"That's it!" cried Bruno. "And I'll tell oo about the caterpillars while we work."

"Ah, let's hear about the caterpillars," I said, as I drew the pebbles together into a heap and began dividing them into colours.

And Bruno went on in a low, rapid tone, more as if he were talking to himself. "Yesterday I saw two little caterpillars, when I was sitting by the brook, just where oo go into the wood. They were quite green, and they had yellow eyes, and they didn't see me. And one of them had got a moth's wing to carry – a great brown moth's wing, oo know, all dry, with feathers. So he couldn't want it to eat, I should think – perhaps he meant to make a cloak for the winter?

"Well, and so he didn't want the other caterpillar to see the moth's wing, oo know – so what must he do but try to carry it with all his left legs, and he tried to walk on the other set. Of course he toppled over and if oo ever saw a caterpillar topple over, oo'd know it's a welly serious thing, and not sit grinning like that – and I shan't tell oo no more!"

"Indeed and indeed, Bruno, I didn't mean to grin. See, I'm quite grave again now."

But Bruno only folded his arms, and said "Don't tell me. I see a little twinkle in one of oor eyes – just like the moon."

"Why do you think I'm like the moon, Bruno?" I asked.

"Oor face is large and round like the moon," Bruno answered, looking at me thoughtfully. "It doosn't shine quite so bright – but it's more cleaner."

I couldn't help smiling at this. "You know I sometimes wash my face, Bruno. The moon never does."

"Oh, doosn't she though!" cried Bruno, and he leant forwards and added in a solemn whisper, "The moon's face gets dirtier and dirtier every night, till it's black. And then, when it's dirty all over," (he passed his hand

across his own rosy cheeks as he spoke) "then she washes it."

"Then it's all clean again, isn't it?"

"Not all in a moment," said Bruno. "What a deal of teaching oo wants! She washes it little by little – only she begins at the other edge, oo know."

By this time he was sitting quietly on the dead mouse with his arms folded, and the weeding wasn't getting on a bit, so I had to say "Work first, pleasure afterwards – no more talking till that bed's finished."

After that we had a few minutes of silence, while I sorted out the pebbles, and amused myself with watching Bruno's plan of gardening.

It was quite a new plan to me, he always measured each bed before he weeded it, as if he was afraid the weeding would make it shrink, and once, when it came out longer than he wished, he set to work to thump the mouse with his little fist, crying out "There now! It's all gone wrong again! Why don't oo keep oor tail straight when I tell oo!"

"I'll tell you what I'll do," Bruno said in a half-whisper, as we worked. "Oo like fairies, don't oo?"

"Yes," I said, "of course I do, or I should have gone to some place where there are no Fairies."

Bruno laughed contemptuously. "Why, oo might as well say oo'd go to some place where there wasn't any air – supposing oo didn't like air!"

This was a rather difficult idea to grasp. I tried a change of subject.

"You're nearly the first fairy I ever saw. Have you ever seen any people besides me?"

"Plenty!" said Bruno. "We see 'em when we walk in the road."

"But they can't see you. How is it they never tread on you?"

"Can't tread on us," said Bruno, looking amused at my ignorance. "Why, suppose oo're walking, here," (making little marks on the ground) "and suppose there's a fairy – that's me – walking here. Very well then, oo put one foot here, and one foot here, so oo doosn't tread on the fairy."

This was all very well as an explanation, but it didn't convince me.

"Why shouldn't I put one foot on the fairy?" I asked.

"I don't know why," the little fellow said in a thoughtful tone. "But I know oo wouldn't. Nobody never walked on the top of a fairy."

By this time we had nearly finished the garden. I had fetched some violets, and Bruno was just helping me to put in the last, when he suddenly stopped and said "I'm tired."

"Rest then," I said, "I can go on without you quite well."

Bruno needed no second invitation. He at once began arranging the dead mouse as a kind of sofa. "And I'll sing oo a little song," he said, as he rolled it about.

"Do," said I, "I like songs very much."

"Which song will oo choose?" Bruno said, as he dragged the mouse into a place where he could get a good view of me. "'Ting, ting, ting' is the nicest."

There was no resisting such a strong hint as this, however, I pretended to think about it for a moment, and then said "Well, I like 'Ting, ting, ting,' best of all."

"That shows oo're a good judge of music," Bruno said, with a pleased look. He seated himself on the dead mouse (he never seemed really comfortable anywhere

else), and, looking up at me with a merry twinkle in his eyes, he began.

He sang the first four lines briskly and merrily, but the last two he sang quite slowly and gently.

"Hush, Bruno!" I interrupted in a warning whisper. "She's coming!"

Bruno checked his song, and, as Sylvie slowly made her way through the long grass, he suddenly rushed out headlong at her, shouting "Look the other way! Look the other way!"

"Which way?" Sylvie asked, in rather a frightened tone.

"That way!" said Bruno, carefully turning her round with her face to the wood. "Now, walk backwards, walk gently – don't be frightened – oo shan't trip!"

But Sylvie did trip notwithstanding, he was far too much excited to think of what he was doing.

I silently pointed out to Bruno the best place to lead her to, so as to get a view of the whole garden at once. It was a little rising ground, about the height of a potato, and, when they had mounted it, I drew back into the shade, that Sylvie mightn't see me.

I heard Bruno cry out triumphantly "Now oo may look!" and then followed a clapping of hands, but it was all done by Bruno himself. Sylvie was silent – she stood and gazed with her hands clasped together. Bruno too was watching her anxiously, and when she jumped down off the mound, and began wandering up and down the little walks, he cautiously followed her about, evidently anxious that she should form her own opinion of it all, without any hint from him.

And when at last she drew a long breath, and gave her verdict, in a hurried whisper, and without the slightest regard to grammar, "It's the loveliest thing as I never saw in all my life before!" the little fellow looked as well pleased as if it had been given by all the judges and juries in England put together.

"And did you really do it all by yourself, Bruno?" said Sylvie. "And all for me?"

"I was helped a bit," Bruno began, with a merry little laugh at her surprise. "We've been at it all the afternoon – I thought oo'd like—" and here the poor little fellow's lip began to quiver, and all in a moment he burst out crying, and running up to Sylvie he flung his arms passionately round her neck, and hid his face on her shoulder.

There was a little quiver in Sylvie's voice too, as she whispered "Why, what's the matter, darling?" and tried to lift up his head and kiss him.

But Bruno only clung to her, sobbing, and wouldn't be comforted till he had confessed. "I tried – to spoil oor garden – first – but I'll never – never," and then came another burst of tears, which drowned the rest of the sentence. At last he got out the words "I liked – putting in the flowers – for oo, Sylvie – and I never was so happy before."

After that they went through the whole garden again, flower by flower, as if it were a long sentence they were spelling out, with kisses for commas, and a great hug by way of a full stop when they got to the end.

"Doos oo know, that was my river-edge, Sylvie?" Bruno solemnly began.

Sylvie laughed merrily. "What do you mean?" she said. And she pushed back her heavy brown hair with both hands, and looked at him with dancing eyes.

Bruno drew in a long breath, and made up his mouth for a great effort. "I mean revenge," he said, "now oo under'tand." And he looked so happy and proud at having said the word right at last, that I quite envied him. I rather think Sylvie didn't 'under'tand' at all, but she gave him a little kiss on each cheek, which seemed to do just as well.

So they wandered off lovingly together, in among the buttercups, each with an arm twined round the other, whispering and laughing as they went, and never once

looked back at poor me. Yes, once, just before I quite lost sight of them, Bruno half turned his head, and nodded me a little goodbye over one shoulder. And that was all the thanks got for my trouble.

The very last thing I saw of them was this – Sylvie was stooping down with her arms round Bruno's neck, and saying coaxingly in his ear, "Do you know, Bruno, I've quite forgotten that hard word. Do say it once more. Come! Only this once, dear!"

But Bruno wouldn't try it again.

The Fiddler in the Fairy Ring

By Juliana Horatia Gatty Ewing

READING TIME: 10 MINUTES

There are many stories about fairy fiddlers, whose music is so sweet that all who hear it must dance, whether they want to or not. In this story, the fiddler is a human, but his music is just as powerful.

There once lived a farmer's son, who had no great harm in him, and no great good either. He always meant well, but he had a poor spirit, and was too fond of idle company.

One day his father sent him to market with some sheep for sale, and when business was over for the day, the rest of the country folk made ready to go home, and more than one of them offered the lad a lift in his cart.

"Thank you kindly, all the same," said he, "but I am going back across the downs with Limping Tim."

Then out spoke a steady old farmer and bade the lad go home with the rest, and by the main road. For Limping Tim was an idle, graceless kind of fellow, who fiddled for his livelihood, but what else he did to earn the money he squandered, no one knew. And as to the sheep path over the downs, it stands to reason that the highway is better travelling after sunset, for the other is no such very short cut, and has a big fairy ring near it.

But the farmer's son would go his own way, and that was with Limping Tim, and across the downs.

So they started, and the fiddler had his fiddle in his hand, and a bundle of marketings under his arm, and he sang snatches of strange songs, the like of which the lad had never heard before. And the moon drew out their shadows over the short grass till they were as long as the great stones of Stonehenge.

At last they turned the hill, and the fairy ring looked dark under the moon, and the farmer's son blessed himself that they were passing it quietly, when

Limping Tim suddenly pulled his cloak from his back, and handing it to his companion, cried, "Hold this for a moment, will you? I'm wanted. They're calling for me."

"I hear nothing," said the farmer's son.

But before he had got the words out of his mouth, the fiddler had completely disappeared. The farmer's son shouted aloud, but in vain, and had begun to think of proceeding on his way, when the fiddler's voice cried, "Ah, this is dancing! Come in, my lad, come in!"

But the farmer's son was not totally without prudence, and he took good care to keep at a safe distance from the fairy ring.

"Come back, Limping Tim! Come back!" he shouted.

Again heard his friend's voice, crying, "Take care of it for me! The money dances out of my pocket." And the fiddler's purse was hurled to the farmer's son, where it fell with a heavy chinking of gold within.

He picked it up, and, after waiting for a long time, he made the best of his way home alone, hoping that the fiddler would follow, and come to reclaim his property.

The fiddler never came. And when at last there was a fuss about his disappearance, the farmer's son, who had but a poor spirit, began to be afraid to tell the truth of the matter.

"Who knows but they may accuse me of theft?" said he.

So he hid the cloak, and the bundle, and the money bag in the garden.

But when three months passed, and still the fiddler did not return, it was whispered that the farmer's son had been his last companion, and the place was searched, and they found the cloak and the money bag and the lad was taken to prison.

Now, when it was too late, he plucked up a spirit, and told the truth, but no one believed him, and it was said that he had murdered the fiddler for the sake of his money and goods. And he was taken before the judge, found guilty, and sentenced to death.

Fortunately, his old mother was a wise woman. And when she heard that he was condemned, she said, "Only follow my directions, and we may save you yet, for I can guess how it is."

So she went to the judge, and begged for her son three favours before his death.

"I will grant them," said the judge, "if you do not ask for his life."

"The first," said the old woman, "is, that he may choose the place where the gallows shall be erected. The second, that he may fix the hour of his execution. And the third favour is, that you will not fail to be present."

"I grant all three," said the judge. But when he learnt that the criminal had chosen a certain hill on the downs for the place of execution, and an hour before midnight for the time, he sent to beg the sheriff to bear him company on this important occasion.

The sheriff placed himself at the judge's disposal, but he commanded the attendance of the jailer as some sort of protection, and the jailer, for his part, implored his reverence the chaplain to be of the party, as the hill was not in good spiritual repute. So, when the time came, the four started together, and the hangman and the farmer's son went before them to the foot of the gallows.

Just as the rope was being prepared, the farmer's son

called to the judge, and said, "If your Honour will walk twenty paces down the hill, to where you will see a bit of paper, you will learn the fate of the fiddler."

"That is, no doubt, a copy of the poor man's last confession," thought the judge.

"Murder will out, Mr Sheriff," said he, and in the interests of truth and justice he hastened to pick up the paper.

But the farmer's son had dropped it as he came along, by his mother's direction, in such a place that the judge could not pick it up without putting his foot on the edge of the fairy ring. No sooner had he done so than he perceived an innumerable company of little people dressed in green cloaks and hoods, who were dancing round in a circle as wide as the ring itself.

They were all about two feet high, and had aged faces, brown and withered, like the knots on gnarled trees in hedge bottoms, and they squinted horribly, but, in spite of their seeming age, they flew round and round like children.

"Mr Sheriff! Mr Sheriff!" cried the judge, "come and see the dancing. And hear the music, too, which is so lively that it makes the soles of my feet tickle."

"There is no music, my Lord Judge," said the sheriff, running down the hill. "It is the wind whistling over the grass that your lordship hears."

But when the sheriff had put his foot by the judge's foot, he saw and heard the same, and he cried out, "Quick, jailer, and come down! I should like you to be witness to this matter. And you may take my arm, jailer, for the music makes me feel unsteady."

"There is no music here, sir," said the jailer, "but your worship doubtless hears the steady creaking of the gallows."

But no sooner had the jailer's feet touched the fairy ring, than he saw and heard like the rest, and he called lustily to the chaplain to come and stop the unhallowed measure.

"It is a delusion of the Evil One," said the parson, "there is not a sound in the air but the distant croaking of some frogs." But when he too touched the ring, he perceived his mistake.

At this moment the moon shone out, and in the middle of the ring they saw Limping Tim the fiddler, playing till great drops stood out on his forehead, and dancing as madly as he played.

"Ah, you rascal!" cried the judge. "Is this where you've been all the time, and a better man than you as good as hanged for you? But you shall come home now."

Saying which, he ran in, and seized the fiddler by the arm, but Limping Tim resisted so stoutly that the sheriff had to go to the judge's assistance, and even then the fairies so pinched and hindered them that the sheriff was obliged to call upon the jailer to put his arms about his waist, who persuaded the chaplain to add his strength to the string. But as ill luck would have it, just as they were getting off, one of the fairies picked up Limping Tim's fiddle, which had fallen in the scuffle, and began to play.

And as he began to play, everyone began to dance – the fiddler, and the judge, and the sheriff, and the jailer, and even the chaplain.

"Hangman! Hangman!" screamed the judge, as he lifted first one leg and then the other to the tune, "come down, and catch hold of his reverence the chaplain. The prisoner is pardoned, and he can lay hold too."

The hangman knew the judge's voice, and ran towards it, but as they were now quite within the ring he could see nothing, either of him or his companions.

The farmer's son followed, and warning the hangman not to touch the ring, he directed him to stretch his hands forwards in hopes of catching hold of someone. In a few minutes the wind blew the chaplain's cassock against the hangman's fingers, and he caught the parson round the waist. The farmer's son then seized him in like fashion, and each holding firmly by the other, the fiddler, the judge, the sheriff, the jailer, the parson, the hangman, and the farmer's son all got safely out of the fairy circle.

"Oh, you scoundrel!" cried the judge to the fiddler, "I have a very good mind to hang you up on the gallows without further ado."

But the fiddler only looked like one possessed, and upbraided the farmer's son for not having the patience to wait three minutes for him.

"Three minutes!" cried he, "why, you've been here three months and a day."

This the fiddler would not believe, and as he seemed in every way beside himself, they led him home, still upbraiding his companion, and crying continually for his fiddle.

As to the farmer's son, it is said that thenceforward he went home from market by the high road, and spoke the truth straight out, and was more careful of his company.

The Fairy Wife

By Patrick Kennedy

READING TIME: 8 MINUTES

In the story Fairy Ointment *by Joseph Jacobs, the ointment makes everything appear more beautiful than it really is, but in this story it makes everything look worse. This is one of the many stories in which a person is stolen away by the fairies, and another person hopes to rescue them, which usually takes great courage and steadfastness. In Irish fairy stories, people who neglect their prayers or don't go to church are always at more risk of being stolen by the fairies. In this story, 'fairy man' means a man who claims to have skill in curing the illnesses and disorders that fairies cause.*

*T*here was once a little farmer and his wife living near Coolgarrow. They had three children, and my story happened while the youngest was a baby. The wife was a good wife enough, but her mind was all on her family and her farm, and she hardly ever went to her knees to pray without falling asleep, and she thought the time spent in the chapel was twice as long as it need be. So, friends, she let her husband and her two children go before her one day to Mass, while she called to consult a fairy man about a disorder one of her cows had. She was late at the chapel, and was sorry all the day after, for her husband was in grief about it.

Late one night the farmer was wakened up by the cries of his children calling out, "Mother! Mother!"

When he sat up and rubbed his eyes, there was no wife by his side, and when he asked the little ones what was become of their mother, they said they saw the room full of nice little men and women, dressed in white and red and green, and their mother in the middle of them, going out by the door as if she was walking in her sleep.

Out he ran, and searched everywhere round the house but, neither tale nor tidings did he get of her for many a day.

Well, the poor man was miserable enough, for he was as fond of his wife as she was of him. It used to bring the salt tears down his cheeks to see his poor children neglected and dirty, as they often were, and they'd be bad enough only for a kind neighbour that used to look in whenever she could spare time.

About six weeks after – just as he was going out to his work one morning – a neighbour, that used to mind

women when they were ill, came up to him, and kept step by step with him to the field, and this is what she told him:

"Just as I was falling asleep last night, I heard a horse's tramp on the grass and a knock at the door, and there, when I came out, was a fine-looking dark man, mounted on a black horse, and he told me to get ready in all haste, for a lady was in great want of me. As soon as I put on my cloak and things, he took me by the hand, and I was sitting behind him before I felt myself stirring. 'Where are we going, sir?' said I. 'You'll soon know,' said he, and he drew his fingers across my eyes, and not a ray could I see. I kept a tight grip of him, and I little knew whether he was going backwards or forwards, or how long we were about it, till my hand was taken again, and I felt the ground under me. The fingers went the other way across my eyes, and there we were before a castle door, and in we went through a big hall and great rooms all painted in fine green colours, with red and gold bands and ornaments, and the finest carpets and chairs and tables and window curtains, and grand ladies and gentlemen walking about.

"At last we came to a bedroom, with a beautiful lady

in bed, with a fine bouncing boy beside her. The lady clapped her hands, and in came the dark man and kissed her and the baby, and praised me, and gave me a bottle of green ointment to rub the child all over.

"Well, the child I rubbed, sure enough, but my right eye began to smart, and I put up my finger and gave it a rub, and then stared, for never in all my life was I so

frightened. The beautiful room was a big, rough cave, with water oozing over the edges of the stones and through the clay, and the lady, and the lord, and the child weazened, poverty-bitten creatures – nothing but skin and bone – and the rich dresses were old rags. I didn't let on that I found any difference, and after a bit said the dark man, 'Go before me to the hall door, and I will be with you in a few moments, and see you safe home.'

"Well, just as I turned into the outside cave, who should I see watching near the door but your poor wife Molly. She looked round all terrified, and said she to me in a whisper, 'I'm brought here to nurse the child of the king and queen of the fairies, but there is one chance of saving me. All the court will pass the cross near Templeshambo next Friday night, on a visit to the fairies of Old Ross. If my husband John can catch me by the hand or cloak when I ride by, and has courage not to let go his grip, I'll be safe. Here's the king. Don't open your mouth to answer.'

"The dark man didn't once cast his eye towards Molly, and he seemed to have no suspicion of me. When we came out I looked about me, and where do you think we were but in the dyke of the Rath of Cromogue. I was on the horse again, which was nothing but a big ragweed, and I was in dread every minute I'd fall off, but nothing happened till I found myself in my own cabin. The king slipped five guineas into my hand as soon as I was on the ground, and thanked me, and bade me good night. I hope I'll never see his face again. I got into bed, and couldn't sleep for a long time, and when I examined my five guineas this morning, that I left in the table drawer the last thing, I found five withered leaves of oak – bad luck to the giver!"

Well, you may all think the fright, and the joy, and the grief the poor man was in when the woman finished her story. They talked and they talked, till Friday night came, when both were standing where the mountain road crosses the one going to Ross. There they stood, looking towards the bridge of Thuar, in the dead of the night, with a little moonlight shining.

At last she gave a start, and said she, "Here they come, bridles jingling and feathers tossing!" He looked, but could see nothing, and she stood trembling and her eyes wide open, looking down the way to the ford of Ballinacoola.

"I see your wife," said she, "riding on the outside. We'll walk on quietly, as if we suspected nothing, and when we are passing I'll give you a shove. If you don't do your duty then, woe be with you!"

Well, they walked on easy, and the poor hearts beating in both their breasts, and though he could see nothing, he heard a faint jingle and trampling and rustling, and at last he got the push that she promised. He spread out his arms, and there was his wife's waist within them, and he could see her plain, but such a hullabulloo rose as if there was an earthquake, and he found himself surrounded by horrible-looking things, roaring at him and striving to pull his wife away. But he made the sign of the cross and bid them begone in God's name, and held his wife as if it was iron his arms were made of. In one moment everything was as silent as the grave, and the poor woman lying in a faint in the arms of her husband and her good neighbour. Well, all in good time she was minding her family and her business again, and I expect, after the fright she got, she spent more time praying, and avoided fairies all the days of the week, and particularly on Sunday.

The Treasure Stone
of the Fairies

By William Elliot Griffis

READING TIME: 10 MINUTES

Long ago, when London was a village and Cardiff only
a hamlet, there was a boy who tended sheep on the
hillsides. His father was a hardworking farmer, who
every year tried to grow out of the stony ground some
oats, barley, leeks and cabbage. In summer, he worked
hard, from the first croak of the raven to the last hoot of
the owl, to provide food for his wife and baby daughter.
When his boy was born, he took him to the church to be

christened Gruffyd, but everybody called him 'Gruff'.

In time, several little sisters came to keep the boy company. His mother always kept her cottage, which was painted pink, very neat and pretty, with vines covering the outside, while flowers bloomed indoors. These were set in pots and on shelves near the latticed windows. They seemed to grow finely, because so good a woman loved them. The copper doorframe was kept bright, and the broad borders on the clay floor, along the walls, were always fresh with whitewash. The pewter dishes on the sideboard shone as if they were moons, and the china cats on the mantelpiece, in silvery lustre, reflected both sun and candle light. Daddy often declared he could use these polished metal plates for a mirror when he shaved his face. Puss, the cat, was always happy purring away on the hearth, as the kettle boiled to make the sour oat jelly, which daddy loved so well.

Mother Gruffyd was always neat, with her striped apron, her high peaked hat, with its scalloped lace and quilled fastening around her chin, her little short shawl, with its pointed, long tips, tied in a bow, and her bright red petticoat folded back from her frock. Her white collar and neck cloth knotted at the top, and fringed at the ends, added fine touches to her picturesque costume.

In fact, young Gruffyd was proud of his mother and he loved her dearly. He thought no woman could be quite as sweet as she was.

Once, at the end of the day, on coming back home, from the hills, the boy met some lovely children. They were dressed in very fine clothes, and had elegant manners. They came up, smiled, and invited him to play with them. He joined in their sports, and was too much interested to take note of time. He kept on playing with them until it was pitch dark.

Among other games, which he enjoyed, had been that of 'The king in his counting house, counting out his money,' and 'The queen in her kitchen, eating bread and honey,' and 'The girl hanging out the clothes,' and 'The saucy blackbird that snipped off her nose.' In playing these, the children had aprons full of what seemed to be real coins, the size of crowns, or five-shilling pieces, each worth a dollar. These had 'head and tail,' beside letters on them and the boy supposed they were real.

But when he showed these to his mother, she saw at once from their lightness, and because they were so easily bent, that they were only paper, and not silver.

She asked her boy where he had got them. He told her what a nice time he had enjoyed. Then she knew that these, his playmates, were fairy children. Fearing that some evil might come of this, she charged him, her only son, never to go out again alone, on the mountain. She mistrusted that no good would come of making such strange children his companions.

But the lad was so fond of play, that one day, tired of seeing nothing but byre and garden, while his sisters liked to play girls' games more than those which boys cared most for, and the hills seeming to beckon him to come to them, he disobeyed, and slipped out and off to the mountains. He was soon missed and search was made for him.

Yet nobody had seen or heard of him. Though inquiries were made on every road, in every village, and at all the fairs and markets in the neighbourhood, two whole years passed by, without a trace of the boy.

But early one morning of the twenty-fifth month, before breakfast, his mother, on opening the door, found him sitting on the steps, with a bundle under his arm, but dressed in the same clothes, and not looking a day older or in any way different, from the very hour he disappeared.

"Why my dear boy, where have you been, all these months, which have now run into the third year – so long a time that they have seemed to me like ages?"

"Why, mother dear, how strange you talk. I left here yesterday, to go out and to play with the children, on the hills, and we have had a lovely time. See what pretty clothes they have given me for a present." Then he opened his bundle.

But when she tore open the package, the mother was all the more sure that she was right, and that her fears

had been justified. In it she found only a dress of white paper. Examining it carefully, she could see neither seam nor stitches. She threw it in the fire, and again warned her son against fairy children.

But pretty soon, after a great calamity had come upon them, both father and mother changed their minds about fairies.

They had put all their savings into the venture of a ship, which had for a long time made trading voyages from Cardiff. Every year, it came back bringing great profit to the owners and shareholders. In this way, his father was able to eke out his income, and keep himself, his wife and daughters comfortably clothed, while all the time the table was well supplied with good food. Nor did they ever turn from their door anyone who asked for bread and cheese.

But in the same month of the boy's return, bad news came that the good ship had gone down in a storm. All on board had perished, and the cargo was totally lost in the deep sea, far from land. In fact, no word except that of dire disaster had come to hand.

Now it was a tradition, as old as the days of King Arthur, that on a certain hill a great boulder could be

seen, which was quite different from any other kind of rock to be found within miles. It was partly imbedded in the earth, and beneath it, lay a great, yes, an untold treasure. The grass grew luxuriantly around this stone, and the sheep loved to rest at noon in its shadow. Many men had tried to lift, or pry it up, but in vain. The tradition, unaltered and unbroken for centuries, was to the effect, that none but a very good man could ever budge this stone. Any and all unworthy men might dig, or pull, or pry, until doomsday, but in vain. Till the right one came, the treasure was as safe as if in heaven.

But the boy's father and mother were now very poor and his sisters now grown up wanted pretty clothes so badly, that the lad hoped that he or his father might be the deserving one. He would help him to win the treasure for he felt sure that his parent would share his gains with all his friends.

Though his neighbours were not told of the generous intentions credited to the boy's father, by his loving son, they all came with horses, ropes, crowbars, and tackle, to help in the enterprise. Yet after many a long days' toil, between the sun's rising and setting, their end was failure. Everyday, when darkness came on, the stone lay

there, as hard and fast as ever. So they gave up the task.

On the final night, the lad saw that his father and mother were holding hands, while their tears flowed together, and they were praying for patience.

Seeing this, before he fell asleep, the boy resolved that on the morrow, he would go up to the mountains, and talk to his fairy friends about the matter.

So early in the morning, he hurried to the hill tops, and going into one of the caves, met the fairies and told them his troubles. Then he asked them to give him again some of their money.

"Not this time, but something better. Under the great rock there are treasures waiting for you."

"Oh, don't send me there! For all the men and horses of our parish, after working a week, have been unable to budge the stone."

"We know that," answered the principal fairy, "but do you yourself try to move it. Then you will see what is certain to happen."

Going home, to tell what he had heard, his parents had a hearty laugh at the idea of a boy succeeding where men, with the united strength of many horses and oxen, had failed.

Yet, after brooding for a while, they were so dejected, that anything seemed reasonable. So they said, "Go ahead and try it."

Returning to the mountain, the fairies, in a band, went with him to the great rock.

One touch of his hand, and the mighty boulder trembled, like an aspen leaf in the breeze. A shove, and the rock rolled down from the hill and crashed in the valley below.

There, underneath, were little heaps of gold and silver, which the boy carried home to his parents, who became the richest people in the country round about.

Guleesh

By Joseph Jacobs

READING TIME: 20 MINUTES

The fairies in Ireland are tricksters who love to work mischief on the human world, but just occasionally a human manages to outwit them. Fairies are often called the good people or sheehogue and live inside raths (ancient hillforts).

There was once a boy in the County Mayo, Guleesh was his name. There was the finest rath a little way off from the gable of the house, and he was often in the habit of seating himself on the fine grass bank that was running round it. One night he stood, looking up into the sky, and watching the beautiful white moon over his head when he heard a great noise coming like the sound of many people running together, and talking, and laughing, and the sound went by him like a whirl of wind, and he was listening to it going into the rath. "By my soul," said he, "ye're merry enough, and I'll follow ye."

What was in it but the fairy host, and he followed them into the rath. It's there he heard every man of them crying out as loud as he could:

"My horse, and bridle and saddle! My horse, and bridle and saddle!"

"By my hand," said Guleesh, "my boy, that's not bad. I'll imitate ye," and he cried out as well as they:

"My horse, and bridle, and saddle!" And on the moment there was a fine horse with a bridle of silver, and a saddle of gold, standing before him. He leaped up on it, and the moment he was on its back he saw clearly that the rath was full of horses, and of little people going riding on them.

Said a man of them to him, "Are you coming with us tonight, Guleesh?"

"I am surely," said Guleesh.

"If you are, come along," said the little man, and out they went all together, riding like the wind, faster than

the fastest horse ever you saw a-hunting. The cold
winter's wind that was before them, they overtook her,
and the cold winter's wind that was behind them, she
did not overtake them. And stop nor stay of that
full race, did they make none, until they
came to the brink of the sea.

Then every one of them said, "Hie over cap! Hie over
cap" and that moment they were up in the air, and before
Guleesh had time to remember where he was, they were

down on dry land again, and were going like the wind. At last they stood still, and a man of them said to Guleesh "You're in France, Guleesh," said he. "The daughter of the king of France is to be married tonight, the handsomest woman that the sun ever saw, and we must do our best to bring her with us, if we're only able to carry her off, and you must come with us that we may be able to put the young girl up behind you on the horse, for it's not lawful for us to put her behind ourselves. But you're flesh and blood, and she can take a good grip of you, so that she won't fall off the horse."

They got off their horses there, and a man of them said a word that Guleesh did not understand, and Guleesh found himself and his companions in the palace. There was a great feast going on there, and there was not a nobleman or a gentleman in the kingdom but was gathered there, dressed in silk and satin, and gold and silver, and the night was as bright as the day with all the lamps and candles that were lit, and Guleesh had to shut his eyes at the brightness. There were a hundred tables spread out, and on each table of them, cakes and sweetmeats, and wine and ale, and every drink that ever a man saw. Such a feast as there was that day had not been in France for twenty years, because the old king had only the one daughter, and she was to be married to the son of another king that night.

Guleesh and his companions were standing together at the head of the hall, where there was a fine altar dressed up, and two bishops behind it waiting to marry the girl. Now nobody could see the sheehogues, for they said a word as they came in, that made them all invisible,

"Tell me which of them is the king's daughter," said Guleesh.

"Don't you see her there away from you?" said the little man that he was talking to.

Guleesh looked where the little man was pointing with his finger, and there he saw the loveliest woman that was, he thought, upon the ridge of the world. The rose and the lily were fighting together in her face, and one could not tell which of them got the victory. Her form was smooth and slender, and her hair was falling down from her head in buckles of gold. Her garments and dress were woven with gold and silver, and the bright stone that was in the ring on her hand was as shining as the sun.

Guleesh was nearly blinded with all the loveliness and beauty that was in her, but when he looked again, he saw that she was crying, and that there was the trace of tears in her eyes. "It can't be," said Guleesh, "that there's grief in her, when everybody round her is so full of merriment."

"She is grieved," said the little man, "for it's against her own will she's marrying, and she has no love for the husband she is to marry. She is eighteen years old tonight, and it's time for her to marry, but, indeed," said he, and he crooked his mouth in an ugly way, "it's no king's son she'll marry, if I can help it."

Guleesh pitied the young lady greatly when he heard that, and he was heartbroken to think that it would be necessary for her to marry a man she did not like, or, what was worse, to take a nasty sheehogue for a husband. However, he did not say a word, though he could not help giving a curse to his ill luck to be helping the people that were to snatch her away.

He began thinking what it was he ought to do to save her. He was looking on when the king's son came up to her and asked her for a kiss, but she turned her head away from him. Guleesh had such pity for her then, when he saw the lad taking her by the hand, drawing her out to dance. They went round in the dance near where Guleesh was, and he could see that there were tears in her eyes.

When the dancing was over, the old king, and her mother the queen, came up and said that the bishop was ready, and it was time to put the wedding-ring on her and give her to her husband.

When they came near the altar, the little sheehogue stretched out his foot before the girl, and she fell. Before she was able to rise again he said a couple of words, and upon the moment the maiden was gone from amongst the grand folk, for the words had made her invisible. Out of the door of the palace they went, without being stopped or hindered, for nobody saw them, and, "My horse, my bridle and saddle!" said every man of them.

"My horse, my bridle and saddle!" said Guleesh, and on the moment the horse was standing ready before him.

"Now, jump up, Guleesh," said the little man, "and put the lady behind you, and we will be going."

Guleesh raised her up on the horse's back, and leaped up himself before her. "Rise, horse," said he, and his horse, and the other horses with him, went in a full race until they came to the sea.

"Hie over cap!" said every man of them.

"Hie over cap!" said Guleesh, and the moment the horse rose under him, and cut a leap in the clouds, they

came down in Erin. They did not stop there, but rode
to Guleesh's house and the rath. And when
they came as far as that, Guleesh
turned and caught the young girl in
his arms, and leaped off the horse.

"I call and cross you to
myself, in the name of God!"
said he, and on the spot, before
the word was out of his mouth,
the horse fell down, and what
was it but the beam of a plough.

The good people called out
together when they heard what
Guleesh said:

"Oh! Guleesh, isn't that a nice turn you
did us, and we so kind to you? What good have we now
out of our journey to France. You'll pay us another time
for this. Believe us, you'll repent it."

But they had no power at all to carry off the girl, after
Guleesh had consecrated her to himself.

"He'll have no good to get out of the young girl," said
the little man that was talking to him before that, and as
he said the word he moved over to her and struck her on

the side of the head. "Now," said he, "she'll be without talk anymore. It's time for us to go – but you'll remember us, Guleesh!"

When he said that he stretched out his two hands, and he and the rest of them were gone into the rath out of his sight, and he saw them no more.

He turned to the young woman and said to her:

"Thanks be to God, they're gone. Would you not sooner stay with me than with them?" She gave him no answer.

'There's trouble and grief on her yet,' said Guleesh in his own mind, and he spoke to her again:

"I am afraid that you must spend this night in my father's house, lady, and if there is anything that I can do for you, tell me, and I'll be your servant."

The beautiful girl remained silent, but there were tears in her eyes.

"It cannot be," said Guleesh, "that you are dumb. Did I not hear you speaking to the king's son in the palace tonight? Or has that devil made you really dumb, when he struck his nasty hand on your jaw?"

The girl raised her white smooth hand, and laid her finger on her tongue, to show him that she had lost her voice and power of speech, and the tears ran out of her two eyes like streams, and Guleesh's own eyes were not dry.

He began thinking with himself what he ought to do, and he did not like to bring her home with himself to his father's house, for he knew well that they would not believe him, that he had brought back with him the king of France's daughter.

"Glory be to God," said he, "I'll bring her to the priest's house, and he won't refuse me to keep the lady and care her." He turned to the lady again and told her that he was loth to take her to his father's house, but that there was an excellent priest very friendly to himself, who would take good care of her.

She bent her head, to show him she was obliged, and gave him to understand that she was ready to follow him any place he was going.

They went together accordingly to the priest's house, and the sun was just rising when they came to the door. Guleesh beat it hard, and as early as it was the priest was up, and opened the door himself.

"Father," said Guleesh, "I came to you now to ask you, to give a lodging in your house to this young lady."

The priest looked at him as though he had ten heads on him, but without putting any other question to him, he desired him to come in, himself and the maiden, and when they came in, he shut the door, brought them into the parlour, and put them sitting.

"Now, Guleesh," said he, "tell me truly who is this young lady."

"I'm not telling a word of lie, nor making a joke of you," said Guleesh, "but it was from the palace of the king of France I carried off this lady, and she is the daughter of the king of France."

He began his story then, and told the whole of it to the priest, and the priest was so much surprised that could not help calling out at times.

When Guleesh said from what he saw he thought the girl was not satisfied with the marriage that was going take place in the palace before the sheehogue broke it up, there came a red blush into the girl's cheek and he was more certain than ever that she had sooner be as she was – badly as she was – than be the married wife of the man she hated. When Guleesh said that he would be very thankful to the priest if he would keep her in his own house, the kind man said he would do that. They made it up then that the priest should let on that it was his brother's daughter he had, who was come on a visit to him from another county, and that he should tell everybody that she was dumb. Guleesh went home then, and when his people asked him where he had been, he said that he had been asleep at the foot of the ditch.

It was seldom the day went by but Guleesh would go to the priest's house, and have a talk with him, and as often as he would come he used to hope to find the young lady well again, but, alas! She remained dumb and silent, without relief or cure. Since she had no other means of talking, she carried on a sort of conversation by moving her hands and fingers, winking her eyes, opening and shutting her mouth, laughing or smiling, and a thousand other signs, so that it was not long until they understood each other very well. Guleesh was always thinking how he should send her back to her father, but he did not know what road to go, for he had never been out of his own country before the night he brought her away with him. Nor had the priest any better knowledge than he, but when Guleesh asked him, he wrote three or four letters to the king of France, and gave them to buyers and sellers of wares, who used to be going from place to place across the sea, but they all went astray, and never a one came to the king's hand.

This was the way they were for many months, and Guleesh was falling deeper and deeper in love with her every day, and it was plain to himself and the priest that she liked him. The boy feared greatly at last, lest the king should really hear where his daughter was, and take her back from himself, and he besought the priest to write no more, but to leave the matter to God.

So they passed the time for a year, until there came a day when Guleesh was lying by himself on the grass, on the last day of the last month in autumn, and he was thinking over again in his own mind of everything that happened.

He said to himself, "We have November night again today, and I'll stand in the same place I was last year, until I see if the good people come again. Perhaps I might see or hear something that would be useful to me, and might bring back her talk again to Mary" – that was the name himself and the priest called the king's daughter, for neither of them knew her right name.

Guleesh accordingly went to the old rath when the night was darkening, and he stood with his bent elbow leaning on a grey old flag, waiting till the middle of the night should come. The moon rose slowly, and it was like a knob of fire behind him, and there was a white fog which raised up over the fields of grass and all damp places. There were a thousand, thousand bright stars shining over his head, and there was a little frost out, which left the grass under his foot white and crisp.

He was thinking, in his own mind, at last, that the sheehogues would not come that night, when he heard a sound far away from him, coming towards him, and he recognized what it was at the first moment. The sound increased, and at first it was like the beating of waves on a stony shore, and then it was like the falling of a great waterfall, and at last it was like a loud storm in the tops of the trees, and then the whirlwind burst into the rath and the sheehogues were in it.

It all went by him so suddenly that he lost his breath with it, but he came to himself on the spot, and listened to what they would say.

Scarcely had they gathered into the rath till they all began shouting, and talking amongst themselves, and then each one of them cried out, "My horse, and bridle and saddle! My horse, and bridle and saddle!"

And Guleesh took courage, and called out as loudly as any of them. But before the word was well out of his mouth, another man cried out:

"Guleesh, my boy, are you here with us again? There's no use in your calling for your horse tonight. You won't play such a trick on us again."

"Isn't he a prime lad, to take a woman with him that never said as much to him as, 'How do you do?' since this time last year!" said the second man.

"And if the he only knew that there's an herb growing up by his own door, and if he were to boil it and give it to her, she'd be well," said another voice.

"Don't bother your head with him, we'll be going."

And with that they rose up into the air, and they left poor Guleesh standing where they found him, looking after them and wondering.

He did not stand long till he returned back, thinking in his own mind on all he saw and heard, and wondering whether there was really a herb at his own door that would bring back the talk to the king's daughter.

"It can't be," said he to himself, "that they would tell it to me, if there was any virtue in it, but perhaps the sheehogue didn't observe himself when he let the word slip out of his mouth. I'll search well as soon as the sun rises."

He went home, and as tired as he was he did not sleep a wink until the sun rose on the morrow. He got up then, and it was the first thing he did to go out and search through the grass round about the house. And, indeed, he was not long searching till he observed a large strange herb that was growing up just by the gable of the house.

He went over to it, saw that there were seven little branches coming out of the stalk, and seven leaves growing on every branch of them and that there was a white sap in the leaves.

"It's very wonderful," said he to himself, "that I never noticed this herb before."

He drew out his knife, cut the plant, and carried it into his own house, stripped the leaves off it and cut up the stalk, and there came a thick, white juice out of it. He put it in a little pot and a little water in it, and laid it on the

fire until the water was boiling, and then he took a cup,
filled it half up with the juice, and put it to his own
mouth. It came into his head then that perhaps it was
poison that was in it, and that the good people were only
tempting him that he might kill himself with that trick. It
was not bitter, and, indeed, had a sweet, agreeable taste.
He grew bolder then, and drank a thimble of it.

He went over to the priest's house with the drink in
his hand, and he never felt himself so bold and valiant,
and spirited and light, as he was that day, and he was
quite certain that it was the drink he drank which made
him so hearty.

When he came to the house, he found the priest and
the young lady within, and he told them all his news, and
said that he was certain that there was great power in that
herb, and that it would do the lady no hurt, for he tried it
himself and got good from it, and then he made her taste
it, for he vowed and swore that there was no harm in it.

Guleesh handed her the cup, and she drank half of
it, and then fell back on her bed and a heavy sleep came
on her.

Guleesh and the priest sat up the entire night with
her, waiting till she should awake, and they between hope

and unhope, between expectation of saving her and fear
of hurting her.

She awoke at last when the sun had gone half its way
through the heavens. She rubbed her eyes and looked like
a person who did not know where she was.

The two men were in great anxiety waiting to see –
would she speak, or would she not speak, and when they
remained silent for a couple of minutes, the priest said to
her, "Did you sleep well, Mary?"

And she answered him, "I slept well, thank you."

No sooner did Guleesh hear her talking than he put a
shout of joy out of him, and ran over to her and fell on
his knees saying, "Lady of my heart, speak again to me."

The lady answered him that she was obliged to him
from her heart for all the kindness he showed her, and
that he might be certain that she never would forget it.

Guleesh was ready to die with satisfaction and delight.
Then they brought her food, and she ate with a good
appetite, and was merry and joyous, and never left off
talking while she was eating.

Guleesh used after that to come to the house from day
to day, and the friendship that was between him and the
king's daughter increased, because she had no one to

speak to except Guleesh and the priest, and she liked Guleesh best.

So they married one another, and it was a fine wedding they had, and I heard that there was neither sickness nor sorrow, mishap nor misfortune on them till the hour of their death, and may the same be with me, and with us all!

Beautiful as the Day 434

Christmas Every Day 452

Under the Sun 465

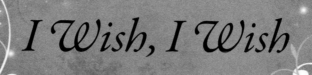

I Wish, I Wish

The Magic Pitcher 471

The Laird and the Man of Peace 488

Peter's Two Wishes 499

Beautiful as the Day

From *Five Children and It* by E Nesbit

READING TIME: 20 MINUTES

*T*he house was three miles from the station, but before the dusty hired fly had rattled along for five minutes the children began to put their heads out of the carriage window to say, "Aren't we nearly there?" And every time they passed a house, which was not very often, they all said, "Oh, is *this* it?" But it never was, till they reached the very top of the hill, just past the chalk quarry and before you come to the gravel pit. And then there was a white house with a green garden and an orchard beyond, and mother said, "Here we are!"

"How white the house is," said Robert.

"And look at the roses," said Anthea.

"And the plums," said Jane.

"It is rather decent," Cyril admitted.

The baby said, "Wanty go walky."

Everyone got their legs kicked or their feet trodden on in the scramble to get out of the carriage that very minute, but no one seemed to mind. The children had explored the gardens and the outhouses thoroughly before they were caught and cleaned for tea, and they saw quite well that they were certain to be happy at the White House. The best part of it all was that there were no rules about not going to places and not doing things. In London almost everything is labelled 'You mustn't touch', and though the label is invisible, it's just as bad, because you know it's there.

Now that I have begun to tell you about the place, I feel that I could go on and make this into a most interesting story about all the ordinary things that the children did – just the kind of things you do yourself, you know – and you would believe every word of it. But children will believe almost anything, and I daresay you will find it quite easy to believe that before Anthea and

Cyril and the others had been a week in the country they had found a fairy. At least they called it that, because that was what it called itself, but it was not at all like any fairy read about.

It was at the gravel pits. Father had to go away suddenly on business, and mother had gone away to stay with Granny, who was not very well. They both went in a great hurry, and when they were gone the house seemed dreadfully quiet and empty. It was Cyril who said:

"I say, let's take our spades and go and dig in the gravel pits. We can pretend it's seaside."

"Father said it was once," Anthea said, "he says there are shells there thousands of years old."

So they went. Of course they had been to the edge of the gravel pit and looked over, but they had not gone down into it for fear father should say they mustn't play there.

Each of the children carried its own spade, and took it in turns to carry the Lamb. He was the baby, and they called him that because 'Baa' was the first thing he ever said. They called Anthea 'Panther', which sounds silly when you read it, but when you say it it sounds a little like her name.

The children built a castle, of course, but castle-building is rather poor fun when you have no hope of the swishing tide ever coming in to fill up the moat.

Cyril wanted to dig out a cave to play smugglers in, but the others thought it might bury them alive, so it ended in all spades going to work to dig a hole through the castle to Australia. The children dug and they dug and they dug, and their hands got sandy and hot and red, and their faces got damp and shiny. The Lamb had tried to eat the sand, and had cried so hard when he found that it was not, as he had supposed, brown sugar, that he was now tired out, and was lying asleep in a warm fat bunch in the middle of the half-finished castle.

This left his brothers and sisters free to work really hard, and the hole that was to come out in Australia soon grew so deep that Jane, who was called Pussy for short, begged the others to stop.

Cyril and Anthea knew that Australia was not quite so near as all that, but they agreed to stop using the spades and go on with their hands. This was quite easy, because the sand at the bottom of the hole was very soft and fine and dry, like sea sand.

The party were just making up their minds that the sand makes you thirstier when it is not by the seaside, and someone had suggested going home for lemonade, when Anthea suddenly screamed:

"Cyril! Come here! Oh, come quick! It's alive! It'll get away! Quick!"

They all hurried back.

"Perhaps it is a snake," said Jane, shuddering.

"Oh, don't be silly!" said Anthea, "it's not a snake. It's got feet, I saw them, and fur! No – not the spade. You'll hurt it! Dig with your hands."

But Cyril merely observed that his sister must have gone off her nut, and he and Robert dug with spades while Anthea sat on the edge of the hole, jumping up and down with hotness and anxiety. They dug carefully, and presently everyone could see that there really was something moving in the bottom of the hole.

Then Anthea cried out, "*I'm* not afraid. Let me dig," and fell on her knees and began to scratch like a dog does when he has suddenly remembered where it was that he buried his bone.

"Oh, I felt fur," she cried, half laughing and half crying. "I did indeed! I did!" Suddenly a dry husky voice in the sand made them all jump back, and their hearts jumped nearly as fast as they did.

"Leave me alone," it said. And now everyone heard the voice and looked at the others to see if they had too.

"But we want to sec you," said Robert bravely.

"I wish you'd come out," said Anthea, also taking courage.

"Oh, well – if that's your wish," the voice said, and the sand stirred and spun and scattered, and something brown and furry and fat came rolling out into the hole and the sand fell off it, and it sat there yawning and rubbing the ends of its eyes with its hands.

"I believe I must have dropped asleep," it said, stretching itself.

The children stood round the hole in a ring, looking at the creature they had found. It was worth looking at. Its eyes were on long horns like a snail's eyes, and it could move them in and out like telescopes. It had ears like a bat's ears, and its tubby body was shaped like a spider's and covered with thick soft fur. Its legs and arms were furry too, and it had hands and feet like a monkey's.

"What on earth is it?" Jane said. "Shall we take it home?"

The thing turned its long eyes to look at her, and said, "Does she always talk nonsense, or is it only the rubbish on her head that makes her silly?"

It looked scornfully at Jane's hat as it spoke.

"She doesn't mean to be silly," Anthea said gently, "We none of us do, whatever you may think! Don't be frightened."

It said. "*Me* frightened? Upon my word! Why, you talk as if I were nobody in particular." All its fur stood out like a cat's when it is going to fight.

"Well," said Anthea, still kindly, "perhaps if we knew who you are in particular we could think of something to say that wouldn't make you cross."

"You don't know?" it said. "Well, I knew the world had changed – but – well, really – do you mean to tell me seriously you don't know a Psammead when you see one? Or, in plain English, then, a *sand-fairy*. Don't you know a sand-fairy when you see one?"

Of course no one could think of anything to say, but at last Robert thought of 'How long have you lived here?' and he said it at once.

"Oh, ages – several thousand years," replied the Psammead.

"Was the world like this then?"

It stopped digging.

"Not a bit," it said, "it was nearly all sand where I lived, and coal grew on trees. We sand-fairies used to live on the seashore, and the children used to come with their little flint-spades and flint-pails and make castles for us to live in. That's thousands of years ago, but I hear that children still build castles on the sand. It's difficult to break yourself of a habit."

"Why did you stop living in castles?" asked Robert.

"It's a sad story," said the Psammead gloomily. "It was because they *would* build moats to the castles, and the nasty wet bubbling sea used to come in, and of course as soon as a sand-fairy got wet it caught cold, and generally died. And so there got to be fewer and fewer."

"And did *you* get wet?" Robert inquired.

The sand-fairy shuddered. "Only once," it said, "the end of the twelfth hair of my top left whisker – I feel the place still in damp weather. I scurried away to the back of the beach, and dug myself a house deep in warm dry sand, and there I've been ever since. And the sea changed its lodgings afterwards. And now I'm not going to tell you another thing."

"Just one more, please," said the children. "Can you give wishes now?"

"Of course," said it, "didn't I give you yours a few minutes ago? You said, 'I wish you'd come out,' and I did."

"Oh, please, mayn't we have another?"

"Yes, but be quick about it. I'm tired of you."

I daresay you have often thought what you would do if you had three wishes given you. These children had often talked this matter over, but, now the chance had suddenly come to them, they could not make up their minds.

"Quick," said the sand-fairy crossly.

No one could think of anything. Only Anthea did manage to remember a private wish of her own and Jane's which they had never told the boys. "I wish we were all as beautiful as the day," she said in a great hurry.

The children looked at each other, but each could see that the others were not any better looking than usual. The Psammead pushed out its long eyes, and seemed to be holding its breath and swelling itself out till it was twice as fat and furry as before. Suddenly it let its breath go in a long sigh.

"I'm really afraid I can't manage it," it said apologetically, "I must be out of practise."

The children were horribly disappointed.

"Oh, *do* try again!" they said.

"Well," said the sand-fairy, "the fact is, I was keeping back a little strength to give the rest of you your wishes with. If you'll be contented with one wish a day amongst the lot of you I daresay I can screw myself up to it. Do you agree to that?"

"Yes, oh yes!" said Jane and Anthea. The boys nodded.

It stretched out its eyes farther than ever, and swelled and swelled and swelled.

"I do hope it won't hurt itself," said Anthea.

"Or crack its skin," Robert said anxiously.

Everyone was very much relieved when the sand-fairy, after getting so big that it almost filled up the hole in the sand, suddenly let out its breath and went back to its proper size.

"That's all right," it said, panting heavily. "It'll come easier tomorrow. It'll last till sunset."

"Did it hurt much?" asked Anthea.

"Only my whisker, thank you," said he. "Good day."

It scratched suddenly and fiercely with its hands and feet, and disappeared in the sand. Then the children

looked at each other, and each child suddenly found itself alone with three perfect strangers, all radiantly beautiful.

They stood for some moments in perfect silence. Each thought that its brothers and sisters had wandered off, and that these strange children had stolen up while it was watching the swelling form of the sand-fairy.

Anthea spoke first, "Excuse me," she said very politely to Jane, who now had enormous blue eyes and a cloud of russet hair, "but have you seen two little boys and a little girl anywhere about?"

"I was just going to ask you that," said Jane. And then Cyril cried:

"Why, it's *you*! I know the hole in your pinafore! You *are* Jane, aren't you? Crikey! The wish has come off, after all. I say, am I as handsome as you are?"

"If you're Cyril, I liked you much better before," said Anthea decidedly. "You look like the picture of the young chorister, with your golden hair, you'll die young, I shouldn't wonder. And if that's Robert, he's like an Italian organ grinder. His hair's all black."

"You two girls are like Christmas cards, then – that's all – silly Christmas cards," said Robert angrily.

"Well, it's no use finding fault with each other," said Anthea, "let's get the Lamb and lug it home to dinner. The servants will admire us most awfully, you'll see."

Baby was just waking when they got to him, and not one of the children but was relieved to find that he at least was not as beautiful as the day, but just the same as usual.

"I suppose he's too young to have wishes naturally," said Jane. "We shall have to mention him specially next time."

Anthea ran forward and held out her arms.

"Come to own Panther, ducky," she said.

The Baby looked at her disapprovingly, and put a sandy pink thumb in his mouth.

"G'way long!" said the Baby.

"Come to own Pussy," said Jane.

"Wants my Panty," said the Lamb dismally, and his lip trembled.

"Here, come on, Veteran," said Robert, "come and have a yidey on Yobby's back."

"Yah, narky narky boy," howled the Baby, giving way altogether. Then the children knew the worst. *The baby did not know them!*

They looked at each other in despair, and it was terrible to each, in this dire emergency, to meet only the beautiful eyes of perfect strangers, instead of the merry, friendly, little eyes of its own brothers and sisters.

"This is most truly awful," said Cyril. "I can't carry him home screaming like that. Fancy having to make friends with our own baby! It's too silly."

That, however, was exactly what they had to do. It took over an hour, and the task was not rendered any easier by the fact that the Lamb was by this time as hungry as a lion and as thirsty as a desert.

At last he consented to allow these strangers to carry him home by turns, but as he refused to hold on to such new acquaintances he was a dead weight and most exhausting.

"Thank goodness, we're home!" said Jane, staggering through the iron gate to where Martha, the nursemaid, stood at the front door shading her eyes with her hand and looking out anxiously. "Here! Do take baby!"

Martha snatched the baby from her arms.

"Thanks be, *he's* safe back," she said. "Where are the others, and whoever to goodness gracious are all of you?'

"We're *us*, of course," said Robert.

448

"And who's *us*, when you're at home?" asked Martha scornfully.

"I know we *look* different, but I'm Anthea, and we're so tired, and it's long past dinner time."

"Then go home to your dinners, whoever you are, and if our children put you up to this play-acting you can tell them from me they'll catch it, so they know what to expect!" With that she did bang the door. Cyril rang the bell violently. No answer. Presently cook put her head out of a bedroom window and said:

"If you don't take yourselves off, I'll go and fetch the police." And she slammed down the window.

"It's no good," said Anthea. "Oh, do, do come away before we get sent to prison!"

The boys said it was nonsense, and the law of England couldn't put you in prison for just being as beautiful as the day, but all the same they followed the others out into the lane.

"We shall be our proper selves after sunset, I suppose," said Jane.

It was a horrible afternoon. There was no house near where the children could beg a crust of bread or even a glass of water. They were afraid to go to the village, because they had seen Martha go down there with a basket, and there was a local constable. True, they were all as beautiful as the day, but that is a poor comfort when you are as hungry as a hunter and as thirsty as a sponge.

It came at last to their sitting down in a row under the hedge, with their feet in a dry ditch, waiting for sunset.

At last hunger and fright and crossness and tiredness – four very nasty things – all joined together to bring one nice thing, and that was sleep. The children lay asleep in a row, with their beautiful eyes shut and their beautiful mouths open. Anthea woke first. The sun had set, and the twilight was coming on.

"Wake up," she said, almost in tears of joy, "it's all right. Oh, Cyril, how nice and ugly you do look, with your old freckles and your brown hair and your little eyes. And so do you all!" she added, so that they might not feel jealous.

When they got home they were very much scolded by Martha, who told them about the strange children.

"A good-looking lot, I must say, but that impudent."

"I know," said Robert, who knew by experience how

hopeless it would be to try to explain things to Martha.

"And where on earth have you been all this time, you naughty little things, you?"

"In the lane."

"Why didn't you come home hours ago?"

"We couldn't because of *them*," said Anthea.

"'Who?"

"The children who were as beautiful as the day. They kept us there till after sunset. We couldn't come back till they'd gone. You don't know how we hated them! Oh, do, do give us some supper – we are so hungry."

"Hungry! I should think so," said Martha angrily, "out all day like this. Well, I hope it'll be a lesson to you not to go picking up with strange children – down here after measles, as likely as not! Now mind, if you see them again, don't you speak to them – not one word."

"If ever we *do* see them again we'll tell you," Anthea said, and Robert, fixing his eyes fondly on the cold beef that was being brought in on a tray by cook, added in heartfelt undertones, "And we'll take jolly good care we never *do* see them again."

And they never have.

Christmas Every Day

By W D Howells

READING TIME: 12 MINUTES

*T*he little girl came into her papa's study and asked for a story. He tried to beg off that morning, for he was very busy, but she would not let him. So he began:

"Well, once there was a little pig—"

She put her hand over his mouth to stop him, saying that she had heard pig stories till she was sick of them.

"Well, what kind of story shall I tell, then?"

"About Christmas. It's getting to be the season. It's past Thanksgiving already."

"It seems to me," her papa argued, "that I've told as often

452

about Christmas as I have about little pigs."

"Christmas is more interesting."

"Well, then, I'll tell you about the little girl that wanted it to be Christmas every day in the year. How would you like that?"

"First-rate!" said the little girl, and she nestled into comfortable shape in his lap, ready for listening...

Once there was a little girl who liked Christmas so much that she wanted it to be Christmas every day. As soon as Thanksgiving was over she began to send letters to the Christmas Fairy to ask if she could, and – just the day before Christmas – she got a letter from the fairy, saying she might have Christmas every day for a year, and then they would see about having it longer.

The little girl was a good deal excited already,
preparing for the old-fashioned, once-a-year Christmas
that was coming the next day, and perhaps the fairy's
promise didn't make such an impression on her as it
would have made at some other time. She just resolved
to keep it to herself, and surprise everybody with it as
it kept coming true, and then it slipped out of her
mind altogether.

She had a splendid Christmas. She went to bed early,
so as to let Santa Claus have a chance at the stockings,
and in the morning she was up the first of anybody and
went and felt them, and found hers all lumpy with
packages of candy, and oranges and grapes, and books
and rubber balls, and all kinds of small presents. Then
she waited around till the rest of the family were up, and
she was the first to burst into the library when the doors
were opened, and look at the large presents laid out –
books, and boxes of stationery, and dolls, and little
stoves, and skates, and photograph-frames, and little
easels, and boxes of water-colours, and Turkish paste,
and nougat, and candied cherries, and dolls' houses –
and the big Christmas tree, lighted and standing in a
waste basket in the middle.

She had a splendid Christmas all day. She ate so much candy that she did not want any breakfast, and she went round giving the presents she had got for other people, and came home and ate turkey and cranberry for dinner, and plum-pudding and nuts and raisins and oranges and more candy, and then went out sledging, and came in with a stomach-ache, crying, and her papa said he would see if his house was turned into that sort of fool's paradise another year, and they had a light supper, and pretty early everybody went to bed cross.

The little girl slept very heavily, and she slept very late, but she was wakened at last by the other children dancing round her bed with their stockings full of presents in their hands.

"What is it?" said the little girl, and she rubbed her eyes and tried to rise up in bed.

"Christmas! Christmas! Christmas!" they all shouted, and waved their stockings.

"Nonsense! It was Christmas yesterday."

Her brothers and sisters just laughed. "We don't know about that. It's Christmas today, anyway. You come into the library and see."

Then all at once it flashed on the little girl that the fairy was keeping her promise, and her year of Christmases was beginning. She was dreadfully sleepy, but she sprang up like a lark – a lark that had overeaten itself and gone to bed cross – and darted into the library. There it was again! Books, and boxes of stationery...

"You needn't go over it all, papa, I guess I can remember just what was there," said the little girl.

Well, and there was the Christmas tree blazing away, and the family picking out their presents, but looking pretty sleepy, and her father perfectly puzzled, and her mother ready to cry.

"I don't see how I'm to dispose of all these things," said her mother, and her father said it seemed to him they had had something just like it the day before, but he supposed he must have dreamt it. This struck the little girl as the best kind joke, and so she ate so much candy she didn't want breakfast, and went round carrying presents, and had turkey and cranberry for dinner, and then went out sledging, and came in with a...

"Papa!"
"Well, what now?"
"What did you promise, you forgetful thing?"
"Oh! Oh yes!"

Well, the next day, it was just the same thing over again, but everybody getting crosser, and at the end of a week's time so many people had lost their tempers that you could pick up lost tempers anywhere, they perfectly strewed the ground. Even when people tried to recover their tempers they usually got somebody else's, and it made the most dreadful mix.

The little girl began to get frightened, keeping the secret all to herself. She wanted to tell her mother, but she didn't dare to, and she was ashamed to ask the fairy to take back her gift, it seemed ungrateful and ill-bred, and she thought she would try to stand it, but she hardly knew how she could, for a whole year. So it went on and on, and it was Christmas on St Valentine's Day and Washington's birthday, just the same as any day, and it didn't skip even the first of April, though everything was counterfeit that day, and that was some little relief.

After a while turkeys got to be about a thousand dollars apiece and they got to passing off almost anything for turkeys – half-grown humming-birds, and even rocs out of the *Arabian Nights* – the real turkeys were so scarce. And cranberries – well, they asked a diamond apiece for cranberries. All the woods and orchards were cut down for Christmas trees, and where the woods and orchards used to be it looked just like a stubble field, with the stumps. After a while they had to make Christmas trees out of rags, and stuff them with bran, like old-fashioned dolls, but there were plenty of rags, because people got so poor, buying presents for one another, that they couldn't get any new clothes, and they just wore their old ones to tatters. They got so poor that everybody had to go to the poorhouse, except the confectioners, and the shopkeepers, and the picture-book sellers, and they all got so rich and proud that they would hardly wait upon a person when he came to buy. It was perfectly shameful!

Well, after it had gone on for about three or four months, the little girl, whenever she came into the room in the morning and saw those great ugly, lumpy stockings dangling at the fireplace, and the disgusting presents around everywhere, used to just sit down and burst out crying. In six months she was perfectly exhausted. She couldn't even cry anymore – she just lay on the lounge and rolled her eyes and panted. About the beginning of October she took to sitting down on dolls wherever she found them she hated the sight of them so, and by Thanksgiving she was crazy, and just slammed her presents across the room.

By that time people didn't carry presents around nicely any more. They flung them over the fence, or through the window, or anything, and, they used to write in the gift books, 'Take it, you horrid old thing!' and then go and bang it against the front door. Nearly everybody had built barns to hold their presents, but very soon the barns overflowed, and then people just let their presents lie out in the rain, or anywhere. Sometimes the police used to come and tell them to shovel their presents off the sidewalk, or they would arrest them.

Well, before Thanksgiving came it had leaked out who had caused all these Christmases. The little girl had suffered so much that she had talked about it in her sleep, and after that hardly anybody would play with her. People just perfectly despised her, because if it had not been for her greediness it wouldn't have happened, and now, when it came Thanksgiving, and she wanted them to go to church, and have squash-pie and turkey, and show their gratitude, they said that all the turkeys had been eaten up for her old Christmas dinners, and if she would stop the Christmases, they would see about the gratitude. Wasn't it dreadful?

And the very next day the little girl began to send letters to the Christmas Fairy, and then telegrams, to stop it. But it didn't do any good. And then she got to calling at the fairy's house, but the girl that came to the door always said, 'Not at home,' or 'Engaged,' or 'At dinner,' or something like that.

And so it went on till it came to the old once-a-year Christmas Eve. The little girl fell asleep, and when she woke up in the morning...

"She found it was all nothing but a dream," suggested the little girl.

"No, indeed!" said her papa. "It was every bit true!"

"Well, what did she find out, then?"

"Why, that it wasn't Christmas at last, and wasn't ever going to be, any more. Now it's time for breakfast."

The little girl held her papa fast around the neck.

"You shan't go if you're going to leave it so!"

"How do you want it left?"

"Christmas once a year."

"All right," said her papa, and he went on again...

Well, there was the greatest rejoicing all over the country, and it extended clear up into Canada. The people met together everywhere, and kissed and cried for joy. The city carts went around and gathered up all the candy and raisins and nuts, and dumped them into the river, and it made the fish perfectly sick, and the whole United States, as far out as Alaska, was one blaze of bonfires, where the children were burning up their gift books and presents of all kinds. They had the best time!

The little girl went to thank the fairy because she had stopped it being Christmas, and she said she hoped she would keep her promise and see that Christmas never came again. Then the fairy frowned, and asked her if she was sure she knew what she meant. The little girl asked her, "Why?" and the fairy said that now she was behaving as greedily as ever, so she'd better look out.

This made the little girl think it all over carefully again, and she said she would be willing to have it Christmas about once in a thousand years, and then she said a hundred, and then she said ten, and at last she got down to one. Then the fairy said that was the good old way that had pleased people ever since Christmas began, and she was agreed.

Then the little girl said, "What're your shoes made of?" And the fairy said, "Leather." And the little girl said, "Bargain's done forever," and skipped off, and hippity-hopped the whole way home, she was so glad.

"How will that do?" asked the papa.

"First-rate!" said the little girl, but she hated to have

the story stop, and was rather sober. However, her mamma put her head in at the door, and asked her papa:

"Are you never coming to breakfast? What have you been telling that child?"

"Oh, just a moral tale."

The little girl caught him around the neck again. "*We* know! Don't you tell *what*, papa! Don't you tell *what*!"

Under the Sun

By Juliana Horatia Gatty Ewing

READING TIME: 6 MINUTES

There once lived a farmer who was so greedy and miserly, and so hard in all his dealings that, as folks say, he would skin a flint. It is needless to say that he never either gave or lent.

Now, by thus scraping, and saving, and grinding for many years, he had become almost wealthy, though, indeed, he was no better fed and dressed than if he had not a penny to bless himself with. But what vexed him sorely was that his next neighbour's farm prospered in all matters better than his own, and this, although the owner was as generous as our farmer was stingy.

Now on the lands of the liberal farmer (whose name was Merryweather) there lived a fairy or hillman, who made a wager that he would both beg and borrow of the envious farmer, and out-bargain him as well. So he went one day to his house, and asked him if he would kindly give him half a stone of flour to make hasty pudding with, adding, that if he would lend him a bag to carry it into the hill, this should be returned clean and in good condition.

The farmer saw with half an eye that this was the fairy from his neighbour's estate, and as he had always laid the luck of the liberal farmer to his being favoured by the good people, he resolved to treat the little man with all politeness.

"Look you, wife," said he, "this is no time to be saving half a stone of flour when we may make our fortunes at one stroke. I have heard my grandfather tell of a man who lent a sack of oats to one of the fairies, and got it back filled with gold pieces. And as good measure as he gave of oats so he got of gold." Saying which, the farmer took a canvas bag to the flour bin, and began to fill it.

Meanwhile the fairy sat in the larder window and

cried, "Give us good measure, neighbour, and you shall have anything under the sun that you like to ask for."

When the farmer heard this he was nearly out of his wits with delight, and his hands shook so that the flour spilled all about the larder floor.

"Thank you, dear sir," he said, "It's a bargain, and I agree to it. My wife hears us, and is witness. Wife! Wife!" he cried, running into the kitchen, "I am to have anything under the sun that I choose to ask for. I think of asking for neighbour Merryweather's estate, but this is a chance never likely to happen again, and I should like to make a wise choice."

"You will have a week to think it over in," said the fairy, who had come in behind him. "I must be off now, so give me my flour, and come to the hill behind your house seven days hence at midnight."

"Not for seven days, did you say, sir? You know, dear sir, when amongst each other we men have to wait for the settlement of an account, we expect something over and above the exact amount. Interest we call it, my dear sir."

"And you want me to give you something extra for waiting a week?" asked the fairy. "What do you expect?"

"Oh, dear sir, I leave it to you," said the farmer.

"I will give you something over and above what you shall choose," said the fairy, "but, as you say, I shall decide what it is to be." With which he shouldered the flour-sack, and went his way.

For the next seven days, the farmer had no peace for thinking and scheming how to get the most out of his one wish. His wife made many suggestions to which he did not agree, but he was careful not to quarrel with her, "For," he said, "we will not be like the foolish couple who wasted three wishes on black puddings."

And so, after a week of sleepless nights and anxious days, he came back to his first thought, and resolved to ask for his neighbour's estate.

At last the night came. It was full moon, and the farmer looked anxiously about, fearing the fairy might not be true to his appointment. But at midnight he appeared, with the flour bag neatly folded in his hand.

"You hold to the agreement," said the farmer, "of course. I am to have anything under the sun that I ask for, and I am to have it now."

"Ask away," said the fairy.

"I want neighbour Merryweather's estate," said the farmer.

"What, all this land below here, that joins on to your own?"

"Every acre," said the farmer.

"Farmer Merryweather's fields are under the moon at present," said the fairy, coolly, "and thus not within the terms of the agreement. You must choose again."

But the farmer could choose nothing that was not then under the moon. He soon saw that he had been outwitted, and his rage knew no bounds at the trick the fairy had played him.

"Give me my bag, at any rate," he screamed, "and the string – and your own extra gift that you promised. For half a loaf is better than no bread," he muttered, "and I may

yet come in for a few gold pieces."

"There's your bag," cried the fairy, clapping it over the miser's head like an extinguisher, "it's clean enough for a nightcap. And there's your string," he added, tying it tightly round the farmer's throat. "And, for my part, I'll give you what you deserve." Saying which he gave the farmer such a hearty kick that he kicked him straight down from the top of the hill to his own back door.

"If that does not satisfy you, I'll give you as much again," shouted the fairy, and as the farmer made no reply, he went chuckling back to his hill.

The Magic Pitcher

By S M Mitra

READING TIME: 20 MINUTES

Long ago there lived far away in India a woodcutter called Subha Datta and his family, who were all very happy together. The father went every day to the forest near his home to get supplies of wood, which he sold to his neighbours, earning by that means quite enough to give his wife and children all that they needed. Sometimes he took his three boys with him, and now and then, as a special treat, his two little girls were allowed to trot along beside him. The boys longed to be allowed to chop wood for themselves, and their father told them that as soon as they were old enough he would give each of them a little axe of his own. The girls, he said, must be content with breaking off small twigs from the branches he cut down, for he did not wish them to chop their own fingers off.

All went well with Subha Datta for a long time. Each of the boys had his own little axe at last, and each of the girls had a little pair of scissors to cut off twigs, and very proud they all were when they brought some wood home to their mother to use in the house.

One day, however, their father told them they could none of them come with him, for he meant to go a very long way into the forest, to see if he could find better wood there than nearer home. Vainly the boys entreated him to take them with him.

"Not today," he said, "you would be too tired to go all the way, and would lose yourselves coming back alone. You must help your mother today and play with your sisters." They had to be content, for although Hindu children are as fond of asking questions as English boys and girls, they are obedient to their parents and do all they are told without making any fuss.

When Subha Datta started for the forest, he fully

intended to come back the same evening, but as he was busy cutting down a tree, he suddenly had a feeling that he was no longer alone. He looked up, and there, quite close to him, in a little clearing where the trees had been cut down by some other woodcutter, he saw four beautiful young girls looking like fairies in their thin summer dresses and with their long hair flowing down their backs, dancing round and round, holding each other's hands. Subha Datta was so astonished at the sight that he let his axe fall, and the noise startled the dancers, who all four stood still and stared at him.

The woodcutter could not say a word, but just gazed and gazed at them, till one of them said to him:

"Who are you, and what are you doing in the very depths of the forest where we have never before seen a man?"

"I am only a poor woodcutter," he replied, "come to get some wood to sell, so as to give my wife and children something to eat and some clothes to wear."

"That is a stupid thing to do," said one of the girls. "You can't get much money that way. If you will only stop with us we will have your wife and children looked after for you much better than you can do it yourself."

Subha Datta, though he certainly did love his wife and children, was so tempted at the idea of stopping in the forest with the beautiful girls that, after hesitating a little while, he said, "Yes, I will stop with you, if you are quite sure all will be well with my dear ones."

"You need not be afraid about that," said another of the girls. "We are fairies, you see, and we can do all sorts of wonderful things. It isn't even necessary for us to go where your dear ones are. We shall just wish them everything they want, and they will get it. And the first thing to be done is to give you some food. You must work for us in return, of course."

Subha Datta at once replied, "I will do anything you wish."

"Well, begin by sweeping away all the dead leaves from the clearing, and then we will all sit down and eat together."

Subha Datta was very glad that what he was asked to do was so easy. He began by cutting a branch from a tree, and with it he swept the floor of what was to be the dining-room. Then he looked about for the food, but he could see nothing but a great big pitcher standing in the shade of a tree, the branches of which hung over the clearing. So he said to one of the fairies, "Will you show me where the food is, and exactly where you would like me to set it out?"

"We don't have to bother about fetching this and fetching that. You see that big pitcher. Well, we get all our food and everything else we want out of it. We just have to wish as we put our hands in, and there it is. It's a magic pitcher – the only one there is in the whole wide world. You get the food you would like to have first, and then we'll tell you what we want."

Subha Datta could hardly believe his ears when he

heard that. Down he threw his axe, and hastened to put
his hand in the pitcher, wishing for the food he was used
to. He loved curried rice and milk, lentils, fruit and
vegetables, and very soon he had a beautiful meal spread
out for himself on the ground. Then the fairies called
out, one after the other, what they wanted for food.

The next few days passed away like a dream, and at
first Subha Datta thought he had never been so happy in
his life. The fairies often went off together leaving him
alone, only coming back to the clearing when they
wanted something out of the pitcher. The woodcutter
got all kinds of things he fancied for himself, but
presently he began to wish he had his wife and children
with him to share his wonderful meals. He began to miss
them terribly, and he missed his work, too. It was no
good cutting trees down and chopping up wood when
all the food was ready cooked. Sometimes he thought he
would slip off home when the fairies were away, but
when he looked at the pitcher he could not bear the
thought of leaving it.

Meanwhile his poor wife was at her wits' end how to
feed her dear children. If it had not been that the two
boys were brave, plucky little chaps, she really would

have been in despair. When their father did not come back and all their efforts to find him were in vain, these boys set to work to help their mother. They could not cut down trees, but they could climb them and chop off small branches with their axes, and this they did, making up bundles of faggots and selling them to their neighbours. These neighbours were touched by the courage they showed, and not only paid them well for the wood but often gave them milk and rice and other little things to help them. In time they actually got used to being without Subha Datta, and the little girls nearly forgot all about him. Little did they dream of the change that was soon to come into their lives.

A month passed peacefully away in the depths of the forest, Subha Datta waiting on the fairies and becoming every day more selfish and bent on enjoying himself. Then he had a dream, in which he saw his wife and children in the old home with plenty of food, and evidently so happy without him that he felt quite determined to go and show them he was still alive.

When he woke he said to the fairies, "I will not stop with you any longer. I have had a good time here, but I am tired of this life away from my own people."

The fairies saw he was really in earnest this time, so they consented to let him go, but they were kind-hearted people and felt they ought to pay him in some way for all he had done for them. They consulted together, and then one of them told him they wished to make him a present before he went away, and they would give him whatever he asked for.

Directly the woodcutter heard he could have anything he asked for, he cried, "I will have the magic pitcher."

You can just imagine what a shock this was to the fairies! You know, of course, that fairies always keep their word. If they could not persuade Subha Datta to choose something else, they would have to give him their beloved, precious pitcher and would have to seek their food for themselves. They all tried all they could to persuade the woodcutter to choose something else. They took him to their own secret treasure house, in an old, old tree with a hollow trunk, even the entrance to which no mortal had ever been allowed to see. They blindfolded him before they started, so that he could never reveal the way to anyone, and one of them led him by the hand, telling him where the steps going down from the tree began.

When at last the
bandage was taken from
his eyes, he found himself
in a lofty hall with an
opening in the roof
through which the light
came. Piled up on the
floor were sparkling stones
worth a great deal of gold
and silver money, and on
the walls hung beautiful
robes. Subha Datta was
quite dazed with all he
saw, but he was only an
ignorant woodcutter and
did not realize the value
of the jewels and clothes.
So when the fairies, said
to him, "Choose anything
you like here and let us
keep our pitcher," he
shook his head, saying,

"No! No! No! The pitcher! I will have the pitcher!" And at last they had to give it up.

So Subha Datta took the pitcher, carrying it very, very carefully, lest he should drop it and break it before he got home. He did not think at all of what a cruel thing it was to take it away from the fairies, and leave them either to starve or to seek for food for themselves. The poor fairies watched him till he was out of sight, and then they began to weep and wring their hands.

"He might at least have waited whilst we got some food out for a few days," one of them said.

"He was too selfish to think of that," said another. "Come, let us forget all about him and go and look for some fruit."

So they all left off crying and went away hand in hand. Fairies do not want very much to eat. They can live on fruit and dew, and they never let anything make them sad for long at a time. They go out of this story now, but you need not be unhappy about them, because you may be very sure that they got no real harm from their generosity to Subha Datta in letting him take the pitcher.

You can just imagine what a surprise it was to Subha

Datta's wife and children when they saw him coming along the path leading to his home. He did not bring the pitcher with him, but had hidden it in a hollow tree in the wood near his cottage, for he did not mean any one to know that he had it. He told his wife that he had lost his way in the forest, and had been afraid he would never see her or his children again, but he said nothing about the fairies. When his wife asked him how he had got food, he told her a long story about the fruits he had found, and she believed all he said, and determined to make up to him now for all she thought he had suffered. When she called the little girls to come and help her get a nice meal for their father, Subha Datta said, "Oh, don't bother about that! I've brought something back with me. I'll go and fetch it, but no one is to come with me."

Subha Datta's wife was sorely disappointed at this, because she loved her husband so much that it was a joy to her to work for him. The children too wanted, of course, to go with their father, but he ordered them to stop where they were. He seized a big basket which was full of fuel for the fire, tumbled all the wood in it onto the floor, and went off alone to the pitcher. Very soon he was back again with his basket full of all sorts of good things, the very names of which his wife and children had no idea of.

"There!" he cried, "what do you think of that? Am I not a clever father to have found all that in the forest? Those are the 'fruits' I meant when I told your mother about them."

Life was now, of course, completely changed for the family in the forest. Subha Datta no longer went to cut wood to be sold, and the boys also left off doing so. Every day their father fetched food for them all, and the greatest desire of each one of the family was to find out where it came from. They never could do so, for Subha Datta managed to make them afraid to follow him when he went forth with his basket.

The secret he kept from the wife to whom he used to tell everything soon began to spoil the happiness of the home. The children who had no longer anything to do quarrelled with each other. Their mother got sadder and sadder, and at last decided to tell Subha Datta that, unless he would let her know where the food came from, she would go away from him and take her little girls with her. She really did mean to do this, but something soon happened to change everything again.

Of course, the neighbours in the wood, who had bought the fuel from the boys and helped them by giving them fruit and rice, heard of the return of their father and of the wonderful change in their lot. Now the whole family had plenty to eat every day, though none of them knew where it all came from. Subha Datta was very fond of showing off what he could do, and sometimes asked his old friends amongst the woodcutters to come and have a meal with him. When they arrived they would find all sorts of good things spread out on the ground and different kinds of wines in beautiful bottles.

This went on for some months, Subha Datta getting prouder and prouder of all that he could do, and it seemed likely that his secret would never be discovered. Everybody tried to find it out, and many followed him secretly when he set forth into the woods, but he was very clever at dodging them, hiding his treasure in a new place in the dead of the night. If he had only been content with getting food out of his pitcher and drinking pure water, all would most likely have been well with him. But that was just what he could not do. Till he had his pitcher he had never drunk anything but water, but now he often took too much wine.

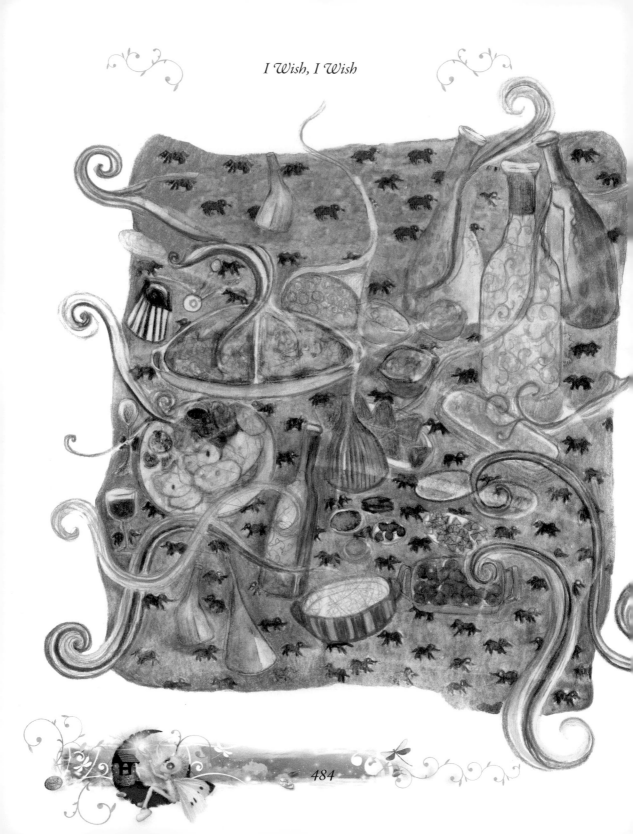

He began to boast of his cleverness, telling his friends there was nothing they wanted that he could not get for them, and one day when he had given them a very grand feast, in which were several rare kinds of food they had asked for, he drank too much wine – so much that he no longer knew what he was saying.

This was the chance his guests wanted. They began teasing him, telling him they believed he was really a wicked robber, who had stolen the food or the money to buy it. He got angry, and at last was actually silly enough to tell them all to come with him, and he would show them he was no robber.

When they all got very near the place, however, some idea began to come into Subha Datta's head that he was doing a very foolish thing. He stopped suddenly, turned round facing the crowd that followed him, and said he would not go a step further till they all went back to the cottage. His wife begged him to let her at least go with him, and the children all clamoured not to be sent back, but it was no good. Back they all had to go, the woodcutter watching till they were out of sight.

When the woodcutter was quite sure that everyone was gone and nobody could see where he had hidden the

pitcher, he took it from the hole in which it lay and carried it carefully to his home. You can imagine how everybody rushed out to meet him when he came in sight, and crowded round him, so that there was danger of the pitcher being thrown to the ground and broken. Subha Datta however managed to get into the cottage without any accident, and then he began to take things out of the pitcher and fling them on the ground, shouting, "Am I a robber? Am I a robber? Who dared to call me a robber?"

Then, getting more and more excited, he picked up the pitcher, and holding it on his shoulder began to dance wildly about. His wife called out to him, "Oh, take care, take care! You will drop it!" But he paid no attention to her. Suddenly, however, he began to feel giddy and fell to the ground, dropping the pitcher as he did so. It was broken to pieces, and a great cry of sorrow went up from all who saw the accident. The woodcutter himself was broken hearted, for he knew that he had done the mischief himself, and that if only he had resisted the temptation to drink the wine he would still have his treasure.

He was going to pick up the pieces to see if they

could be stuck together, but to his very great surprise he could not touch them. He heard a silvery laugh, and what sounded like children clapping their hands, and he thought he also heard the words, "Our pitcher is ours again!"

One by one the friends went away, leaving Subha Datta alone with his family.

This is the end of the story of the magic pitcher, but it was the beginning of a new chapter in the lives of Subha Datta and his family. They never forgot the wonder-working pitcher, and the children were never tired of hearing the story of how their father came to get it. They often wandered about in the forest, hoping that they too would meet with some wonderful adventure, but they never saw the fairies or found a magic pitcher. By slow degrees the woodcutter returned to his old ways, but he had learnt one lesson. He never again kept a secret from his wife, because he felt sure that if he had told her the truth about the pitcher when he first came home, she would have helped him to save the precious treasure.

The Laird and the Man of Peace

By Juliana Horatia Gatty Ewing

READING TIME: 10 MINUTES

In Scotland, fairies were often called Daoiné Shi (pronounced dheen-ya-shee), meaning men of peace. A laird is an important landowner, always known by the name of his estate. Cairngorms are a type of smoky quartz, much prized for making jewellery, especially in Scotland, where kilt pins are often decorated with them.

In the Highlands of Scotland there once lived a Laird of Brockburn, who would not believe in fairies. Not that he

bore any ill-will to the Good People, or spoke uncivilly
of them. Indeed he always denied any feeling of
disrespect towards them if they existed, saying that he
was a man of peace himself, and anxious to live
peaceably with whatever neighbours he had, but that till
he had seen one he could not believe in them.

Now one afternoon, between Hallowmas and Yule, it
chanced that the laird, being out on the hills looking for
some cattle, got parted from his men and dogs and was
overtaken by a mist, in which, familiar as the country
was to him, he lost his way.

In vain he raised his voice high, and listened low, no
sound of man or beast came back to him through the
thickening vapour.

Then night fell, and darkness was added to the fog, so
that Brockburn needed to sound every step with his
stick before he took it.

Suddenly light footsteps pattered beside him, then
something rubbed against him, then ran between his
legs. The delighted laird was sure that his favourite collie
had found him once more.

"Wow, Jock, man!" he cried, "but ye needn't throw
me on my face. What's got ye this night, that you should

lose your way in a bit of mist?"

To this a voice from the level of his elbow replied, in piping but patronizing tones:

"Never did I lose my way in a mist since the night that Finn crossed over to Ireland in the dawn of history. Eh, laird! I'm well acquainted with every little path on the hillside these hundreds of years, and I'll guide ye safe home, never fear!"

The hairs on Brockburn's head stood on end till they lifted his broad bonnet, and a damp chill broke out over him that was not the fog. But, for all that, he stoutly resisted the evidence of his senses, and only felt about him for the collie's head to pat, crying:

"Bark! Jock, my mannie, bark! Then I'll recognize your voice, ye ken. It's not canny to hear ye speak like a Christian, my wee doggie."

"I'm nae your doggie, I'm a man of peace," was the reply. "Don't miscall your betters, Brockburn – why will ye not credit our existence, man?"

"Seeing's believing," said the laird, stubbornly, "but the mist's over thick for seeing this night, ye ken."

"Turn round to your left, man, and ye'll see," said the dwarf, and catching Brockburn by the arm, he twisted

him swiftly round three times, when a sudden blaze of
light poured through the mist, and revealed a crag
of the mountain well known to the laird,
and which he now saw to be a kind of
turret, or tower.

Lights shone gaily through the
crevices or windows of the tower, and
sounds of fiddling came forth. Blinded
by the light, and amazed at what he
saw, the laird staggered, and was
silent. Then stepping up to the
door of the tower, the
strange man stood
so that the light
from within fell
full upon him, and
the astonished
laird saw a tiny,
well-proportioned
man, with delicate
features, and golden
hair flowing over
his shoulders.

He wore a cloak of green cloth, lined with daisies. His beautiful face quivered with amusement, and he cried triumphantly, "D'ye see me? D'ye see me now, Brockburn?"

"Aye, aye," said the laird, "and seeing's believing."

"Then round with ye!" shouted the man of peace, and once more seizing the laird by the arm, he turned him swiftly round – this time, to the right – and at the third turn the light vanished, and Brockburn and the man of peace were once more alone together in the mist.

"Aweel, Brockburn," said the man of peace, "I'll allow ye're honest, and have a convincible mind. I'm not ill disposed towards ye, and ye shall get safe home, man."

As he spoke he stooped down, and picking up half-a-dozen big stones from the mountainside, he gave them to the laird, saying, "If the goodwife asks ye about the stones, say ye got them as a compliment."

Brockburn put them into his pocket, briefly saying, "I'm obliged to ye," but as he followed the man of peace down the hillside, he found the obligation so heavy, that from time to time he threw a stone away, unobserved, as he hoped, by his companion. When the first stone fell,

the man of peace looked sharply round, saying:

"What's that?"

"It'll be me striking my rung upon the ground," said the laird.

"You're mad," said the man of peace, and Brockburn felt sure that he knew the truth, and was displeased. But as they went on, the stones were so heavy, and bumped his side so hard, that he threw away a second, dropping it as gently as he could. But the sound of its fall did not escape the ears of the man of peace, who cried as before:

"What's that?"

"It's just a nasty cough that I have," said the laird.

"'Man, you're daft," said the dwarf, contemptuously, "that's what ails ye."

The laird now resolved to be prudent, but the heaviness of his burden was so great that after a while he resolved to risk the displeasure of the man of peace once more, and gently slipped a third stone to the ground.

'Third time's lucky,' he thought. But the proverb failed him, for the dwarf turned as before, shouting:

"What's that?"

"It'll be my new shoes that ye hear stumbling upon the big stones," said the laird.

"Ye're drunk, Brockburn, I tell ye so. Ye're drunk!" growled the man of peace, angrily, and the laird dared not drop any more of the gifts. After a while his companion's good humour seemed to return, and he became talkative and generous.

"Ye shall not have to say that ye've been with the Daoiné Shi and are not the better for it," he said. "I'm thinking I'll grant ye three wishes. But choose wisely, man, and don't throw them away."

The laird at once began to cast about in his mind for three wishes sufficiently comprehensive to secure his lifelong prosperity, but the more he beat his brains the less could he satisfy himself.

How many miles he wandered thus, the dwarf keeping silently beside him, he never knew, before he sank exhausted on the ground, saying:

"I'm thinking, man, that if ye could bring home to me, in place of bringing me home, I'd doubt your powers no more. It's a far cry to Loch Awe, ye know, and it's a weary long road to Brockburn."

"Is this your wish?" asked the man of peace.

"This is my wish," said the laird, striking his rung upon the ground.

The words had scarcely passed his lips when the whole homestead of Brockburn, house and farm buildings, was planted upon the bleak hillside.

The astonished laird now began to bewail the rash wish which had removed his home from the sheltered and fertile valley where it originally stood to the barren side of a bleak mountain.

The man of peace, however, would not take any hints as to undoing his work of his own accord. All he said was:

"If ye wish it away, so it'll be. But then ye'll only have one wish left."

"To leave the steading in such a spot is no to be thought on," sighed the laird, as he spent his second wish in undoing his first. But he cannily added the provision:

"And ye may take me with it."

The words were no sooner spoken than the homestead was back in its place, and Brockburn himself was lying in his own bed, Jock, his favourite collie, barking and licking his face by turns for joy.

"Whisht, whisht, Jock!" said the laird. "Ye would not bark when I begged, so ye may hand your peace now."

And pushing the collie from him, he sat up in bed and looked anxiously but vainly round the chamber for the man of peace.

"Lie down, lie down," cried his good wife from beside him. "Ye're surely out of your wits. Would ye go wandering about the country again tonight?"

"Where is he?" cried the laird.

"There's not a soul here but your lawful wife and your own dear doggie. Was there anybody that ye expected?" asked his wife.

"The man o' peace, woman!" cried Brockburn. "I've one of my wishes to get yet, and I must have it."

"The man's mad!" was his good wife's comment.

"Ye've surely forgotten yourself. Ye never believed in the Daoiné Shi before."

"Seeing's believing," said the laird. "I forgathered with a man of peace tonight on the hill, and I wish I just saw him again."

As the laird spoke the window of the chamber was lit up from without, and the man of peace appeared sitting on the window ledge in his daisy-lined cloak, his feet hanging down into the room, the silver shoes glittering as they dangled.

"I'm here, Brockburn!" he cried. "But eh, man! Ye've had your last wish."

And even as the stupefied laird gazed, the light slowly died away, and the man of peace vanished also.

On the following morning the laird was roused from sleep by loud cries of surprise and admiration.

His wife had been stirring for some hours, and in emptying the pockets of her good man's coat she had found huge cairngorms of exquisite tint and lustre. Brockburn thus discovered the value of the gifts he had thrown away.

But no subsequent visits to the hillside led to their recovery. Many a time did the laird bring home a heavy pocketful of stones, at his thrifty wife's bidding, but they only proved to be the common stones of the mountainside. The tower could never be distinguished from any other crag, and the Daoiné Shi were visible no more.

Yet it is said that the Laird of Brockburn prospered and throve thereafter, in acre, stall, and steading, as those seldom prosper who have not the good word of the people of peace.

Peter's Two Wishes

From *Peter Pan in Kensington Gardens* by J M Barrie

READING TIME: 15 MINUTES

Peter Pan is a human boy who was left behind in a London park called Kensington Gardens by mistake. He has lived there ever since, a friend of the fairies.

*I*t is frightfully difficult to know much about the fairies, and almost the only thing known for certain is that there are fairies wherever there are children.

I have heard of children who declared that they had never once seen a fairy. Very likely if they said this in the Kensington Gardens, they were standing looking at a fairy all the time. The reason they were cheated was that she pretended to be something else. This is one of their best tricks. They usually pretend to be flowers, because there are so many flowers there, so a flower is the thing least likely to attract attention. They dress exactly like flowers, and change with the seasons, putting on white when lilies are in and blue for bluebells, and so on. They like crocus and hyacinth time best of all, as they are partial to a bit of colour, but tulips (except white ones, which are the fairy cradles) they consider garish, and they sometimes put off dressing

like tulips for days, so that the beginning of the tulip weeks is almost the best time to catch them.

When they think you are not looking they skip along pretty lively, but if you look and they fear there is no time to hide, they stand quite still, pretending to be flowers. Then, after you have passed without knowing that they were fairies, they rush home and tell their mothers they have had such an adventure.

There are also numbers of them along the Baby Walk, which is a famous gentle place, as spots frequented by fairies are called. Once, twenty-four of them had an extraordinary adventure. They were a girls' school out for a walk with the governess, and all wearing hyacinth gowns, when she suddenly put her finger to her mouth, and then they all stood still on an empty bed and pretended to be hyacinths. Unfortunately, what the governess had heard was two gardeners coming to plant new flowers in that very bed. They were wheeling a handcart with flowers in it, and were quite surprised to find the bed occupied.

"Pity to lift them hyacinths," said the one man.

"Duke's orders," replied the other, and, having emptied the cart, they dug up the boarding school and put the poor, terrified things in it in five rows. Of course, neither the governess nor the girls dare let on that they were fairies, so they were carted far away to a potting shed, out of which they escaped in the night without their shoes, but there was a great row about it among the parents, and the school was ruined.

As for their houses, it is no use looking for them, because they are the exact opposite of our houses. You can see our houses by day but you can't see them by dark. Well, you can see their houses by dark, but you can't see them by day, for they are the colour of night, and I never heard of anyone yet who could see night in the daytime. This does not mean that they are black, for night has its colours just as day has, but ever so much brighter. Their blues and reds and greens are like ours with light behind them. Their palace is entirely built of many-coloured glasses, and is the loveliest of all royal residences, but the queen sometimes complains because the common people will peep in to see what she is doing. They are very inquisitive folk, and press quite hard against the glass, and that is why their noses are mostly snubby.

One of the great differences between the fairies and us is that they never do anything useful. When the first baby laughed for the first time, his laugh broke into a million pieces, and they all went skipping about. That was the beginning of fairies. They look tremendously busy, you know, as if they had not a moment to spare, but if you were to ask them what they are doing, they could not tell you in the least. They are frightfully ignorant, and everything they do is make-believe. It is a very noticeable thing that, in fairy families, the youngest is always chief person, and usually becomes a prince or princess.

The fairies are exquisite dancers, and hold their great balls in the open air, in what is called a fairy ring. For weeks afterward you can see the ring on the grass. It is not there when they begin, but they make it by waltzing round and round. Sometimes you will find mushrooms inside the ring, and these are fairy chairs that the servants have forgotten to clear away. The chairs and the rings are the only tell-tale marks these little people leave

behind them, and they would remove even these were
they not so fond of dancing that they toe it till the very
moment of the opening of the gates.

If on such a night we could remain behind in the
gardens, we might see delicious sights, hundreds of
lovely fairies hastening to the ball, the married ones
wearing their wedding rings round their waists, the
gentlemen, all in uniform, holding up the ladies' trains,
and linkmen running in front carrying winter cherries,
which are the fairy lanterns, the supper table, with
Queen Mab at the head of it, and behind her chair the
Lord Chamberlain, who carries a dandelion on which he
blows when her majesty wants to know the time.

The tablecloth varies according to the seasons, and in
May it is made of chestnut blossom. The way the fairy
servants make them is this. Scores of the men climb up
the trees and shake the branches, and the blossom falls
like snow. Then the lady servants sweep it together by
whisking their skirts until it is exactly like a tablecloth,
and that is how they get their tablecloth.

You know, without my telling you, that Peter Pan is
the fairies' orchestra. He sits in the middle of the ring,
and they would never dream of having a dance nowadays

without him. They are grateful little people, too, and at the coming-of-age ball of the princess (they come of age on their second birthday and have a birthday every month) they gave him the wish of his heart.

The way it was done was this. The queen ordered him to kneel, and then said that for playing so beautifully she would give him the wish of his heart. Then they all gathered round Peter to hear what was the wish of his heart, but for a long time he hesitated, not being certain what it was himself.

"If I chose to go back to mother," he asked at last, "could you give me that wish?"

Now this question vexed them, for were he to return to his mother they should lose his music, so the queen tilted her nose contemptuously and said, "Pooh, ask for a much bigger wish than that."

"Is that quite a little wish?" he inquired.

"As little as this," the queen answered, putting her hands near each other.

"What size is a big wish?" he asked.

She measured it off on her skirt and it was a very handsome length.

Then Peter reflected and said, "Well, then, I think

I shall have two little wishes instead of one big one."

Of course, the fairies had to agree, though his cleverness rather shocked them, and he said that his first wish was to go to his mother, but with the right to return to the gardens if he found her disappointing. His second wish he would hold in reserve until he thought of something really worth wishing for. They tried to dissuade him, and even put obstacles in the way.

"I can give you the power to fly to her house," the queen said, "but I can't open the door for you."

"The window I flew out at will be open," Peter said confidently. "Mother always keeps it open in the hope that I may fly back."

"How do you know?" they asked, quite surprised, and, really, Peter could not explain how he knew.

"I just know," he said.

So as he persisted in his wish, they had no choice but to grant it, and the way they gave him power to fly was this. The fairies tickled him on the shoulder, and soon he felt a funny twitching in that part. Then up he rose, higher and higher till he flew away out of the gardens and over the house tops.

It was so delicious that instead of flying straight to his

old home he skimmed away over St Paul's to the Crystal Palace and back by the river and Regent's Park, and by the time he reached his mother's window he had quite made up his mind that his second wish should be to become a bird.

The window was wide open, just as he knew it would be, and in he fluttered, and there was his mother lying asleep. Peter alighted on the wooden rail at the foot of the bed. She lay with her head on her hand, and the hollow in the pillow was like a nest lined with her brown wavy hair. He was very glad she was a pretty mother. But she looked sad, and he knew why she looked sad. One of her arms moved as if it wanted to go round something, and he knew what it wanted to go round.

"Oh, mother," said Peter to himself, "if you just knew who is sitting on the rail at the foot of the bed."

Very gently he patted the little mound that her feet made, and he could see by her face that she liked it. He knew he had but to say 'Mother' ever so softly, and she would wake up. They always wake up at once if it is you that says their name. Then she would give such a joyous cry and squeeze him tight.

But why does Peter sit so long on the rail, why does he not tell his mother that he has come back?

I quite shrink from the truth, which is that he sat there in two minds. Certainly it would be pleasant to be her boy again, but, on the other hand, what times those had been in the gardens! Was he so sure that he would enjoy wearing clothes again? He opened some drawers to have a look at his old garments. They were still there, but he could not remember how you put them on. The socks – were they worn on the hands or feet? He was about to try one on his hand, when he had a great adventure. His mother woke up, for he heard her say "Peter," as if it was the most lovely word in the language. He held his breath, wondering how she knew that he had come back. If she said 'Peter' again, he meant to cry 'Mother' and run to her. But she spoke no more, and when next he peeped at her she was once more asleep, with tears on her face.

It made Peter very miserable, and what do you think was the first thing he did? Sitting on the windowsill, he played a beautiful lullaby to his mother on his pipe. He had made it up himself out of the way she said 'Peter,' and he never stopped playing until she looked happy.

He thought this so clever of him that he could scarcely resist wakening her to hear her say, 'Oh, Peter, how exquisitely you play.' However, as she now seemed comfortable, he again cast looks at the window. You must not think that he meditated flying away and never coming back. He had quite decided to be his mother's boy, but hesitated about beginning tonight. It was the second wish which troubled him. He no longer meant to make it a wish to be a bird, but not to ask for a second wish seemed wasteful, and, of course, he could not ask for it without returning to the fairies. Also, if he put off asking for his wish too long it might go bad.

And in the end, you know, he flew away. Twice he came back from the window, wanting to kiss his mother, but he feared the delight of it might waken her, so at last he played her a lovely kiss on his pipe, and then he flew back to the gardens. Many nights and even months passed before he asked the fairies for his second wish, and I am not sure that I quite know why he delayed so long. One reason was that he had so many goodbyes to say, not only to his particular friends, but to a hundred favourite spots. Then he had his last sail, and his very last sail, and his last sail of all, and so on.

But, mind you, though Peter was so slow in going back to his mother, he was quite decided to go back. The best proof of this was his caution with the fairies. They were most anxious that he should remain in the gardens to play to them, and to bring this to pass they tried to trick him into making such a remark as 'I wish the grass was not so wet,' and some of them danced out of time in the hope that he might cry, 'I do wish you would keep time!' Then they would have said that this was his second wish. But he smoked their design, and though on occasions he began, "I wish," he always stopped in time. So when at last he said to them bravely, "I wish now to go back to mother for ever and always," they had to tickle his shoulders and let him go.

He went in a hurry in the end because he had dreamt that his mother was crying, and he knew the great thing she cried for, and that a hug from her splendid Peter would quickly make her to smile. Oh, he felt sure of it, and so eager was he to be nestling in her arms that this time he flew straight to the window, which was always to be left open for him.

About the artists

Zdenko Basic Born in Zagreb, Croatia, Zdenko graduated from the School of Applied Art and Design, and later the Zagreb Academy of Fine Arts. He uses a mixture of photography and illustration in his artwork, and also works in costume and set design, puppetry and animation. He has won several awards for his artwork, most recently the *Grigor Vitez Award* (2008) for Best Illustration in Children's Books.

Billy Beg, Tom Beg, and the Fairies ∗ *Fairy Ointment*
A Boy That Visited Fairyland ∗ *Iktomi and the Ducks*
Connla and the Fairy Maiden ∗ *The Phantom Vessel*
Iktomi and the Muskrat ∗ *The Smith and the Fairies*
The Laird and the Man of Peace

Jasmine Foster As a child, Jasmine was drawn to illustrations with a dreamlike quality, and now strives to capture that same sense of imagination in her own work. She enjoys reading myths and folk stories and loves having the opportunity to explore weird and wonderful characters through her illustrations.

A French Puck ∗ *The Fairy Wife* ∗ *Rosanella* ∗ *Murdoch's Rath* ∗ *The Prince with the Nose* ∗ *Sweet-One-Darling and the Dream-Fairies* ∗ *Under the Sun* ∗ *Paddy Corcoran's Wife* ∗ *Mrs Bedonebyasyoudid and Mrs Doasyouwouldbedoneby*

Patricia Moffett After 15 years of working as a designer and art buyer, Patricia decided to re-kindle her desire to be an illustrator. She found the developments in image-making software exciting and liberating, and loves the fact that she can paint in virtual watercolour and then send her pictures off across the world through the ether.

Eva's Visit to Fairyland ∗ *Graciosa and Percinet*
The Boy Who Wanted More Cheese ∗ *Peter's Two Wishes*
Christmas Every Day ∗ *The Fairy Blackstick*
The Fairies and the Envious Neighbour

Christine Pym Since studying illustration for children's publishing in Wales, Christine has illustrated two children's books and several greetings cards, all in watercolour and pencil crayon, which is her preferred choice of media. When she is not illustrating, Christine helps to run a small post office and general store in Derbyshire with her partner, and lives with a Yorkshire terrier called Cindy and two goldfish called Athos and Aramis.

Beautiful as the Day ∗ *Betty and the Wood Maiden*
Drak, the Fairy ∗ *The Fiddler in the Fairy Ring*
Melisande ∗ *Master and Man* ∗ *The Touch of Iron*

Elena Selivanova A graduate of Moscow State University of Printing Arts, Elena has been working as an illustrator with major publishing houses for more than 20 years. Her style and technique have changed over this time, but her desire to make her illustrations for each new book moving and amusing is unchangeable.

The Fairy Fluffikins ∗ *Farmer Mybrow and the Fairies*
The Hillman and the Housewife ∗ *The Fairy Cure*
The Man Who Would Not Scold ∗ *Puck of Pook's Hill*
The Treasure Stone of the Fairies

Katy Wright Growing up on a farm and then studying illustration at University College Falmouth in Cornwall, UK, gave Katy a background rich in nature and mythology that has provided her with inspiration for her work as an illustrator. After graduating, Katy packed up her belongings and moved to France, where she can now be found sketching in her little studio in the heart of the beautiful city of Bordeaux.

My Own Self ∗ *A Midsummer Night's Dream*
Adventures of a Brownie ∗ *Bruno's Revenge* ∗ *Guleesh*
The Fairy Cow ∗ *The Maiden of the Green Forest*
The Story of Wali Dad, the Simple-Hearted
The Magic Pitcher